# HALSEY FAMILY TREE

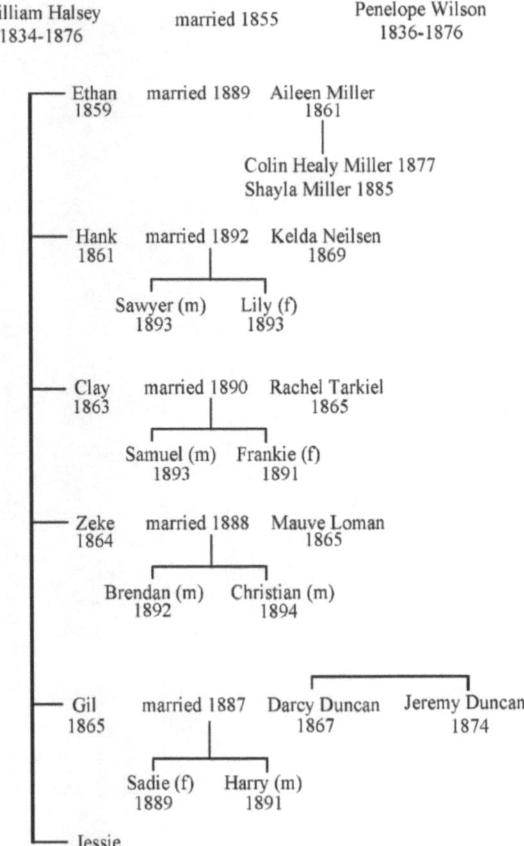

**Halsey Homecoming Series**

Laying Claim
Staking Claim
Claiming a Heart

# CLAIMING A HEART

**Halsey Homecoming Series**

by
**Paty Jager**

Windtree Press
Hillsboro, OR

CLAIMING A HEART



Contact Information: info@windtreepress.com

Windtree Press

Oregon

Visit us at http://windtreepress.com

Cover Art by Covers by Karen

Published in the United States of America

ISBN 9781940064475

# Acknowledgement

This book would not have been possible if not for my daughter's basketball team taking a tour of the Pendleton Underground and her enthusiasm pushing me to take the same tour. Once I participated in the tour my brain started coming up with many possibilities for stories set in the tunnels.

Also many thanks to Keith F. May a fellow author and historian of the Pendleton area. Our conversation one afternoon in his store put me onto some great historical information that played into this story.

## *Chapter One*

Pendleton, Oregon 1900

Harnesses jangled, voices shouted, horses and mules snorted and brayed, and behind all of that was the hiss of steam and the metal on metal rumble of a train pulling out of the station. Donny Kimball fidgeted beside the wagon he and Jasper had brought to Pendleton to pick up supplies. He'd spent the last fourteen of his twenty-two years in the dark. Using only sounds and smells, he could tell what a town was like better than a person using their sight.

This one smelled of smoke, horses, unwashed men, and liquor. Every other person who passed had the smell of alcohol wafting from them. He knew liquor meant there'd be brawls, shootouts, and lawlessness. If Jasper didn't hurry up, their chances of getting caught in the middle of one of those messes increased. It was the kind of place he tried to avoid. While he didn't consider his blindness a handicap, he knew his limits and navigating in this mass of moving bodies would be difficult.

"Found out where we's need to go." Jasper's voice fell on Donny's ears at the same time a large hand settled on his shoulder.

"Good. I don't like the sounds of this place," said Donny. "Why did Clay have to use a tannery in this town?" Clay Halsey, his mentor, was getting more orders for his writing book for the blind every day and had added fancy ones with tooled covers.

"He likes this man's work. We's just have to find him. Never seen so many peoples in the streets other than at Fourth o' July. Climb on before you gets pulled away in the swarm o' peoples." Jasper's voice high above Donny's head said he'd already climbed aboard the wagon.

Donny grabbed the side of the buckboard and joined him.

"Hup!" Jasper ordered over the din of the street. The wagon lurched then moved forward.

He'd helped harness the horses this morning when they'd left Pilot Rock. He wondered how the two geldings felt about pulling their load through what sounded like a tangle of teams.

"The man at the depot says this tannery is over the other side o' the river."

"I suppose that's on the other side of town." Donny didn't know the layout of this town. He wasn't even sure why Clay had insisted he go with Jasper to pick up the covers. Jasper had run errands to Pendleton before without needing someone along.

"Shore 'nuff. We're goin' down Main Street right now. There's a heap o' cowboys hangin' out down the side streets." Jasper let out a laugh. Not the loud gut laugh he made when he found humor in something. This laugh was more restrained and held a note of embarrassment.

"What's that laugh for?" Donny asked.

"There's women hangin' out winders down that last street."

"Is the building on fire?" Donny knew he wasn't much help in a situation like a fire unless they put him in a line to hand buckets along, but he felt compelled to do something if there was a fire.

"Naw, they's alright. Just tryin' to catch the eye of a cowboy's all."

"Why would they have to hang out a window to do that?" Donny had been taught a lot by the Halsey brothers, and the younger members of the family, Jeremy and Colin, but he was pretty sure he'd never heard them say anything about women hanging out windows to get attention.

"They's painted up ladies. The kind can't be seen on the streets."

"They're soiled doves. Why didn't you just say that?" Donny knew a little about soiled doves. He'd been on a couple trips with Jeremy when they'd had some ladies, none-too-subtlety, ask them if they'd like to sow their oats.

"I didn't—"

The wagon stopped abruptly.

"Hey! Let go dat horse!" Jasper yelled.

"What's happening?" Donny leaned forward, trying to hear what had caused them to stop.

"I's got this handled." Jasper said under his breath. "We ain't lookin' for trouble. Let my horse go and there won't be no trouble."

"Lookie here, we have us a darkie. We don't let Chiney walk our streets, I don't think we should allow you either." The deep voice held menace.

"Let us pass. We're only here on an errand," Donny said, hoping that by entering the conversation the man would know Jasper wasn't on his own.

"You a darkie lover?" The voice came from directly below him.

"I'm a friend of the man sitting next to me," he said.

A hand grabbed his arm and yanked him off the wagon. Donny scrambled to his feet and listened. The sound of a body being struck, oofs, groans, and cussing came from the other side of the wagon.

"Leave him alone!" Donny felt the wagon, crawled under it, and grabbed the first leg he found.

Using the man as a ladder, he pulled himself to his feet and started swinging. A hand smashed his face, another shoved air out of his lungs. He landed on the ground. Toes of boots struck his body over and over again until one last blow brought on the darkness of unconsciousness.

Callie MacPherson cowered in the stairwell to the underground tunnels. She knew better than to step onto the street when the liquored-up cowboys were riled. The young man Murphy pulled off the wagon had guts to take on the four men pounding on his Negro friend. Her stomach churned at the sound and sight of the men kicking him. He'd curled up, but not before a boot connected with his skull. From her position she was nearly face to face with the man as he lay in a heap against the railing.

"Help me," he whispered.

The men had gone back to beating on the Negro. Shouts and a couple of shots sent the cowboys running down the street.

Callie bit her lip and peered into the face of the man. He needed medical help. When the lawmen arrived, they'd haul him to jail and wait for him to wake up and tell his story. The law would believe the man deserved to be beaten until he could say otherwise.

She peered over the stairwell. The spectators were walking away. The big Negro lay in a bloody pile in the street. She couldn't help him. He was too big and out in the open.

Callie scooted up the wood stairs, grabbed the young man by the legs, and pulled him to the stairs. He didn't need any more damage to his body or head, but he weighed nearly double her weight and was a good foot taller. She pulled his legs until his backside was on the first step.

Pushing his back to put him in a sitting position, she straddled his body from behind, placing her wool clad legs on the outside of his. She slid him down the steps, bouncing her backside step by step downward. At the bottom, she opened the door, grasped his arms, and tugged.

"Missy Mac, what you find?" her friend Yi Wu asked.

"A man who has been badly beaten. Can you help me take him to Mr. Cai?" She released her hold on one of the arms, and together they tugged and pulled the man down the stone tunnel. His boot heels scraped along the hard-packed floor. The sound of boot heels on the board walkway above echoed in the tunnel along with their straining breaths.

The heat and steam of Mr. Wu's laundry entered the tunnel as they passed his business. Yi called out to her father in Chinese. Callie only caught a couple of the words. "Helping Missy Mac" and "back."

Callie and Yi grunted and tugged, dragging the man through the communal kitchen under the Josh house. The scent of fish and spices clung to her nostrils. Several men playing with small tiles at a table glanced up but didn't offer to help.

Finally, they passed the opium parlor. Smoke furled out of the door releasing a cloying, sweet, herbal scent.

The next doorway led to Mr. Cai's apothecary. He was the resident doctor for the Chinese of Pendleton and anyone else who didn't want to be seen going to a regular doctor.

He chattered in Chinese to Yi. She shrugged and stared at Callie.

"Mr. Cai. He was beat up on the street for riding in a wagon with a Negro. I could tell he needed help fast." She and Yi slowly lowered the man to the floor.

Mr. Cai knelt beside the man. Callie's stomach churned at the sight of the blood and bruising on the man's face.

Yi nudged Callie with her pointy elbow.

Callie frowned at the girl the same height and weight as she. They were both small boned. Frail was the word her mother used to say when her father took Callie hunting and fishing. There was nothing frail about either Callie or Yi. They both worked in Wu's laundry, washing heavy, wet clothes and bedding.

Yi giggled and leaned toward Callie. "Missy Mac, you found one fine cowboy."

Callie shook her head. Yi thought about men all the time. Even though she couldn't marry anyone until her father said she could marry and to whom, Yi talked nonstop about being a wife.

Callie had watched her mother waste away to nearly nothing when her husband, Callie's father, died. Then her mother had remarried. Callie's stomach soured with disgust. The man had made it perfectly clear he'd be sneaking into her bed. When he did, she'd killed the man and ran away.

She'd figured on getting a job and living just fine. Not having any skills other than hunting, fishing, and wrangling horses, she couldn't find work. No one believed a woman the size of a boy could tame a horse or bring in game. When the men had started saying things like her stepfather, she'd put on mens clothing and ducked into the underground tunnels of Pendleton. She called herself Mac and had the people on the streets and half the people living underground believing she was a young man. Yi, Yi's father, and Mr. Cai knew the truth. She lived with the Wu family and had been in need of doctoring. That was how Mr. Cai discovered her true nature.

"Him concussed. Need clean injuries and watch him." Mr. Cai stood. "Help get him on bed in back."

Callie and Yi each grabbed an arm and pulled the injured man to a small room behind a curtain. A narrow bed barely wide enough for the man's shoulders and shorter than his length stood at the back of the room.

"Here." Mr. Cai pointed to the small bed. "Put."

Callie tugged and managed to get her side of the man's back onto the bed. She shoved her hands under his other shoulder and helped lift his upper body onto the cot. Then she put his legs one by one onto the bed. His boots hung over the end.

"I mix medicine." He pointed to Yi. "Go work." Mr. Cai pointed to the man. "You. Take off clothes."

Callie's face burned. She'd seen a few men half-dressed staggering through the alleys, but she'd never undressed a man.

"Not all. Leave johns." Mr. Cai spun around and disappeared behind the curtain.

"Undress him." She bit her bottom lip and stared at his feet. Boots. They were safe.

She stood with one of the boots between her legs, bent, and tugged. "Uhhhg. Come on boot." She urged the footwear to release from the man's foot.

Slowly, the boot started to release. Rocking the boot back and forth, the socked foot slowly appeared. She placed the boot by the end of the bed and went to work on the second one. The man stirred and called out as she worked on this boot, but he didn't wake up. She worried she'd injured him, but didn't know what to do other than follow Mr. Cai's orders. When the two boots sat at the end of the bed, she stared down at the man.

Neckerchief. That was also safe.

The warmth of his neck surprised her as her fingers worked at the knot in the fabric. She stuffed the garment into the boots.

He had on a jacket, a vest, and a chambray shirt. Staring at the clothing she determined to unbutton all three. Then slip them all off at the same time and only have to lift him up once. Working the coat and vest buttons gave her a chance to study the face underneath the blood and bruises. She hadn't seen his features before the beating, but from what she could tell, he'd be pleasing to look at. The light brown color of his hair reminded her of caramel candy she'd seen in a store once.

The top two layers of buttons were done. She swallowed, pulled the warm tails of his shirt out of his wool britches and unbuttoned the bottom button. The heat that had built in her cheeks ebbed when her fingers rubbed against flannel. He was wearing a full set of long johns. Knowing he had a layer she didn't have to remove made the task go faster and with less embarrassment.

She struggled to get his first arm out of the

three garments, but once it was free, she rolled him and drew the clothing off his other arm. Folding the garments, she was surprised by the scents she encountered. Wood, leather, and only a faint trace of horse. He wasn't a cowboy. He wasn't dressed like a farmer either.

"What do you do?" she asked as she pulled his socks off his feet. She ran a finger up the underside of his left foot. His toes didn't even wiggle. If she didn't see the slow rise and fall of his chest she'd think he was dead.

She stood by the cot staring at the last piece of clothing she had to remove. Wool trousers. Drawing in a deep breath, she steeled herself for the task. The red flannels he wore would cover his lower body, but she wasn't sure she wanted to touch him so intimately. After all, she'd have to slide the britches over his hips and down.

"Lookin' at him ain't gettin' the job done." She leaned down and unbuttoned the waist button. Working the other buttons under the flap loose required her fingers to touch a part of a man's body she shouldn't be touching.

She held her breath and worked the buttons loose as quickly as her dry, cracked fingers would go. A whoosh of air relaxed her lungs when the buttons were all free of the holes. Sliding her hands inside the pants and down his hips, she worked the garment down and eventually off his legs.

Sweat beaded her brow when she stood at the end of the cot holding his trousers.

The curtain fluttered, and Mr. Cai hustled in

carrying a tray with a steaming tea pot and several tiny bowls.

Callie folded the trousers and laid them over the other clothing and boots. "Do you have a blanket to cover him?" she asked, staring down at the tray Mr. Cai placed on the small table at the head of the cot.

"We give medicine, then cover, wait."

He handed her a wet cloth and a small bowl with salve in it. "Clean face. Spread wounds."

She gently wiped at the dried and congealed blood on his face. Most of the blood had come from his nose and a cut on his forehead. She'd never administered to anyone. But this man brought out a nurturing instinct she hadn't experienced before. Setting the cloth down, she picked up the bowl and dipped a finger into the cool ointment. Her hand shook. She'd never touched a man so intimately. Her chest squeezed. He needed her help. Cautiously, she dabbed the ointment onto the open cuts on his face.

Mr. Cai poured the steaming tea into a cup and added herbs from the various bowls on his tray. He stirred the tea and took the bowl from her.

"Hold him. I make drink." Mr. Cai held the cup up in front of the man.

Callie put her hands under the man's back and raised him enough Mr. Cai could drip the tea into the man's mouth. He stroked the man's neck, making him swallow the liquid.

"Enough." Mr. Cai placed the drink on the tray, picked up the tray, and left the room.

She lowered the man's upper body back to the bed and stood watching him.

Mr. Cai returned. "You watch." He placed a stool against the wall at the head of the bed.

"I can't. I was just getting fresh air when I discovered him. I need to get back to work." Mr. Wu paid her twenty-five cents a week to work in the laundry along with a place to eat and sleep. It was a generous offer, especially, considering what she would have to do if she lived above the tunnels.

"I watch when you deliver laundry. Now you watch. I busy." Mr. Cai left the room and returned with a bowl of broth for her.

"Tell Mr. Wu I'll be there to make my deliveries. And tell him you're the one making me stay here." She narrowed her eyes at the man the same height as her only stockier.

He grinned, showing off small, smoke-stained teeth. "Dwee, dwee. I tell him. You find man. You watch man."

Callie sat on the stool and leaned her head against the cold stone wall. She sure did find the man. What was she going to do with him when he woke?

# Chapter Two

Each breath sent shards of pain piercing through his chest. Donny's head pounded and burning spasms shot up his left leg.

His eyelids felt like they were nailed to his cheeks. He couldn't open them. Why did he hurt so bad? The scents reminded him a bit of Rachel's front parlor. The one she used to take care of patients. But the air wasn't as medicinal smelling, it had an earthy aroma.

He raised a hand to touch his face. A creak, like someone getting up from a chair, filled the silence. A whoosh of air fluttered across his hand.

"Mister? Mister are you awake?"

The voice sounded young, and he was pretty sure feminine.

He drew in a breath to say yes and winced instead.

"Don't talk. I'll get Mr. Cai."

Soft footsteps and air fluttering around him proved the person had left. He hadn't heard the sound of skirts rustling. It must be a young boy.

"In here. He moved and tried to talk." The same voice drew closer.

Two sets of soft footsteps drew near the bed.

A small pair of hands touched his neck and moved down each arm feeling and testing the parts that should move.

Donny steeled himself for the pain and said, "Chest. Hurt."

The hands deftly moved to his chest and found the spot that radiated the pain.

"Ahhh!" Donny couldn't stop the agony-filled cry as the man pressed on the spot.

"Rib broke." The man moved his hands down Donny's legs. "Other pain?" The man asked in a funny way Donny hadn't heard before.

"Left leg. Head." Donny forced the words and found the pain wasn't near what he'd experienced when the man pushed on his ribs.

The hands moved down his left leg. "Broke."

He heard one of the people move away from the cot. "Who is he and who are you?" he asked.

"That's Mr. Cai. He's the Chinese healer. I'm Mac. I found you in the street and brought you here."

He listened intently. He was pretty sure the person talking was a girl. But Mac was a boy's name. His head pounded harder trying to hear more.

"Where am I?" He vaguely remembered being

pulled off a wagon, and then being beaten.

"You're in the underground tunnels in Pendleton."

Underground? That's why he smelled dirt and dankness.

A rustle and footsteps revealed the doctor returning.

"Chest first," the man said.

Hesitant fingers worked the buttons on his long johns. They weren't the nimble, knowledgeable fingers that had inspected his body for injuries. It must be the young person. His body heated when the small, cold fingers touched his skin as the garment was opened. The hands slid toward his shoulders, sliding the garment down his arms.

"Lift. All off," the man ordered.

The small hands slipped under his back and raised him to a sitting position.

He gasped for air as the strain on his ribs added to the pain.

"Sorry," the young voice whispered in his ear, as his flannels were drawn off his arms and settled around his waist.

"Arms up," the doctor said.

Donny tried to raise his arms, but he couldn't hold both up at the same time. The pain was too much.

"I'll help," said the young person. The small hands grasped his arms at the elbow.

Something wide wrapped around his chest as one arm was raised and then the other. The pressure of the bandage on his ribs helped ease the pain a bit.

His leg hurt worse than his ribs now. He grimaced as the doctor leaned him forward before the small, hesitant hands lowered him back to the bed.

"Fix leg, then more medicine," the doctor said.

His flannels on his left leg tugged. The shrill sound of ripping material and cool air hitting his throbbing leg meant the doctor had opened the flannels in the area of his leg that was broken.

He heard a sharp intake of breath.

"No faint," the doctor admonished.

"I-I won't. I've never seen a broken leg before it was set." The shaky voice made Donny wonder if the young person would be able to help the doctor.

While he hadn't actually seen a broken leg, he had helped Rachel set one. She was the perfect wife for Clay. She helped her blind husband do things most blind people wouldn't even consider doing, and she had opened Donny's mind to doing things he hadn't thought possible either. The day Donny tripped over Clay Halsey at the blind school had started Donny's life to a better situation than he'd been headed. Clay had helped him leave the school and become a businessman. Both things Donny thought he'd never be able to do.

"Ahhh!" He shouted as pain radiated up his leg. "What're you doing?"

"Set leg." Small strong hands grasped his leg just below the knee. "Mac, put hands here."

The firm hands were replaced with the small, cold hands.

The doctor grasped his leg below the pain. "Hold tight!" he said.

"Ahhh!" Donny exclaimed as pain ripped through his lower leg, shot up his thigh, and landed as a nauseous spiral in his gut.

"Mac. Hold here. Man. No move." The doctor ordered both of them.

If the man's voice hadn't been so insistent, Donny didn't think he would have heard it through the pain radiating in his body.

He remained still, fearful of more pain if he moved. The small hands dug into his leg above his ankle.

The doctor pressed on the sore place on his leg then began wrapping the leg.

Donny felt the pressure of something long and hard pressing on four sides of his leg. The sound and rhythm of the wrapping started again.

"Nothing for head," the doctor said. "Make more tea."

The sound of the man leaving the room was followed by movement around the bed.

"What are you doing?" Donny asked.

The person stopped. "It's pretty plain to see I'm cleanin' up."

"It would be plain if I could see."

"Oh! Mr. Cai! Come quick he can't see!" The voice rose an octave.

He was pretty sure it was a young woman and not a boy.

"Shhh… don't raise a ruckus."

"That kick you took must have injured your eyes." The small hand fluttered across his forehead.

"I couldn't see before I was attacked."

Air whooshed out of the young woman. "You mean you flung yourself into that fight not seein' a thing?" She made a snort sound. "You're either foolish or brave. I'm not sure which."

Talking about the beating started things coming back to him. "Jasper. My friend. Is he here too?"

"No. He was too big and out in the middle of the street. I couldn't get to him without bein' seen. You were layin' right next to the stairwell where I was sittin'."

Donny tried to sit up. The pain seared through his body, but not as piercing as the fear in his heart. "We have to help Jasper."

"Lay down. You can't go anywhere until you heal. I'll go by the jail and see if that's where he's at. That's usually where they take men who get in fights."

"But we didn't start the fight. Someone stopped us when all we were trying to do was cross town." He relaxed onto his back but wasn't content to lie around here while Jasper could need help. "Get the doctor in here. I need to know how soon I can get out of here and help Jasper."

The sound of footsteps faded.

Callie was pretty sure Mr. Cai wouldn't let the man leave until he was healed. But let the two of them talk it out, she needed to make deliveries for the laundry. She walked up and stood beside Mr. Cai as he measured herbs into the small bowls. "The man wants to know when he can leave. He's worried about a friend who was also beaten." She shot a glance to the curtain separating the two rooms.

"He's blind. Can't see."

"I check."

"No. He was that way before he was beaten." She took two steps toward the door leading to the tunnels. "I have to deliver the laundry now."

"When finish, come back. Sleep here."

"He's your patient, not mine." She held up her hands as if she could ward off the power Mr. Cai had over people to make them do his bidding.

"He not mine. You found. You responsibility he not cause trouble."

Callie sighed. She knew the unspoken rule. If an outsider, like herself when she first arrived, was brought in by someone, in her case Yi Wu, that person was responsible for the actions of the outsider.

"I'll bring my sleeping pad." She wasn't looking forward to sleeping in the small room with the injured man, but she also didn't want to get tossed out of the underground refuge she'd found.

Callie followed the tunnel back to Wu's laundry.

"How your man?" Yi asked, glancing up from the bedding she was folding.

"He isn't my man." Callie was getting tired of people calling the blind, foolish man hers.

"You found, you keep." Yi giggled and continued folding the bedding.

Mr. Wu glared at his daughter, as was usual. Yi must have received her good spirits and playfulness from her mother. Yi said she didn't know because her mother had died when she was born. Her father and mother had paid to come to America to live better before the Chinese Exclusion Act of 1882.

"Mac deliveries." Mr. Wu waved his hand toward the four bundles wrapped in brown paper and tied with a string sitting inside the door. "Golden Rule. Pendleton Hotel. Academy. St. George."

Callie mentally fixed the routes she would take to deliver the bundles of bedding. The Academy was the farthest away and the Golden Rule was the closest to the courthouse and jail.

She picked up the bundle for the St. George Hotel and headed down the tunnels to the stairwell closest to the street she would travel to deliver the laundry. Not being Chinese or a soiled dove, she could have popped out anywhere and carried the laundry down the street like anyone else. But she didn't like anyone taking particular notice of her.

Her picture could be on a wanted poster. When Ma found her husband stabbed to death in her daughter's bed, Callie was pretty sure Ma would have sent the law after her.

# Chapter Three

Donny drank the nasty-tasting tea the man gave him. He knew the man was of another culture, but he'd never heard the words the man said or the way he said them. Even his English words had a funny sound to them.

"When can I get out of here?" he asked, when the cup pressed to his lips disappeared.

"Leg two months. Chest one month."

He heard the scoot, clink, and thunk of the man placing items on a tray.

"I can't stay here that long. I have a friend who was beaten up like me. I have to make sure he's getting help." Donny tried to sit up and fell back against the bed as pain shot through his chest and leg.

A hand rested on his shoulder. "Rest. Quicker heal."

"Mac isn't like you. What is she doing down here? Why are you hiding underground?" Donny needed to learn all he could about this underground living. Without sight he had to rely on other senses to get him out and help Jasper.

"Missy Mac story. She tell when return."

The shuffling gait and fading herbal scents told him the man had left him alone.

He couldn't even get up and check out the room. He had to rely on the muffled voices in the language he'd heard the doctor mutter to know he wasn't alone. He ran a hand over the wall. Rough square stones made the wall he laid next to and above his head. Dangling an arm over the edge of the cot, he winced but touched a cold, dirt-packed floor.

Maybe he wasn't underground. But why would the girl say so if they weren't? He searched his mind to try and remember everything he'd heard about Pendleton. It was wild and unruly most of the time. He placed a hand on his swollen face. Why had those men stopped them? And why hadn't anyone stepped in and helped? Where was the law in this town?

Callie dropped the last bundle of laundry at the back door of the Golden Rule and set out at a brisk pace toward the courthouse. The jail was in the bottom of the courthouse. She didn't like walking around out in the open, but would feel guilty if she didn't help the friend of the man on Mr.Cai's cot.

Dr. Vincent walked out of the courthouse. He

was stopped by the sheriff. She walked up the path to the front of the courthouse, listening intently.

"That Negro insists he didn't do anything and I believe him. He's big enough if he'd started something there would be more than one person needing medical attention," Dr. Vincent said.

"He insists he had someone with him. I sent a deputy back down to see if he could find anyone," the sheriff said.

She hurried on toward the courthouse then ducked around to the side. The Negro had doctoring. She could relay that news. Now to get back to the tunnels without anyone taking notice of her.

Callie trotted through the alleys and cautiously crossed the main streets. While she looked like a boy from a distance, she had a hard time looking like one when someone took the time to peer under her hat brim. Yi told Callie, her face reminded Yi of a doll she'd seen in a store window. Pink cheeks, big blue eyes with long eyelashes, and pretty bow-shaped lips. That wasn't how you'd describe a boy. Her hands were rough, red, and cracked from doing the laundry. They didn't give her away.

One block from the tunnel entrance and ten feet from the entrance to one of the saloons, a fight broke out. Three men were shoving another man around.

"Where is it, Hubert?" one man asked, slamming Hubert in the mouth. The man stumbled backwards.

"I don't have—" Before he could finish the sentence another fist sunk into the man's belly.

He staggered, turned, and started to run toward Callie. She tried to dodge the man but stumbled. The man lurched forward and fell on top of her.

"Get off me!" she huffed and shoved at the man. He smelled of liquor and sweaty male. Just like her step-father the night he…She screamed and shoved. Her mind leapt back to that night. His hands grabbing, pinching. His nasty breath. His body pushing against her. She tried to reach down, but she wasn't on a bed. There wasn't a knife hidden under the mattress. Her hand grasped something small and round. She clutched it in her fisted hand.

The weight lifted off her, and she rolled into a ball, crying.

A rough shake pulled her out of her memory.

"Hey, boy. Nothin' to fret about. Hubert's just had too much to drink."

She sprang to her feet, but before they could carry her away, the same hand that shook her shoulder, grabbed her arm.

"Ain't you the boy that delivers laundry for the Chiney Wu?"

She ducked her head. Dusk had settled in, but the light from the open door of the establishment spread across the steps and the man's back. Her face would be drenched in light if she raised her head.

"Yes. I need to get goin'." She struggled to pull her jacket free of the man's grip.

"The boss has been wantin' to visit with you." The man hauled her up the steps. He turned back to the street. "Take care of him," he told the other two.

She glanced over her shoulder as the man

hauled her into the building. The men were digging through Hubert's pockets.

Callie hadn't set foot in a saloon before. There was a bordello upstairs and a gambling hall in the basement. She delivered laundry to the back steps of two places similar to this one. Mr. Wu only dealt with the two. He said he owed the owners, since they'd helped him when he first arrived in the area.

The man hauled her across the room by the back collar of her jacket. The large room had tables and chairs, a long bar, and a small stage where a woman, in a short dress with too much of her bosoms showing, was singing and kicking up her legs, showin' her lacy underdrawers. Cowboys, merchants, and businessmen puffed on cigars and lifted mugs of beer and shots of whiskey. Sweat, stale smoke, and stench of tobacco spit assaulted her nose. The man continued through the noisy room without anyone so much as glancing their way. The next door he opened had a half-dozen scantily-clad women standing and sitting about the room. Men were scattered among the ladies. They all held glasses with amber liquid. Smoke hung in the air just like the opium den in the tunnel. But this smoke wasn't sickly sweet, it was the opposite. Between the acrid smoke and sweet perfume her nose started to tickle and burn.

She didn't get a good look at the people or the room before the man stopped at a door. He knocked and went in, dragging her behind, without waiting for an invite.

A man sat in a chair with a girl not much older

than Callie sitting on his lap. The dark-haired girl showed off more skin than was proper. Callie ducked her head and shoved her fisted hand in her trouser pockets. She released the object she'd picked up in the street.

The man's probing gaze landed on her.

"I thought you were taking care of a matter for me, Mort?" The man's deep booming voice was riddled with accusation.

"Mr. Bentine, I took care of that problem. This is that boy that works for Wu. The other day you said to grab him if I seen him." Mort shoved her toward the man with the girl on his lap.

Keeping her brim tilted downward, all she could see of the man and woman were their feet and legs. The man had on shiny brown shoes and brown wool trousers. The girl had fancy slippers and bare legs.

The girl slid off Mr. Bentine's lap and walked toward her.

Callie gulped and continued to stare at the floor.

"He's shy," the girl said, walking in a close circle around her. She sniffed. "Smells funny too."

"Go find something to do Iris," Mr. Bentine's deep-voice ordered.

The girl left the room.

"What's your name, boy?" Mr. Bentine asked.

"Mac." She tried to make her voice sound huskier.

Mr. Bentine laughed. "I think we got us a boy that's not quite a man."

Mort joined the laughter.

"I want you to tell Wu, I'll be dropping off laundry tomorrow morning. And I expect it back here tomorrow night." The deep voice lowered to a near growl.

"He can't get your laundry back in one day. We've others to do as well."

A hand snaked out and grabbed her wrist. He turned the hand palm up. "You work in the laundry too?"

She nodded. No sense lying, her hands gave her away.

He didn't let loose of her wrist. He pulled her closer. "Look at me when I talk to you." He whipped her hat off her head.

Callie cursed Yi for talking her into not cutting her hair. It had grown since she started working in the laundry. It fell below her shoulders. She glared up into the face of Raymond Bentine. She'd watched him from a distance, listening to what others had to say about him.

His eyes widened in surprise before his mouth twisted into a smirk. "You look like a china doll. Men are going to pay good money to bed you." His grip tightened.

She curled her lips back. "I killed the last man that tried to bed me." She bit his hand.

He roared and released her wrist. She snatched her hat from his hand, smashed it on her head, and dashed by Mort, using the door the girl had left open. Dodging through the shrieking women and stunned men, she grabbed the door and swung it open. She heard hollering behind her as she dashed around tables in a direct line for the door.

The cold night air stung her lungs as she drew in gulps of air. She ducked around the corner and down an alley. Her legs pumped as fast as she could make them go, carrying her to the safety of a stairwell leading to the tunnels.

Inside the tunnel, she slid down the wall, clutched her knees to her chest, and gulped the moist, earthy scent of the sanctuary. She was of no use to Mr. Wu now. She couldn't deliver the laundry. Mr. Bentine would have men waiting for her. One of the stories she'd heard about him was the fact when he set his mind to getting a woman in his house, he got her by any means. He'd been linked to the murder of a pretty woman's husband. When she could no longer pay her debts, he paid them, then put her to work in his bordello.

She had to remain in the tunnels or move on.

Once her breathing was normal, she stood. Using the moonlight shining through the metal grids on the boardwalk above, she scurried down the tunnel to the communal kitchen. Her belly had been aching since before she hauled the last bundle of laundry to the Golden Rule.

The scents of fish, spices, and tea wafted to her as she neared the large area with a wood cookstove and long table. Mr. Wu paid to have his food cooked by Lin Huang, the cook. Mr. Wu didn't want Yi to socialize with the single men who ate in the communal kitchen and slept in the three high bunk beds in a dormitory-type area under the Josh house, a building the Chinese used as a place to worship. He also paid for food for Callie. She liked to eat in the kitchen area. It gave her time away from her employer and time to learn what was happening up on the streets.

Tonight, her heart beat in her throat as she approached the area. After her encounters, she really didn't feel like eating with the others, but she also didn't want to be alone.

Mr. Cai walked out of the kitchen carrying a tray.

He thrust the tray at her. "Eat. Feed man." He turned and walked back into the kitchen area.

She smiled at his abrupt manner and giving her the perfect situation to stay away from the others, yet not have to eat alone.

# Chapter Four

Donny smelled food and heard the swish of fabric.

"Doc, I need to know more about this place."

"I'm not Mr. Cai."

Mac's voice put a smile on his face. She was easier to talk to than the abrupt doctor.

"Do I smell food?" he asked, to ease her into a conversation. She hadn't acted friendly during their last conversation.

"Yes. I hope you like Chinese food. It's a bit different from what you're probably used to."

Dishes rattled and the sound of something scooting across the floor tilted his head toward the sound.

"Help me sit up. I can feed myself," he said, starting to push up with his hands. The twinge in his side reminded him that he couldn't move like before the beating.

Small, rough-skinned hands lifted his back, tucking scratchy wool blankets behind him until he was halfway propped up.

"That's all the blankets."

"I'll figure it out." He held his hands up, waiting for a plate or bowl.

The weight and roundness of a bowl settled in his hands. He raised it to his lips and sipped. The broth was close to the chicken soup his ma made but with a fishy taste. Chunks of something bumped his lips, but he continued drinking until no more broth slid between his lips.

"You have a spoon?" he asked.

"No. Down here we use chopsticks."

He released one hand from the bowl. A small hand cupped his hand. He felt two wooden sticks about the size of Kelda's knitting needles placed in his hand.

"How do I use these?" He tried stabbing the sticks into the bowl, but when he put the end in his mouth there was nothing on them.

Smothered giggles tittered in the air beside him. "For you it would be best to put the bowl to your mouth and use the sticks to scoop it in."

He tried several times and finally found the right angle to get the food into his mouth and operate the sticks. When three tries brought nothing into his mouth he decided the bowl was empty.

"Is there anything to drink?" he asked, enjoying the soft slurping as Mac ate her food.

"Yes, tea with your healin' herbs."

The bowl lifted from his hands. The sticks were removed, and a warm small cup nested against his right palm. He closed his fingers around the cup. The medicinal smell of the tea wasn't the refreshment he was looking for.

"From the way you're scrunchin' your nose, that tea doesn't taste too good."

"It's not as bad as some of the medicine Rachel gave me. The smell is actually worse than the taste." Donny held his breath and gulped down the whole cup at once. Better to get it over with.

"Who's Rachel and what's your name?" The question didn't sound curious, more like conversation.

"I'm Donny Kimball. Rachel is the wife of my boss, Clay Halsey." Donny's chest clenched with emotion thinking about how Rachel and Clay had brought him to Sumpter and allowed him to be treated like a whole man and not a man without sight.

"Your boss? How can you hold a job when you can't see?"

He bristled at the young woman's assumption he was worthless without his sight. "I can do just as much as most men. I taught others how to make brooms at the blind school since I lost my sight at the age of eight. Then Clay gave me a job at his business making writing tablets for the blind." He shoved his cup at her. "Soon as I can stand on this leg, I'll find Jasper and get back to Sumpter."

"Jasper the name of the Negro you were with?"

"Yes."

"He's at the jail. I heard the doc talking to the sheriff. They're tryin' to figure out who started the fight." Mac's tone told him something else had happened.

"You can tell them who started the fight. You saw it. Then bring Jasper here. He'll get me back to Sumpter." This was the first good news he'd heard since waking up from his beating.

"I can't talk to anyone. Especially the sheriff." The finality in her words struck him.

"What do you mean you can't talk to the sheriff? That's how you can get rid of me." He didn't understand anything. "Why are you and the doctor hiding under the ground?"

"It's not just me and Mr. Cai. There is a community of Chinese people who use the tunnels and some who live down here. The soiled doves use the tunnels to get about town too."

That was why he heard voices on the other side of the wall.

"Why are you all living down here?"

"The Chinese are here because the cowboys get liquored up and beat them, like they did you, if they walk the streets during the daylight hours. All a Chinese man has to do is look at a woman or cross the path of the wrong person and they find themselves dead or almost dead. The tunnels allow them to move about without being harmed."

"You made it sound like they live down here."

"Some do. There are a few families who have businesses and living space and there are single men who live in a dorm under the Josh house. There is a kitchen and bath for those of us who choose to live here. There are businesses, both Chinese and a few of our kind, down here. Laundries, baths, milliners, and gaming halls." Mac's voice hardened at the last comment.

"What do you do down here?" He wondered at her not being able to talk to the sheriff and hiding out with the Chinese.

"I work for and live with Mr. Wu's family. They took me in when I arrived. I help with the laundry and make the deliveries."

He heard hesitation in the last comment. "What about the deliveries?"

"What do you mean?" Her tone was defensive.

"I could tell by the way you said deliveries something happened." He moved his hand the direction of her voice. She flinched when he touched her. His fingers grazed the softness of flannel. Settling his hand, he discovered a small arm under the fabric. He hadn't been one for touching until Clay taught him it was the best way to connect with a person when you couldn't look in their eyes.

"Why are you nervous about making deliveries?"

She jerked her arm. He didn't tighten his grip, but didn't let go either. She pulled her arm far enough his ribs started to sear with pain. He wanted to keep contact but couldn't think with the pain. He released her arm.

"Don't touch me," she hissed.

The sound of her moving away from him made him regret his actions. "I didn't mean to scare you.

Without sight, touching is the way I see how a person is reacting."

"You don't need to know my reactions." Her voice came from lower down.

"What are you doing?" he asked.

"Spreading out my bedroll."

"Why?" He was in no shape to hobble around yet and couldn't see where to go anyway.

"I brought you to the tunnels and it's my responsibility to see you don't cause any trouble." Her statement sounded like a death sentence.

"I won't be going anywhere until this leg heals. You should go to your room." Even though the young woman was standoffish and being alone with him all night would ruin her reputation, he welcomed the idea of another person close by.

"I don't have a room. I have this bedroll. I sleep where I put it."

He heard rustling of clothing and a sigh.

"Good-night," he offered.

She grunted.

Donny smiled. If she had to keep an eye on him, he'd have time to figure out why she was down here and scared to make her deliveries. But he also had to get a telegraph to Clay in Sumpter, telling him what had happened.

*Chapter Five*

Callie listened until the man, Donny's, breathing evened and he snored just a bit before she pulled the object she'd found in the street out of her pocket. A pocket watch. She rubbed the dust off the watch and ran her fingers over the raised picture on the front. It was a locomotive. She turned the watch over. On the back was an inscription. *Raymond Bentine.* This was Mr. Bentine's watch! Was this what the men were looking for in Hubert's pockets? Had he stolen it from Mr. Bentine?

She opened the watch. Three numbers, *67-35-92*, were etched inside the lid and a small key sat in a metal cradle in the lid. Tick-tock. Tick-tock. It wasn't an old watch. Someone recently wound it and still used it. *Bentine!* She dropped the time piece onto her bedding. She couldn't take it to the man, he wanted her for his bordello. But she couldn't keep the watch either. It wasn't hers. She had to find a way to get it back to Bentine without him knowing she had it.

Callie scooped up the watch and dropped it into her trouser pocket. She'd figure out how to get it back to Mr. Bentine tomorrow.

The lantern light cast a glow on the face of the man on the cot. She turned her thoughts to him. Even knowing he was blind, she couldn't stare at him when he was awake. The man had an uncanny way of knowing things, and she was afraid he'd know if she stared at him. Which wasn't a polite thing to do.

His one eye was nearly swollen shut from his beating. There were bruises on his chest above the white bandage wrapped round his ribs. He was lucky the men hadn't killed him. From what the doctor had said about the Negro, Jasper, he was still alive. But by how much?

Her gaze rose back to Donny's face. *What am I going to do with him?* Once he was well enough to walk on his own, she couldn't set him loose out on the streets. But after getting caught by Mr. Bentine, and discovering she had his watch, she couldn't be seen on the streets for a while. He now knew she was the boy who delivered Wu's laundry. Or rather the girl.

She groaned.

*I have to tell Mr. Wu I can't deliver the laundry. He'll have to do it.* She smacked her forehead with her hand. She couldn't do nothin' about nothin' tonight. She turned the lantern down and settled onto her bedroll. Hopefully, tomorrow would look a bit brighter than things seemed tonight.

Callie heard Mr. Cai in the other room. She stretched, looked over at Donny—it was impossible to tell if he was sleeping or awake with his eyes swollen shut. She quickly pulled on trousers and a flannel shirt over her long johns.

"I've been thinking."

She jumped at the sound of the voice. "Criminy! You like scarin' people?"

He chuckled. "No. I heard you were awake and started talking."

"I thought you were asleep." She quickly buttoned her shirt and glared at the bed. The fool had a smile on his lips.

"I'm going to get bored lyin' here in bed all day. Is there anything I can do with my hands to keep me busy?"

The honesty of his words whisked her anger away.

"I don't have anythin'. Maybe Mr. Cai needs help with somethin'."

The curtain moved, and Mr. Cai carried in a tray with food, tea, and herbs.

"Mr. Cai, do you have something I can do with my hands to keep me from going crazy lyin' here?" Donny asked.

Callie peered down at the man. How did he know someone else entered the room?

"Yes. I find work." The firm and happy reply glinted in Mr. Cai's eyes.

She had no doubt Mr. Cai could find many things for Donny to do.

"Looks like you have his breakfast. I'll go get mine and get to work." Callie ducked out the curtain before either man could say a word. She had to make it up to Mr. Wu for not being able to handle the deliveries. And she had to figure out a way to get the watch back to Mr. Bentine.

The table was full in the kitchen. She smiled at the men sitting around it. They all thought of her as a boy. Which was exactly how she planned to keep it as long as she lived in the tunnels.

Lin Huang handed her a plate and motioned for her to sit on a chair by the stove.

She studied his face as she thanked him. His lips tipped in a gentler smile than usual, and his eyes held a softness they hadn't when he'd looked at her before. Her cheeks heated. He knew she wasn't a boy. How had he found out? She stole a furtive glance at the table. *They all knew!*

Instead of ignoring her, they stared. A lump caught in her throat. Will I still be safe down here?

Even though her stomach rumbled, she couldn't swallow the food. She'd only been this scared twice. The night her stepfather came to her room and last night when Bentine realized she wasn't a boy.

Lin Huang moved his body between her and the men at the table. "No worry. Missy Mac safe."

She peered up into his eyes. He'd seen her fear. "How did you find out?"

"Man came gambling halls look for Mac. Girl

deliver laundry." He spread his hands and shrugged. "Words travel."

Bentine sent his man looking for her. Why? There were more girls out on the streets who'd work for him. Or did he know she had the watch? "Did anyone tell him where to find me?"

Lin shook his head. "We not like on street. They not like in tunnel."

She was safe as long as she stayed in the tunnels. "Thank you." Callie ate the food, set her plate in the tub of water by the stove, and hurried to Wu's Laundry.

Yi met her at the door. "You hear?"

Callie had an idea what Yi meant but acted like she didn't. "What?"

"Man look for you. What happen yesterday?" Yi tugged on her shirt sleeve, leading her to her father by the fire that heated the wash water.

Mr. Wu shoved a piece of wood into the fire and faced them. "Tell what happen."

"I delivered the laundry and went to the jail to learn about the friend of the man I brought down here yesterday." The scene at the saloon flashed in her mind. She couldn't drag her friends into the trouble she'd found. "Coming back from the jail a drunk ran into me in front of Mr. Bentine's saloon. Bentine's big man pulled me into the building. Bentine wanted me to agree you would do his laundry. When I didn't, he grabbed me and figured out I'm not a boy. He wants me to work for him. I won't do it, but I can't deliver your laundry or even set foot on the streets now."

"True!" Yi said. "Man come gambling halls find Missy Mac." She put an arm around Mac's shoulders. "No worry. You stay us."

Mr. Wu stared at his daughter then at Callie. "Trouble come with man."

She understood he meant Donny. "He's blind. Can't see. What I did was right. But now I will have to get him well and move on." She ducked her head. "I'm sorry I brought trouble to your house."

Mr. Wu put a hand on her shoulder. "No trouble. Good worker." He waved his hand.

His gesture meant they should get to work. She hung her coat and hat on the hook by the door and rolled up her sleeves. Today she would work harder than ever. She owed it to these two people. While she worked, she'd figure out a way to get the watch back to Bentine. Maybe make him a deal. She'd give him his watch and in return, she wanted him to leave her alone.

Donny finished the food and drank the tea the doctor gave him. He felt the man's presence. "Do you want to ask me something?"

"You no see? Not just fight?"

"I can't see. I've been blind since I was eight." He drew in a breath. Even after all these years, the anger of how it happened hadn't diminished. "My pa hit me in the head, causing the blindness."

"Not right."

"Yes, that's how it happened." He knew what happened. The doctor hadn't been there.

"Not right father hit son."

Donny let out a whoosh of air. "Yeah. But there's not a lot a kid can do."

"Where mother?"

"He'd already knocked her unconscious. I was trying to keep him from hurting her worse." The day his father beat his mother and slammed him against a wall played out vividly in his mind when he lamented on his blindness.

"Father alive?"

"I'm not sure. He left and I've never seen him."

"Him dead."

Donny turned his head toward the voice. He couldn't see the man, but the finality of the words struck him. "How do you know?"

"Women allow be beat save children. Children hurt, mother make sure not happen again."

He'd never thought about Ma's reaction to his father hitting him. Had she taken care of him? He'd been lost in darkness and self-pity for several months after the incident. And his sister was too small to ask if she knew anything. The next time Ma came to Sumpter he'd ask her if she knew what happened to Pa.

"Do you have children?" he asked the doctor.

"No. I have mother." His voice held admiration.

"Is she here? With you?" Donny hadn't heard any female voices other than Mac's.

"No. Send money home." The man's movements came from the foot of the bed.

"Is there someone I can send to a telegraph office?" Lying awake waiting for Mac to wake this morning, he'd decided the best way to get out of here was to send a telegraph to Clay. Telling him they were in trouble and needed someone to come get them.

"Missy Mac."

"Why doesn't she want to talk to the sheriff?" Donny had pondered that while lying awake as well.

"Missy Mac have demons. Not ready share."

Something soft landed on Donny's chest. "Here. Make long."

"What's this?" He sunk his hands into soft fabric.

"Make bandage."

The shuffle and swish followed by quiet proved the man had left.

Donny moved the fabric through his hands until he found an edge. He was a burden on the man. The least he could do was make his own bandages.

What kind of demons did Mac have? And who would give a girl a name like Mac?

## Chapter Six

As much as Callie hated to admit it, not having to hide her face and duck away from people in the tunnel would be nice. Now that everyone knew she was a girl, she could go about like a normal person, instead of hiding in the shadows in fear they would discover her secret. Well, one of her secrets.

Yi straightened, pressing her red hands to the small of her back. "One day, I find man to marry. No more laundry."

Callie stared at Yi. She was five years older. "Why haven't you married?"

"Father no find man he like here. He save money to bring a husband to me." Yi dunked a sheet into the washtub.

"You'd marry a man you've never met?" Callie didn't plan to marry, but to marry a man you'd never met and find out he was as vile as her stepfather… Her stomach soured.

"Better husband than be alone." Yi scrubbed the sheet on the washboard.

Callie scrubbed the sheet in her tub. "I don't agree. What if he beats you, or—" she lowered her voice, "—takes your body without your consent?"

"Wife duty give her body to husband." Yi stared at her. "It is gift."

"What if he takes other women to bed, not just you?" She squeezed her eyes closed blocking out the angry, drunk face of her stepfather.

"If wife give gift, husband not find other." Yi stopped scrubbing, wiped her hands on her apron, and walked over to Callie. "What happen? Husband find another?"

She shook her head. "No. No husband. Step-father came to my bed." She scrubbed the sheet hard on the boards. Her hands clenched so tight her knuckles ached.

"No take out on sheet." Yi grabbed her hands, halting her frantic scrubbing. "Him win. You bitter."

Callie stared at her. "Bitter? You think I'm bitter? I'm more than bitter." She flung the sheet into the tub and stalked out of the room. She walked blindly through the tunnel with nowhere to go. Tears streamed down her face. Yi was the first person she'd told about her stepfather and she didn't get angry. What was wrong with her? How could a woman not get angry over a man taking advantage of another woman? Especially one that he was sup-posed to protect?

She stopped, slammed her fist against the cold

stone wall, slid down the wall into a crouch, and cried.

"Who's out there?" Donny called. "I can hear you crying. Who is it?"

*Dang!* She'd stopped outside Mr. Cai's. Callie sniffed and worked to control the anger and the sobs. The only other time she'd cried was after she'd thrown some clothes in a bag, climbed out her window, and ran to the train station. Once she was on the train and headed west, she'd cried for an hour. The other passengers had stared at her, but she didn't care. All the pent up fear and feelings had to come out if she were to survive.

A crash thrust her to her feet. She dashed through the first room, shoved the curtain to the side, and found Donny face down on the floor, the small table by the bed overturned.

"You are a fool. I thought so when I found out you were blind and jumped in the middle of the fight and this just proved it." Ignoring the pain in the hand she'd slammed against the wall, she tugged on his arm, drawing him up onto his knees.

His hands grasped her shoulders, steadying him. Then his hand brushed against her cheek.

"It was you crying."

He placed the palm of his hand against her cheek. "What made you cry?"

She jerked her face away but not before her soul welcomed the comforting contact.

"Nothin' you'd care to hear." She stood, pulling him up. "Tryin' to get out of bed was foolish."

"I understand you think I'm a fool. But I heard

someone in pain and wanted to help." He sat. His bruised face had turned all the colors of a sunset. Purple, blue, gray, orange, red.

"You're lookin' colorful today." She giggled.

"Glad I can entertain you." Donny remained sitting on the edge of the cot. "Any chance you can prop me up. Doc left a pile of bandages for me to tear into strips. It's hard to do layin' on my back."

She toed the pile of cloth on the floor. "When you asked for work, Mr. Cai found you some."

"Yeah."

Callie rolled up the blankets and her bedroll, placing it against the wall at the head of the bed. "Scoot to your right a little more. There." She put her hands on his shoulders guiding him against the padding.

"Thank you. Can you hand that cloth to me?" He held his hands out.

She scooped up the fabric and set it on his lap. Fascinated, she watched him pick up a piece and work his hands around the edges then move his fingers to a corner and start tearing a strip about four inches wide. He then rolled the strip into a tight roll. When he finished that one, he found the cloth on top of the pile and did the same thing. He was good with his hands for not seeing what he was doing.

"You gonna tell me why you were crying?" he asked, moving his fingers over the cloth and tearing.

"You don't need my troubles." She found a stool and plopped down on it when she should have headed back to the laundry. Running out like that wasn't proving to her or anyone else she was a grown woman. She'd stormed out like a child.

"I owe you for dragging me off the street and getting me a doctor." His hands continued working. "Least I can do is listen. By the way you were crying, I think you need to talk to someone."

"Talk about what?" Again, his insight into her made her balk when moments before she'd liked the idea of telling her trouble to someone.

He chuckled. "I have a feeling you've never told anyone a thing about you." His face tipped her way. "Is Mac really your name?"

By the intake of air, Donny knew he'd been right about Mac not being her name. "It's not Mac. I didn't think the name fit with your soft voice." He was going to say angelic but had heard enough conversations between the Halsey brothers to know when to push a woman and when to wait them out.

"Mac fits me for where I live and how I live." Defiance punctuated each word.

He ran his fingers along the cloth and pulled the fabric, tearing it into another bandage. "How do you live?" He'd let the name go for now. Something had caused her to sob as if every inch of her was in pain. He planned to find out the reason.

"Here in the tunnels with the Chinese, I dress like a boy and pass myself off as a boy, here and… in the streets."

She hesitated before in the streets.

"Why do you live down here and pretend to be a boy?"

"It's safer. You were beat up for driving down the street with a Negro. Think what would happen to a girl with no one to protect her."

He didn't like to think what some liquored up cowboy would do to the small woman. Each time she'd helped him, he had a better impression of her size. She was tiny. Darcy, Gil's wife, was small, but Mac was even tinier. She could easily pass herself off as a boy as long as no one heard her speak. I wonder what her face looks like? He pondered that a moment. Was she plain enough to pass as a boy or did she have to hide a face as angelic as her voice? That thought conjured up images in his mind that heated his body a different way than a good wood fire.

"How do you deliver the laundry if you don't like to be on the streets?" As small as she was, he hoped she delivered small items to fancy houses.

"I'd follow the tunnel that opened closest to the hotel and take the laundry when everyone is hurrying home from the end of the day and the cowboys are getting dinner."

"Hotel? You carry large bundles?" He tried to frown but it hurt his face.

"Bedding. Mr. Wu washes the bedding for four hotels." Pride echoed in her words.

"You think a lot of Mr. Wu." He wasn't sure he liked how she favored the Chinaman.

"He and his daughter Yi took me in when I arrived. They've been good friends." The defiant tone returned.

Donny smiled. "I see. Is Yi a young girl?"

A soft laugh lightened the mood in the room. "No. She's older than me by five years. She's my size and loves to laugh. We work together in the laundry."

Air stirred and he heard her footsteps moving toward the door. "Where are you going?"

"Back to work. I owe the Wu's everything. I shouldn't have took off like I did."

"Will you be back later?" He needed to ask her to telegraph Clay, but didn't want to appear as if he only conversed with her to get her to do things for him.

"At the end of the day."

"How long till then?" Being blind the concept of time was lost. He never knew when it was day or night unless someone told him or he could feel the heat of the sun.

"Six hours." Her footsteps faded.

That's a long time to spend with my own thoughts. He ripped the cloth and rolled the bandages. Rolling the last strip of fabric, he heard voices in the other room. They spoke in what he now knew was Chinese. He detected the doctor's voice and another man. The conversation sounded genial. Then a voice rose and the room went silent.

Donny held the rolled bandage and listened intently.

Fabric swished and the footsteps of the doctor entered the room.

"Unhappy patient?" Donny asked.

His body tensed. He had the feeling the man was staring at him.

"No patient. Suitor."

Dishes clanked and he caught a whiff of the

soup the doctor fed him.

"Suitor? A man wants to marry you?" He'd not heard of such a thing but he didn't know much about Chinese customs.

"Not me. Missy Mac."

Donny shoved to a little straighter sitting position. "She said everyone thought she was a boy."

"Mean man learn different yesterday. Come looking for Mac last night. Now all tunnel know she girl."

The bandages disappeared from his lap. The smell of the broth close to his nose brought his hands up, and the bowl was placed in his palms.

"Who is the mean man?" Donny took a sip of the soup.

"Him have house with many women." The man's tone showed his disapproval.

"A bordello?" How had she run into a man who ran a house of ill-repute?

"Man also have saloon and gambling hall."

The clink and smell of sweet tea leaves told Donny the doctor was preparing his healing tea.

He drank the rest of his soup and thought. Could that be why Mac was crying? The Chinese man had asked her to marry him?

"What's the Chinese man's name who wants to marry Mac?"

"Lin Huang. He cook."

The bowl disappeared from his hands and was replaced with a teacup with no handle.

Donny drank the tea and pondered the information. He finished and asked, "I take it from the way the man was upset, this Lin Huang, you told him he couldn't marry Mac."

"Told him she make her own decision. She American not Chinese." The doctor took his empty cup.

He smiled. Then frowned. "He wanted you to tell her to marry him?"

"Chinese have arranged marriage. Man of high station in village say who get married."

"That's wrong. Two people marry because they are in love not because someone says they should." He may not be looking for a wife, but he'd witnessed the marriages of the Halsey brothers. Even Jeremy and Colin had found the perfect wives for them. They had all married women they were head-over-heels in love with. And from what he could tell, they were all about as happy as a group of people could be.

"Here, yes. China, no." The clinking of dishes meant the doctor was getting ready to leave.

"Will this man force Mac to marry him?" He didn't know why he was so worried about her, but he didn't like the idea of her not being able to pick the man she wanted.

"No. I refuse marriage, he mad but not ask." The doctor put his hands on Donny's shoulder. "Check bandages."

Donny relaxed against the bedding behind him and let his thoughts wander to the small young woman who'd saved him as the doctor unwrapped and re-wrapped his ribs and wiggled the toes on the foot of his broken leg.

# *Chapter Seven*

Callie worked beside Yi the rest of the day. They said very little to one another. Yi had smiled when Callie returned. She'd nodded but went straight to work. After hours of bending over the washtub, Callie wished she could deliver the baskets of laundry Mr. Wu stacked by the door. She knew it was foolish to think she could make the deliveries without running into one of Mr. Bentine's men.

Mr. Wu straightened. "Missy Mac."

She faced him, crossing her arms. Was he going to make her do the deliveries?

He motioned to the two stools she and Yi sat on when taking a break mid-day. Callie took her usual seat. Mr. Wu sat on the one Yi usually sat on. Yi moved to stand behind her father.

"Missy Mac, many know you girl."

She nodded. "I'm not much use to you now that Mr. Bentine is looking for me."

Mr. Wu nodded. "Dwee, dwee. Lin Huang asked to marry Missy Mac."

Lin Huang? Marry? She shook her head. "No. I don't want to marry anyone. He's nice, but no." She put her hands out as if to ward off an unseen attack.

Mr. Wu peered into her face. "I not your father. I not say yes."

"Thank you!" She sprang off the stool and hugged the man around the neck.

He patted her arm and she straightened.

The serious expression on his face and the sadness in his eyes squeezed her chest. Something more was about to be said.

"We think you family. Others say you not belong here. Trouble follow you."

Staring into his face, she saw the words pained him. They pained her too. Her chest squeezed. She couldn't catch her breath.

Yi ran to her side. She put an arm around Callie's shoulders. "Get man well. He protect you."

She shook her head. "He can't see. He can't protect me." Callie didn't believe in begging. But she knew to set foot outside the tunnels meant she'd end up either dead or wishing she was dead.

Dropping to her knees, she grabbed Mr. Wu's hands.

"Let me stay until the man is well. When he leaves I will too. I promise." Mr. Cai said it would take a month for Donny to heal well enough to walk on his own with crutches. That would give her time to make a plan.

Mr. Wu tugged his hands from hers and nod-ded.

"Xia xia!" she said. "Thank you!"

"Go to man. Get him well." Mr. Wu walked over to the deliveries and picked one up. He disappeared out the door.

Yi hugged her. "Help your man. He will help you."

She didn't see how he could help her, but at least he gave her more time.

Donny heard Mac speaking to the doctor before he caught the scent of lye soap. Her footsteps entered the room along with the clank of dishes.

"Is it dinner time?" he asked.

"Yes, how did you know?" Her skepticism made him smile.

"I can smell the soup and hear the clank of the dishes."

"Did you know it was me?" she asked.

"Yes. I smelled lye soap. The doctor smells like herbs." He wanted to ask her about the cook who asked to marry her. But he knew better than to blurt it out.

"Soup," she said.

He held out his hands palms up. She placed the bowl in them.

"I see you finished the bandages."

Donny swallowed the soup in his mouth. "I also tied knots in string. Makes me wonder what he'll give me to do after a couple weeks."

Mac laughed. "I'm sure Mr. Cai has all kinds of things you can do."

"That's what I'm afraid of." He finished his soup while Mac chuckled.

"Are you going to eat?" he asked when he didn't hear sounds of her eating.

"There isn't enough for me and you. I'll have Mr. Cai bring me something from the kitchen."

Was she avoiding the cook? "I can be trusted to eat alone. I won't drown in my bowl of soup."

"No. I'll wait."

"Are you avoiding the cook because he wants to marry you?" He mentally slapped himself for saying exactly what he'd planned to wait to ask.

"No! How did you know he—and what business is it of yours!" Her footsteps paced the room. Six across, six footsteps back. As tiny as she was, she must be pacing at a lengthened stride.

"I heard the doc and some man talking. Then the other man got loud and left. I asked Doc what they were talking about. He said the man asked him to arrange a marriage between you two."

The pacing stopped. "He what?" The pacing resumed. "That low-life pot scrubber. What the heck makes him think I'd agree to an arranged marriage? I'm not Yi. Why the lousy, no-good—"

"I'd think you'd be flattered a man wanted to marry you." Donny held out the bowl. It whipped from his hands, and he was left holding air.

A loud thunk echoed through the small room.

"What woman would be flattered to have men decide who they should or shouldn't marry?" Her tone held more anger than the topic warranted.

"Is that why you're mad? Cuz he didn't ask you?" Was she sweet on the Chinaman?

"No! I don't want him or anyone else to ask if I'll marry him. I'm not marrying anyone. Men can't be trusted. They leave or they carouse. There's not a faithful bone in their bodies."

"Wait a minute! Not all men are unfaithful. I know seven men who have always been faithful to their wives." Donny had witnessed the kindness and love the Halsey men had for their wives. Just being in the room with one of the happy couples left a person feeling happy.

"Seven out of how many in the world!" She grasped his hand and shoved the teacup in his palm.

Liquid sloshed onto his bare chest. "Hey! Don't burn me with tea because some other man hurt you. We aren't all bad."

"Says you! A man!" A rough cloth rubbed the wet spot on his chest.

"Stop. Just stay back so I can drink the tea instead of wear it."

"Hmmph!" The lye scent disappeared and the swish of the curtain left the room silent.

She was one prickly woman. He sipped his tea and waited. Someone had to return to get the dishes. He hoped it was Mac, but she could very well tell the doc she was through with him.

He placed the cup on the floor by the cot and dissected her words and actions. She didn't think men could be faithful. What gave her that idea? Her pa? A beau? Both? She was feisty. But vulnerable.

Her sobbing outside the door earlier in the day had made his heart ache. What had caused that? Thinking of the woman only brought on question after question.

Callie stood in Mr. Cai's main room. He sat in a chair smoking an opium pipe and smiling. She wanted to say something but didn't want big-ears in the other room to know she was only on the other side of the curtain. She'd stormed out before remembering she wasn't wanted anywhere else.

She stood by the door, her arms crossed, trying to decide how to get dinner and how to remain hidden.

Mr. Cai motioned to the table where he mixed his medicine. There was a steaming bowl of soup and chopsticks in the middle of the table.

She glanced back at the Chinaman. He motioned for her to eat.

Her stomach grumbled. She picked up the bowl and sticks and sat on a small padded stool. The food helped settle her mind and her temper. *I have to make friends with Donny. He may be blind, but he's my only hope of getting out of here safely. When he leaves, I'll go with him and light out from there.*

She finished the soup and set the bowl and sticks back on the table. She needed a clean set of flannels and a bath. It had been over a month since she'd washed with more than a rag. She'd had her monthly between that time. Her cheeks heated. The way the man in the next room said he could smell her, she wondered if he noticed more than the lye soap.

The next problem was getting to the bath and back without running into anyone. And she needed a guard. There was only a curtain across the bathing room. I could pay Mr. Lee Ting double and he would watch for me. She stared at the curtain. I have to sneak in and get my clean pair of flannels out of my bed roll that's under Donny.

## Chapter Eight

Donny sensed someone at the same time a slight breeze fluttered against his cheek. The scent of lye grew stronger. She was sneaking back. He nestled deeper into his back rest. If she wanted to go to sleep, she'd have to make her presence known to get her bedroll.

The roll under his back tugged. He grabbed her wrist, holding her next to his head.

"Ask if you want your bedroll." There was something about the feisty woman that made him want to challenge her.

"I need my bedroll," she said.

"That's not asking." He locked his fingers around her wrist not allowing her to retreat, but not hurting her either. His years of using his hands to make brooms and now handle woodworking tools had given him a good grip.

"Don't see why I have to ask for my own bed-roll."

Her belligerence only fueled his desire to squabble with her.

"Because it's the polite thing to do. You generously used your things to prop me up, you could at least ask nice to get them back." He released her wrist. "Not sneak in here and yank it out from behind me."

"I wasn't sneaking. I thought you were asleep."

"And I wouldn't notice when my body flopped back against the wall?"

The bedroll yanked from under him. His body and head smacked into the cold, solid stone wall.

"Ouch!" He rubbed the back of his head. "I would have let you have your bedroll, you didn't have to do that."

"Why do you test my good sense?" Her voice lowered an octave.

"Can't figure out why you have such a grudge against everyone." Donny countered. He didn't want to tell Callie, he poked at her to get a rise because it kept her around longer than giving in and her rushing away from him.

"I don't have a grudge against everyone. Just most men I come across. Only a few have been honest."

This added credence to his earlier thoughts about a man hurting her.

"Well, I'm honest," he said, easing his body down to settle his head on the folded blankets she left on the cot.

"I haven't seen you anywhere but in that bed and out on the street getting beat up. Hard to tell if you're honest."

He heard the shuffle of her feet headed to the door. "Where're you going?" She sure had a way of vanishing.

"I'll be back."

The room was still. Only the faint scent of lye hung in the air with the doctor's smoke and herbs.

I have to ask her to send the telegraph tomorrow. There's no telling how bad off Jasper is.

Callie hurried down the tunnels to the bath house run by the old Chinaman, Ting Lee. He sat on a stool at the opening of the small rock room. A lantern on a wall hanger fluttered from the breeze she made.

He stood. "Missy Mac. Not be here."

"I need a bath." She held up two nickels. "I'll give you double to sit here and keep others away."

He glanced up and down the tunnel, shoved her in, and closed the curtain.

Callie dipped her fingers into the water in the tub. It was the end of the day and the water had a grayish tint to it. She didn't want to ask how many others had used the water before her. She would get all wet and scrub, then stand and pour the fresh bucket of water over her to sluice off the dirty water.

Knowing her presence made Ting Lee nervous, she hurriedly undressed, stepped into the tepid water, quickly scrubbed, and stood. She picked up the bucket and slowly poured it over her head and down her body. Stepping out, she picked up a rough cloth and dried.

Donning her clean flannels, she then put a clean shirt and pants on. She stuffed her wet hair under her hat, her feet into her boots, and picked up her bedroll and dirty clothes.

She exited the small room.

"Thank you," she said to Ting Lee and hurried back to Mr. Cai's.

Mr. Cai was curled on a bed roll in his main room. She tiptoed past him and into the room she now shared with Donny.

The lantern flickered as she entered.

"Mac, is that you?" Donny questioned, his nostrils flaring as he inhaled.

"Yes." She spread her bedroll on the floor, tied her dirty clothes into a bundle, and sat, drawing a comb out of the small bag where she kept her personal items.

"Where'd you go? You smell different." He remained on his back, but his face turned her direction.

"I took a bath." She pulled the comb through her hair, taking out tangles and preparing it to braid.

"Down here? How do they do that?" The swelling around his eyes was starting to go down.

"There's a well down here everyone draws water from. Mr. Wu hauls the water to his laundry from the well every day."

"How much of the town is above the tunnels?"

His curiosity and conversation away from her released the tension in her shoulders.

"The center of the town is over the tunnels. The tunnels were built originally to transfer gold from the banks to the railroad. They are still used by some of the shopkeepers to move freight to and from their businesses. The tunnels lead to a few of the Chinese houses and businesses above ground, and a couple tunnels go out farther for the Chinese who work in homes to get there safely."

"And the folks of Pendleton know you are all down here?"

"Yes. They prefer the Chinese stay hidden. They want the Chinese to do the work they don't want to do but not to live with them." She had found the Chinese to be hospitable and kind-hearted. She didn't understand the townspeople's hatred or fear of them.

"Seems kind of cowardly of the townsfolk."

His statement echoed her feelings. "Yes." She braided her hair, tied it with a strip of leather, and put her brush away. "And that's why I prefer to stay down here."

"Good night." She turned the lantern off, slipped out of her shirt and pants, and slid into her bedroll. The room was quiet. She couldn't even hear Donny breathing.

"What's your real name?" he asked in a quiet voice.

"How do you know it isn't Mac?" she whispered back.

"It doesn't feel right."

She glanced toward the bed. The room was too dark to see anything. "It doesn't feel right? That's not a good reason to know it isn't really my name."

"So you're admitting Mac isn't your real name?"

The triumph in his voice made her smile. He'd only guessed it wasn't.

"While I'm here my name is Mac." He might not be able to see, but if he said her real name to anyone that might have read about her stepfather's death, they'd know the law was looking for her.

"But I don't like calling you by a name that isn't yours."

His insistent whisper didn't budge her resolve.

"Then don't talk to me." She settled into her bed and closed her eyes.

"I need you to go to the telegraph office tomorrow."

His blunt statement yanked her from any blissful sleep she might have had. "Why?" Not that she'd go waltzing into the telegraph office for any reason.

"I need to send a telegraph to Clay. Let him know we need his help." Donny's cot creaked.

"Stay put. I can't go to the telegraph office. You'll have to find another way to send the message." Her mind raced. If he gets help to get out of here, I could leave earlier. But can I chance going to the telegraph office? It's not far from the end of one of the tunnels.

"Why can't you go?" He no longer whispered.

"For the same reason I can no longer deliver the laundry." She shivered at the thought of Mr. Bentine finding her. Reaching into the pocket of her folded pants, her fingers clutched the watch. Not only did she have something that belonged to him, he wanted her to work in his bordello. She'd never let a man touch her like that again.

# Chapter Nine

Donny didn't understand Mac's reluctance to go out of the tunnels. Was there someone out there looking for her? He heard her moving around. Why wasn't she asleep? If she was awake she could give him an answer.

"I need to contact Clay. He can come get Jasper out of jail and get me home. I can't hobble to the jail and vouch for Jasper." He needed her to see, he was more worried about Jasper than himself. Which was the truth. In the years Donny had worked with Jasper, he'd always put others first and had been a good example. "Given the things the men said before and while beating up Jasper and me, they don't take kindly to Negros any more than they do the Chinese. He needs someone to get him out of here."

"I'll think about it."

The unease in her voice didn't tell him if she would actually think about it or was just stalling.

"Think hard. If he dies in that jail, it will be on your hands because you dragged me down here with people I can't talk to and can't find my way out." He hated to put guilt on her, but he didn't see any other way to get her to do what was right. Get help for Jasper.

"I won't kill another," Mac whispered.

His ears pricked and he listened harder. What did she mean kill another? Did he dare ask? As stubborn and contrary as she was, he'd wait until he knew her better before he asked.

"Why are you scared to walk around the streets?" He waited. No response. "Besides being a girl who's alone? There are lots of other females walking around the streets without escorts." He didn't think that was the whole reason. She could easily scream or duck into a store if someone made advances.

"It's none of your concern," she snapped.

"It is my concern when I need a telegraph sent and you're the only person I know who can do it." He listened. She could sure make herself quiet. "I've got money in my pockets to pay for the telegraph." He waited then added, "And you for your trouble."

"Money won't buy me."

She said the word money as if it were a pile of cow manure.

"What do you have against money? It can get you food when you're hungry, a place to sleep if you're tired. I bet you paid for that bath."

She humphed.

He wished he had sight to see her expressions when she talked. He had a notion, he'd discover more about her if he could watch her. But he couldn't and would have to use conversation and the way she responded to gauge her thoughts.

"You're going to have a tough time in life if you hate money and men."

"I don't hate money. I like money I've made by an honest day's work. Not handed to me asking for favors."

"Taking a message to the telegraph is a favor to me. But it is also an honest way to get a few coins. I can't go, therefore I'll pay you to take my message to be sent."

"I prefer not to go out of the tunnels." Her tone was more wary than firm.

"I don't understand your fear of the streets. I'm blind and I'd walk the streets if I could."

"Where do you live?" She changed the subject.

He didn't mind. Perhaps by talking about him, she'd reveal something about her.

"I live in a small cabin with Jasper."

"The Negro in jail?" she asked.

"Yes. We both moved to Sumpter from the Blind School in Salem ten years ago to work for Clay Halsey. He's blind. That's where we met him, at the blind school."

"You have a blind man for a boss?"

The awe in her voice made him smile. He was proud of Clay, and of himself. They'd both worked hard to not be a burden on anyone and to make their own way after becoming blind.

"Yes. The accident that blinded him happened when he was an adult. Mine happened when I was eight." He swallowed back the bitterness he always felt when reliving that day.

"I thought people were born blind."

"Some are. Some become blind after blows to the head or injuries to the eyes." He thought of Clay and how his best friend had blinded him by throwing dynamite at him in a cave. And his own encounter with his father.

"What caused your blindness?"

It was a simple question. And the answer was simple as well.

"My pa slammed me into a wall."

Her intake of breath and the sound of cloth rustling made his chest clench. He didn't want pity.

"Was he drinkin'?" she softly asked.

"Yeah." He tried hard to not let that day rush in and harden his heart.

"Men folks do mean, vile things when they're drinkin'."

The words were said low but filled with anger.

"Your father drink?" Finally an opening to find out more about her.

"No. He died. Ma remarried a man who came home drunk every night." Her voice was cold and monotone.

"He hurt your ma or you?" Knowing how small Mac was, he couldn't imagine her living through a beating.

"Never touched Ma." The rustling of someone settling into their bedding whispered through the room. "He won't touch anyone again."

The uttered words hung in the darkness before echoing in his head. He had a feeling he knew why Mac was hiding in the tunnels under Pendleton.

Callie remained as still as she could, listening to Donny's even breathing. She had become no longer useful to Mr. Wu and had something that belonged to Mr. Bentine. She had no doubt he'd be looking a lot harder for her when he discovered she was the person with his watch. She had to find a way to get the watch back to him and get out of town. The best thing for her to do would be to send the telegraph for Donny and talk him into taking her with him to Sumpter. From there she could light out as far as the money she'd saved from working for Mr. Wu would take her.

She wasn't sure how she'd get out of the tunnel without being seen. Everyone would be looking for the young-boy disguise.

Maybe she could borrow a dress from the laundry. She'd pull Yi into the plan tomorrow and between them they might be able to come up with a solution to get to the telegraph office without Mr. Bentine's men spotting her. She wasn't under any illusions that anyone would care if one of the gambling hall's thugs picked her up and hauled her through the street. She could pretend she found the watch on the floor of the telegraph office and hand it over to the clerk. She smiled. Yes, that would be the best way to get the watch back to Bentine. She wouldn't have to go near the man, but the watch would be returned.

While she wanted to believe most of the townsfolk were good people, they were also scared of the riffraff that ran the gambling halls and bordellos.

There was law, but it was spread thin in the rapidly growing town. And she didn't want to go anywhere near the law for fear they would discover her identity.

She mentally clicked off the names of the women who had clothes delivered to the Wu laundry. There was a possibility she would fit in dresses of two of the women. But she wouldn't be able to deliver the telegraph until the women sent a dress to be cleaned. She had little to fear until that day.

Then why did her stomach churn thinking about the watch and her trip to the telegraph office?

*Chapter Ten*

Donny had been awake long enough to mentally write a letter to his mother and sister when he heard rustling noises in the room.

"Did sleeping on it help any?" he asked.

"Eeek! I wish you'd stop scarin' me like that." Mac's admonishment was half angry, half joking.

"Sorry. Next time I'll wave my hand." He shifted. His body was tired of laying in the bed but the doc said he couldn't walk on his leg for several weeks. "Well, did you think on taking a telegraph for me?"

"I did."

"And?"

"I'll do it."

The sound of paper rustling buoyed his spirits. She was going to send the telegraph. He'd be out of here in a few days.

"Who and where does it need to go?" she asked.

"Clay Halsey, Sumpter, Oregon."

Scratching of lead on paper was the only sound in the room.

"What do you want it to say?"

"Jasper in Jail. Donny injured. Come right away."

"That's it?" she asked.

"Clay knows where we are. That will get him here and get Jasper out of jail." That was his highest concern. That Jasper was taken care of. The man had been like a father to him since they left the blind school.

"All right. Where did you say the money was to send this?"

"Should find money in the pocket of my trousers." He didn't hesitate to tell her. From what he knew about her so far, he didn't believe she would steal from him.

Sounds of rummaging and the clink of coins came from the head of the bed but down low.

"How much you think this is going to cost? I've never sent a telegraph before," Mac asked. Her soft words warmed the air beside his head.

"Take a dollar. That should cover it for sure. Use the rest to buy me a razor and soap." He ran a hand over his whiskered chin. "This stuff itches."

"You can shave yourself?" The awe in her voice made him smile.

"I can do just about anything any other man can do. Sometimes it takes me a little longer, but I can do it myself."

"Sorry. I didn't mean to sound like you were a dimwit or something." The coins jingled. "I've never been around a blind person before. There's been times I found myself in the tunnels without a lantern and I had to follow the sides with my hands."

Donny tried to sit up. The movement tweaked his ribs and he moaned.

"Here, let me help you."

The small hands he now knew to be Mac's held his back as she stuffed items behind him.

"Thank you. I'm getting tired of layin' around. Wish I hadn't injured my leg." He wouldn't feel sorry for himself. That was one emotion he'd learned didn't do a lick of good. He'd had enough self-pity when he first became blind. It nearly made him crazy. He wasn't going there again.

"Soon as Mr. Cai says you can walk, I'll take you around the tunnels. You'll need to get your strength up for when Clay comes and gets you."

The earthy scents of the room beyond the curtain floated in.

"You leaving?" he asked.

"I have things to do before I help at the laundry."

He heard hesitation in her voice.

"You going to the telegraph office?" He didn't want to be wrong about her stealing from him or lying to him.

"I have to get something from someone first. See you tonight."

The curtain cut off the earthy scents and muffled her words. Donny sat on the bed, wishing he could get Mac to sit next to him and allow him to touch her face and feel her emotions when she talked. From the little he'd learned about her, he had the notion she was hiding from herself as much as from someone else.

Callie hurried down the tunnels using the sunlight filtering in through the iron grates and stopped outside the laundry. She was early. But she had to talk with Yi while her father was hauling the water for the day.

"You early," Yi said, making piles of laundry beside the two wash tubs.

Callie grasped Yi's hands, stalling her movements. "I need your help. You can say no if you don't want to help."

Yi's cat-shaped eyes stared into Callie's. "You sister. I help."

"I need to borrow a dress from either Mrs. Nelding or Mrs. Shield when they send one to be laundered."

"Borrow?" The young woman's brow wrinkled in a frown.

"Use the dress for a short time and give it back." Callie studied Yi. It wasn't like stealing. She only needed to wear the dress long enough to go to the telegraph office and send the message to Donny's boss.

"Why need dress?"

"Donny needs me to send a telegraph. But I can't go on the streets like this. Mr. Bentine has men looking for me. But I could slip past them dressed as a lady. They aren't looking for me in a dress."

Yi's eyes lit up and her lips curved into a large smile. "Dwee, dwee. Missy Mac make very pretty woman."

Callie wasn't as sure of that, but she knew it was the best disguise to stay away from Bentine's thugs. They were looking for a girl posing as a boy not a woman.

"Don't tell anyone. Not even your father. This has to be a secret between us. As soon as one of the ladies drops off laundry, I'll use a dress and send the telegraph." Having the plan in place lessened the jitters in her stomach. At least until she actually had to step onto the street dressed in someone else's clothes.

Donny whittled on a piece of smooth wood the doctor gave him. The man had been in a hurry this morning, giving Donny little chance to ask questions or have a talk. The longer he remained underground, the harder it was to help Jasper. His worry for his friend was as strong as his concern for the young woman who tended him. He wondered at the reason she refused to set foot out of the tunnels and the statement she'd uttered the night before. Could that small woman have killed a man? If so, he had no doubt the man had been in the wrong and not the woman.

She'd shown her honesty by helping and not robbing him and leaving him in the street.

Noise beyond the curtain caught his attention.

Voices speaking in what he now knew to be Chinese. They were low and congenial. Clinking of dishes and the air stirred, inviting in the aroma of the broth he was fed twice a day.

"Do you have time to talk?" he asked, knowing by the herbal scent it was the doctor and not Mac.

"Yes." A chair scooted across the floor.

"Tell me more about the man who has Mac hiding in the tunnels." The man had avoided his questions about her earlier. He hoped the doctor would be more candid now.

"Not my story—"

"I know not your story to tell," Donny cut him off. "I need her to send a telegraph. She was reluctant but finally gave in. I worry she won't get it done in time to help my friend who was also beat up and is in jail." He drew in a breath. "I think I know why she was living down here when I arrived." He was pretty sure she killed a man. But he didn't fear her. He also had the impression it was out of self-defense. But she'd been crying. That was caused by something new. A new fear.

"I want to know about the man who is looking for her. This gambling hall and bordello owner."

"Mr. Bentine has a reputation for getting the prettiest women for his house."

"You mean he pays them well?" Was that why Mac was against being paid for doing a favor?

"No. He see woman he want, he do anything to get her." The monotone delivery of the statement proved the man didn't like talking about Bentine.

"What do you mean anything? Like take her

against her will?"

"Or get rid of anyone in way. For this reason, Mac asked to leave here when you leave."

Donny had stopped whittling when he started the conversation. The stinging of his knuckles drew his attention to the tight grasp he had on both the wood and the knife.

"I don't like the sounds of this Bentine." He had to get her out of here. He couldn't do it alone. Once they contacted Clay, he'd have help. "I'll take Mac with me when I leave. But how do I keep her safe in the meantime?" He didn't know what Bentine looked like or how to keep her safe from men he couldn't see. The sooner they could get help the better.

"She must stay in tunnel where she can hide. Friends keep safe." The doctor rose and relieved Donny's hands of the stick and knife.

The smell of broth wafted before his nose. He raised his hands. The weight of the bowl in his palms meant it was time to stop talking and eat. But he could think as he ate. He'd sent Mac to the streets to send the message to Clay. If Bentine caught her, he'd never forgive himself.

# Chapter Eleven

Donny waited for Mac to return to the room. If she didn't return, he would know his need to save Jasper could have put her in peril. If she did return, he would talk her out of sending the message.

The doctor had settled the stick and knife back in Donny's hands when he'd finished eating. The hours ticked by with only the slight murmuring of voices on the other side of the wall and his own thoughts battling in his head.

He'd drifted to sleep at some point and woke when the point of his knife poked his arm. I need to move, keep my body from getting stiff. He placed the knife and stick on the floor and methodically moved his hands, wrist, arms, and the good foot and leg. Keeping them limber without causing pain to his ribs and broken leg.

Herbs and lye filled the room at the same moment a slight breeze chilled his arms.

"I see if Mr. Cai doesn't give you somethin' to do you make somethin' up."

The humor in Callie's voice made him smile.

"You finished at the laundry today?" he asked, letting the relief he felt at her return warm his voice.

"Yes. Why are you so relieved to see me?" Her curiosity didn't hide the warmth in her words.

He knew what he was going to say would spin the contrary woman to her usual defensive manner. "The doc told me about Bentine today. Did you go to the telegraph office?"

A tray of dishes clattered as they met a table harshly.

"He shouldn't have said anything."

There was the bristly woman he'd been dealing with.

"You didn't answer. Did you go to the telegraph office?" He was more concerned with her being caught than the message.

"No. Yi and I have a plan. I can't go until we can make the plan work." The confidence in her voice almost had him believing she could pull it off.

"I don't want you to risk getting caught by Bentine. I don't want the telegraph sent." Betrayal squeezed his chest and a lump bobbed in his throat. He owed so much to Jasper, but his friend would be the first to say the young woman came first.

"We need the telegraph sent." The urgency in her words startled him.

"We?" He held out a hand and willed her to place her hand in his. The moments dragged on. His arm shook from being held out at such an angle. When his arm dropped a fraction, two small hands grasped it, lowering their clasped hands to the cot beside his hip.

"I've been asked to leave the tunnel. Bentine will stop at nothin' to get me. I can't put the good people down here in jeopardy because I'm hiding among them. I saved you, now you need to save me. Let me go with you when you leave Pendleton."

Donny used this chance to touch her face. Starting at their clasped hands, he ran his left hand up her flannel clad arm, over her collar, and cupped her cheek in his palm. Her head and face were tiny. The skin smooth. He traced the corner of her eye with his thumb. It tipped up slightly at the corners. Were her lashes dark or light? His thumb slid across her cheek bone and over a small nose. Her full lips parted slightly as his thumb skimmed their silkiness.

"I'd be honored to help you leave this town. But I don't want you coming to harm from my actions." Their continued contact started his heart racing and his body heating.

She drew her face away from his hand, but remained with their hands clasped. "I'll get that message sent as soon as I can. We'll need your boss's help to get your friend."

"Tell me your plan to send the telegraph?" Donny didn't want her to pull her hands away and break the bond they'd established.

"You need to eat. The soup is getting cold."

Her hands disappeared. Rustling and clinking revealed she'd picked up his dinner.

Donny raised his hands and a bowl was placed in them.

Callie watched Donny slurp the soup. She rubbed her chest where a small warm flash had struck her when he gently skimmed his thumb over her face. Donny had shown he was gentle and kind by his every action since waking from his beating. His touch had opened a crack in the armor she'd put around her heart where men were concerned.

She reached out and smoothed the long lock of light brown hair away from his forehead. He smiled, and she jerked her hand back. It was as if his touch had opened her emotions, allowing her to feel something besides anger and fear of touching.

He finished his meal and held the bowl out. "I didn't hear you eating."

"I ate before I came in." She took the bowl, placing it on the tray. "Here is the tea." She tried to put the cup in his hands without touching him but it was impossible. The dish was too small. Instead of jerking back, she let her fingers glide down his hands as he held the cup.

He smiled. The act crinkled the skin on the outside of his eyes and made his face even more handsome. The swelling had gone down. All that remained of his beating was the kaleidoscope of colors on his face. The growth of whiskers hid most of it.

"You might want to wait to shave. The whiskers hide the purple and yellow bruises." The words were out before she could stop them. Just because his touch softened her, she couldn't let her guard down when it came to a man. Giving him the idea she cared wasn't good. He'd expect more and more from her. She had no plans to be any man's property.

"If the whiskers get a little longer they won't itch as bad. Down here no one but you and the doc see the bruises. I might as well be comfortable and shave." He frowned and held up the empty cup. "You didn't buy me a razor and shave soap did you?"

"No, but I can borrow one from Ting Lee. He has the bath house down here." She clenched her bottom lip between her teeth. Why did I offer to do that?

"I wouldn't ask you but this is getting itchy." He scratched his chin.

The rasp of the whiskers reminded her of Pa sharpening his razor before shaving. In the summer he'd shave outside by the back door. She'd sat in the branches of the apple tree in the backyard and watched, her old cat, Mouser, on her lap, purring.

"You don't have to do it tonight. I can wait until tomorrow."

His deep voice penetrated her thoughts.

"What?" She put the cup on the tray and picked up the tray.

"You don't have to get the razor and soap tonight."

"I will. Ting Lee is more likely to let me borrow it tonight when he's less likely to have someone want a bath and shave." She hurried out of the room.

Mr. Cai sat on his chair, puffing on a pipe. His gaze followed her. "Man ask questions about you."

"I know."

"Him care about you. Will help you leave."

Callie nodded. The Chinese she'd allowed close were like family to her. She didn't want to leave, but to stay put that family in peril. "He said he would help me leave. But it will take some time for me to get the telegraph sent."

Mr. Cai nodded. "You will know when right."

She wasn't sure what he meant by that. Gathering up all the dishes from the three of them, she headed to the kitchen.

Lin Huang motioned to the dish pan by the stove when she entered the area. She didn't know if the others knew he'd asked to marry her. Placing the dishes in the pan, she avoided eye contact with the man. He also ignored her. Which hurt a little. They'd had an easy camaraderie before everyone discovered she wasn't a boy.

Back in the tunnel, she hurried along to Ting Lee's baths. She heard female voices and giggling in the tunnel ahead. Before she could find a place to hide, three soiled doves turned the corner and walked toward her. They stopped under one of the iron grids that allowed light and air into the tunnels. The light from a street lamp shone down on the three.

"Looky what we have, girls," said a woman a good ten years older than Callie. She had dark brown hair piled on her head and so much charcoal around her eyes she resembled a raccoon. Her clothing was modest compared to what Callie had seen at Bentine's bordello.

Callie ducked her head. Even though she wasn't under the faint lighting from a grid, she didn't want to risk the women getting a good look at her.

"You two go on."

She knew that voice. Tipping her hat slightly, she caught sight of the girl who'd been sitting on Bentine's lap. The one he called Iris.

The other two walked by, filling the air with floral scents that made her sneeze.

"Bless you," Iris said as she stepped in front of Callie.

She placed a finger under Callie's chin, forcing Callie to look up into her face.

"I know you're a girl. It's all Raymond talks about. Finding the girl, Mac, with the porcelain skin and pretty face." She spit the words as if they were vile to her tongue.

"I don't want him to find me." She wasn't about to let the woman think she wanted anything to do with a bordello.

"Then get out of this town." She dropped her hand, jamming both hands onto her hips.

"I can't. I have a telegraph to send to get help for my traveling partner." She'd gone and hooked herself to Donny. She could think of worse people to be relying upon.

"What's keeping you from sending the message?" Iris dug in her handbag.

"I don't need money. I need a dress so I can

walk the streets without Mr. Bentine's men seeing me." She blurted out her plan. If the woman wanted her gone, surely she'd help with a dress.

"That's all you need?" She smiled. "Meet me here tomorrow night, this time. I'll have a dress for you. Then I don't want to see you again." Iris pushed past Callie, sauntering down the tunnel as if she owned it.

Her gut and head started a battle of wills. Her gut said she shouldn't have given away so much. And her head said it made sense the woman would want competition out of the way. The battle between her head and gut raged as she continued to Ting Lee's.

The man sat on a stool by the curtain leading to the wash tubs.

He shook his head when he saw her and put a finger to his lips.

She stopped, staring at the curtain.

Ting Lee stood and padded quietly up to her. He pointed to the curtain and whispered. "Bentine man."

Callie shot a glance at the curtain and whispered, "I only need a razor and shave soap."

Ting Lee stared at her as if she'd asked him for a weapon.

"The man at Mr. Cai's. He wants to shave," she whispered as the man in the bath started singing an off-key bar room song.

Ting Lee nodded and disappeared behind the curtain.

"What you doin' interruptin' my song!" the

man bellowed.

She hoped he didn't do anything mean to the Chinaman.

Ting Lee appeared, clutching the items she'd asked for, including a brush, bowl, and towel.

"Xia xia," she said, gathering the items and walking at a brisk pace back to Mr. Cai's.

She carried everything straight into the room where Donny still reclined on the bed.

"I have the shaving things." She dumped them on his lap.

"Thank you, I think." He ran his fingers over the items. "I'll need hot water."

"Mr. Cai has a small oil stove he uses to heat up the water for his teas." Callie ducked back out to the main room. She placed a pot of water on the burner and asked Mr. Cai to light the stove.

"Man wash?" he asked.

"Yes," she replied. She shouldn't watch him shave. It was an intimate part of a person's routine. But she had to see how a blind man shaved without cutting himself.

Once the water was steaming, she carried the pot and then a bowl along with a rag into the other room.

Donny had the shaving items placed beside him. The towel draped across his chest. "Hand me a warm, wet rag, please."

She dunked the rag into the hot water, nearly scalding her hands. "Ow! This is really hot."

"That's what I want. Place it in my hands and pour a little water into the soap bowl." He scrubbed his face with the rag.

She dipped water out of the pot, adding it to the shaving soap in the bowl with the brush. She swirled the brush around, dissolving the soap so the brush would pick it up.

He ran the wet rag around his neck. "That feels good. I'm getting grungy layin' around here."

She wasn't sure if he wanted a comment. He was puttin' off a muskier scent than he had when she dragged him out of the street.

He placed the wet rag on top of the towel draped across the top of his chest, he held out his hands. "Soap, please."

She placed the cup in his hands.

His left hand cradled the cup while the fingers of his right hand moved up the cup and grasped the handle of the brush. He swirled the brush and frowned. "There's too much water in the cup."

She glared at him. "How can you tell? You can't see." The minute the words hit the air she wanted to suck them back in.

"I can't, but I can tell the brush moves too easily over the soap." He tipped the cup, pouring several spoons worth of water onto the rag on his chest.

He stirred the brush and smiled. "Now it feels right." Raising the brush, he started scrubbing the soap onto his right cheek and jaw. The white film worked up into a lather with the circular motions of the brush.

Spellbound by his rhythmic movements, Callie stood beside the bed watching. The muscles in his forearm moved and grew as he worked his hand.

This was the arm of a man who was used to labor. Casting a glance at his face, she was struck by how normal he looked. The swelling had gone down and his eyes were open. Two dark brown eyes stared forward as he circled the brush over every inch of his face, dipping and swirling the brush in the cup every time before he moved to a different part of his face.

"That should do it." He turned his face toward her. "Did I miss anywhere?"

"No. I'd say you did a better job of covering your face than a man with sight." She meant the statement as a compliment. By the smile bunching the lather at the corners of his mouth, he took it as such.

He held the cup and brush out to her. Callie placed them on the table and held her breath as he picked up the straight razor. Even a sighted man had to be careful when using a straight razor.

# Chapter Twelve

Donny opened the razor. He felt the handle and barely touched the blade to make sure he had the sharp side toward his face. His mind went back to the day Clay had taken it upon himself to show Donny how to shave. The blind leading the blind, Ethan had said. He'd insisted he should be present to make sure Rachel didn't have to stitch anyone up. Clay had started Donny slow, with a butter knife. Teaching him the slant, the pressure, and how to keep track of his motions so Donny didn't cut off something he might regret.

The first week of shaving he'd nicked pretty much every inch of his face. Ethan and Hank had laughed every time they saw him, but shaving had taught Donny to have even more confidence in himself.

A sharp intake of breath made him smile. Had

Mac ever watched a man shave? Her father probably. He'd have to remember to ask her. Right now he needed to concentrate. He angled the blade and took his first stroke down the left side of his face. The whiskers tugged only slightly on the sharp blade. He continued on the left until his fingers only encountered whiskerless skin. He moved the blade to his right side, making sure he didn't nick his nose in the process. With that side cleared of whiskers, he worked on the area under his nose, his chin, and last his throat. One last time he ran the fingers of his left hand over his face.

"Did I get it all?" he asked, wiping the razor on the rag on his chest and closing the lethal grooming tool.

He sensed Mac leaning over him. Her lye and slight floral scent filled his nostrils.

"You did a fine job." Her breathy response tickled his forehead.

"Could you rinse the rag? I'll wipe my face." He hated to have her move. Her scent and nearness comforted unlike anything he'd experienced before.

Cold air fluttered across his chest as the wet weight of the rag disappeared.

The sloshing of water and his heart beating erratically in his ears were the only sounds he registered.

"Here you go." Mac grasped his hand, placing the rag in his palm.

Donny gripped the rag and settled his empty hand on her wrist. "Thank you. I appreciate all you've done for me."

She didn't pull her hand away. He held on. She remained still and silent. He wasn't sure what he was waiting for.

"That soap's gonna dry if you don't wash it off."

He released her wrist and wiped the rag over his face. Air moved around him and her scent grew stronger. She had retrieved the shaving items.

"I'm taking these shave items back to Ting Lee." The whisper of the curtain revealed she'd left the room.

Donny groaned. How was he to get close to this woman and help her if she continually ran away from him?

Callie returned the shaving items to Ting Lee without running into anyone. She was torn between meeting Iris tomorrow night or following through on the plan she and Yi had come up with.

Mr. Cai sat in his chair smoking a pipe when she returned. He was smart and could probably help her. But she didn't like telling him anything that might get him hurt if someone pressed him for information about her. He smiled around the stem of his pipe. She smiled back and ducked into the room she shared with Donny.

The room felt smaller, more intimate after watching him shave.

"Did you get the shaving items back okay?" He sat with his back against the stone wall.

For being blind he didn't show any weakness. Never had she seen him unsure of himself, even when he didn't know where he was or who he was with.

"Yes. Does your face feel better?" She stepped closer to the cot. Their heads were nearly the same height.

"It feels clean and smooth. I was afraid I was going to scratch my skin off the way I was digging at the itchy spots." He patted the cot beside his right thigh. "Sit here a minute."

She hesitated. Was it his way of getting her close enough to grab and…

"I won't hurt you. If you sit we can talk quietly," he nodded his head toward the curtain, "without anyone else hearing us."

His suggestion made sense. She slowly sat on the edge of the bed, one leg up on the mattress and one still on the floor. This way she could face him.

Donny held up his right hand. "May I hold your hand?"

Heat flamed her cheeks. She'd never sat on a man's bed. And to hold hands…"Why?"

"I can't see you. This is my way of connecting with you while we talk."

She let out a deep sigh and placed her hand in his.

His fingers tickled her palm as his thumb skimmed back and forth over her knuckles.

"You have small hands. I noticed earlier your face and head are also small. How old are you?"

"I'm not a child," she said defensively, though that is what she had been trying to make everyone think—she was a boy.

"I know you're not a child. But you are small, right?"

"Yes. I'm twenty. I'm barely five foot and can fit in boy's clothing."

He nodded while his fingers continued to move in her palm. "I thought you wore trousers. I didn't hear skirts swishing."

She stared at him. He missed nothing.

"Where are you from?"

"How do you know I'm not from here?" A shiver slithered up her spine. How did he know so much?

"You wouldn't be hiding in the same town you lived. It would be too easy for someone to spot you." His fingers stopped moving, and he settled their hands on her leg. "Why are you hiding? You made a comment the other night about not killing another. What did you mean?"

She tried to jerk her hand out of his, but he held on. Keeping their hands on her thigh. His grip didn't hurt but it didn't relent either.

"You must have heard wrong." She stopped tugging on her hand.

"I didn't. Is that why you're hiding? Does Mr. Bentine know why you're hiding?" His tone held a note of suspicion.

"No! He knows nothing of me or where I came from. He just wants another woman in his bordello." *And possibly he wants his watch back.* She didn't want Donny to think she consorted with the likes of Mr. Bentine. Why, she didn't know, but his respect meant something to her.

"There are lots of women who are desperate and would like to have a job in his bordello. Why is he set on you?"

She sighed. "I don't know. Iris said he's obsessed with the girl with the porcelain skin and pretty face."

"Who's Iris?" His body leaned toward her a little as if he were listening intently.

"She's a woman who works at Mr.Bentine's bordello. She was sittin' on his lap the night his thug dragged me into his office and he discovered I'm a woman and not a boy."

His hand tightened on hers. "How did he discover you aren't a boy?"

She patted his arm with her other hand, wanting him to relax. "My hat fell off and my hair fell to my shoulders. I have a girly face. The only way I hid who I was from people was by using my hat to shield my face."

He reached up with his left hand, knocking her hat to the floor and running his hands though her hair. "It's soft. What color?"

"Yellow." No one other than her mother had brushed or touched her hair.

His fingers continued to sift the strands. "Pretty."

This time the heat in her cheeks swept down her neck and up to her ears. She wanted to pull her head away but at the same time her body and heart yearned for the physical connection.

"Where did you talk to Iris? At the bordello?" His fingers continued to feel her hair while his other hand continued to hold her hand.

"She and two other soiled doves were using the tunnel tonight. I couldn't duck and hide before they saw me." Callie chewed on her bottom lip. Donny could help me decide what to do. "She sent the other two ahead and threatened me to get out of town."

His hand stopped sifting her hair. He placed his hand on her cheek. "You told her you were leaving didn't you? She sounds like she could be trouble if she threatened you."

"Yes. I told her I needed to get to the telegraph office, but I needed a dress so I could get by Mr. Bentine's thugs."

"That's a good idea. They'll be looking for the boy named Mac not a beautiful woman." He smiled and his thumb caressed her face as he had the night before.

"Yi and I came up with the idea, but I would have to wait until either Mrs. Nelding or Mrs. Shield brought in a dress to be cleaned. They are the only customers we have who are close to my size." She sighed. "But that could be a week before they bring in a dress to be laundered."

"We can wait a week if it keeps you safe."

The sincerity in his words cracked open the hard shell around her heart a bit more.

"Iris offered to bring me a dress tomorrow night."

His brow furrowed. His thumb stopped caressing her face, but his hand remained. "Do you trust her?"

"What do you mean?" She didn't see a reason

to not trust the woman. After the threat she'd made, it would be the quickest way to get rid of Callie.

"Did her threat scare you? If it didn't then she could have just said that to get you to a spot where they could capture you." His hand tightened on hers.

"She seemed threatening. She offered to help me leave. I would have thought she'd have tried to make friends if she was luring me to Mr. Bentine." Callie thought back on the encounter. The woman's face was in shadow, so she couldn't see her face well enough to see if the woman was mad or bluffing.

"You should take someone with you if you insist on meeting her. I would prefer you wait for a dress from a customer. It would be safer than meeting with someone who works for Mr. Bentine." Donny's thumb started caressing her cheek again.

"I could send Mr. Cai or Yi to meet Iris tomorrow night, but if it is a trap, they might get hurt." She was leaving to keep her friends from harm.

"The cook who asked to marry you. He sounded like a big man." Donny's thumb paused and a frown wrinkled his brow.

Talking about the man wanting to marry her bothered him. Why, because he was Chinese?

"He is a big man." She studied Donny. "Why do you say that?"

"You could have him meet Iris." His hand dropped from her face, but he continued to hold her hand.

"Why him?" She was curious to his line of

thinking.

"If it is a set-up, he could handle himself if they tried to beat him up, and he cares enough for you he would never tell where you are."

She could tell by the intensity of the way he said the last words it did bother him that Lin Huang wanted to marry her.

"The Chinese who live here are laborers. They don't fight. His size makes no difference, he won't fight back." She hadn't fully understood why the Chinese hid in the tunnels until Yi and Mr. Cai told her that they were laborers and had never learned how to fight.

"If you don't want anyone down here to come to harm, including you, I suggest no one meets Iris tomorrow night. We'll wait until you can borrow a dress through the laundry." Donny gave her hand a squeeze and released it. "I only wish I knew how Jasper was faring. If they keep him in jail to heal and don't toss him out to be beat up again, that would be good."

Callie saw the worry etched on Donny's face. He cared a good deal for his friend. If she could find out how he was doing that would make her decision for her. She patted his arm and stood. "Good night."

"Night," he said and wiggled his body down to lay flat on the cot.

There was one person who wasn't Chinese who might do her a favor. He didn't care for Mr. Bentine because he'd been kicked out of the two gaming houses the man ran. If she could get him to check on Jasper at the jail, she'd know what to do. Either meet Iris to get a dress and help Jasper or, if he was being taken care of, they could wait for Donny to heal more and she'd borrow a dress from Mrs. Nelding or Mrs. Shield.

# Chapter Thirteen

Donny pretended to sleep after the conversation with Mac. He was worried she might try to meet Iris even though he'd warned her against it. He'd never had a reason to trust a woman who sold her body. From what he'd guessed as an adult from conversations he remembered hearing between his ma and pa, he was pretty sure his father had frequented places like Mr. Bentine ran. He'd get a woman, gamble away their money, get liquored up, and come home to berate and beat up his wife, as if she caused him to be worthless.

He listened to Mac as she slept. She murmured and thrashed about. He'd noticed it the night before too. Whatever was keeping her in hiding was also stealing her rest from her. If she had killed a man, he had a good notion the man deserved it.

He finally dozed off and woke to the sound of

Mac moving about. From the sluggishness of his brain, he couldn't have been asleep for very long.

"Where're you going?" he asked.

"Eek! I wish you'd give warning when you speak." Mac chastised him.

"Why are you getting dressed?" he asked.

"I need to talk to a person who can get to the jail and check on Jasper. See if we can wait to get a dress or have to get the one from Iris."

"We're waiting," he said firmly. "You aren't meeting with someone employed by Mr. Bentine."

Her scent became stronger. A hand touched his arm. "If Swifty finds out Jasper is fine, I'll wait. But if he's not doing well, I'll find a way to get the dress from Iris." She patted his arm.

"Why can't Swifty send the telegraph?" Donny asked.

"He can't be trusted with money. He'd sooner gamble or drink with it than send a telegraph." A moment later the curtain over the door whispered, emitting the herbal scents from the other room.

Donny didn't like her meeting up with other people in the middle of the night. If his dang leg wasn't broke he could go with her. He felt more helpless with the broken leg than being blind.

Callie slipped by the sleeping Chinese healer and into the tunnels. The faint light seeping into the tunnel through the metal grates kept her from running into walls and moving at a steady pace. She'd heard whispers that the gaming hall owner would send men down the tunnels if a loser disappeared without paying his debt. For this reason she pressed her body into the darkest recesses along the wall.

She also knew Swifty liked to hang around the place. He was there for the "rounds on me" shouts from winners. He was allowed to sleep in a corner if he cleaned the floors after the hall shut down for the night.

The swinging door that was put in to help the people in the tunnel avoid being caught by a drunk cowboy was the only thing between her and the short tunnel to the gaming hall. She ducked down, swinging the bottom of the door up, and walked under the door and into the ten- foot tunnel before the door to the hall.

Drawing in a deep breath, she cautiously walked up to the door and listened. She heard Swifty muttering to himself. Was everyone gone? A gentle push on the door opened it several inches. She peered into the dimly-lit room. Two drunks still remained. One sat on the floor leaning against the bar. One was flopped over a table. Swifty was sweeping and muttering to himself.

She slipped through the door and stood beside the grizzled old man she'd helped out of the muddy street the first week she'd arrived in Pendleton. He'd been grateful she'd found him a warm, dry place to spend the night and brought him two rolls from the bakery where she'd received handouts until she'd ducked into the tunnels and found food and shelter here.

"Swifty."

The old man started and stared at her through

watery eyes.

"Mac. What'ch you doin' here." He glanced over his shoulder. "Pete's still here. You better get."

"I need you to do me a favor." She moved closer to him, ignoring the stench of sweat, urine, and whiskey. "I need you to check on a Negro in the jail. Find out how he's faring. I'll be back around noon to learn what you found out."

He nodded. "Go before Pete sees you. I know'd Bentine is lookin' for you." He smiled a three-toothed grin. "I knew you weren't no boy." He winked and waved to the door leading to the tunnel.

"Thank you, Swifty. I'll meet you here at noon tomorrow." Callie would have hugged the man but she didn't want to carry his smell back to Donny who was waiting for her. She hurried down the tunnel and back to Mr. Cai's.

She barely moved the curtain, returning to the back room she shared with Donny. In the dark she tried to be quiet and undress without waking him.

"Where'd you go?" he whispered.

This time she wasn't startled. She had a notion he'd be awake when she returned. "To see a friend. He's going to learn what he can about Jasper."

He sniffed several times. "You smell like liquor and cigar smoke. Where were you?"

"There's a gambling hall on the end of one of the tunnels. Swifty is a drunk who cleans up the hall at the end of the night. I helped him out once."

She slid out of her clothes and back into her bedroll. "Good-night."

"Anyone see you?"

His urgent whisper in the dark made her smile. His protectiveness made her feel like she had some worth.

"No. There were only two passed-out drunks and Swifty." She pulled the blanket up to her chin. "Go to sleep."

"How is he going to tell you what he finds out?"

She rolled her eyes. Should have known he'd ask that question. "I'm meeting him at noon tomorrow."

"Where?"

Do I lie or tell him the truth? He's going to know if I'm not telling the truth. "Same place."

"The gambling hall? There'll be people there."

The cot creaked. "You can't go there during the day."

"What are you doing?" She scrambled to her feet and to the cot. Her hands met his shoulder and arm.

He was leaning toward the edge and about to topple off the cot. She pushed with her hands, making him lie back down.

"Where were you trying to go?" she demanded.

"Thinking of you putting yourself in danger for me and Jasper made me forget I can't get up." The anger and fight in his voice made her smile.

It had been a very long time since she'd had someone who wanted to protect her with such determination.

"I won't be in danger. Swifty will meet me in the tunnel." I hope.

Donny's fingers wrapped around her arms, settling her onto the cot beside him. "You promise you won't put yourself in danger?"

His face was only inches from hers as he asked the question.

"I can't promise. One thing I've learned since taking out on my own. I never know where danger is coming from." A shiver rolled through her body. Not one of fear, but a warm blanket of happiness.

"Are you cold?" Donny moved his hands up and down her arms.

"No."

"But you shivered." His tone reflected he didn't believe her.

"I'm not cold."

His left hand moved up her arm and cupped her face. "If you want, I can hold you and warm you up."

She smiled. "I'm not cold. I'm happy."

The thumb that rested near her lips moved to caress them. "Happy?"

How much did she reveal to this man who she would walk away from once he helped her get out of this town? Something about him made her feel she could talk to him. "I'm lookin' forward to leavin' here. The Chinese have been good friends, but I'm tired of hiding out in these tunnels. I'd like to smell fresh air and feel the sun on my face."

"I wondered if you were content here. There were times when you talked about the people and your life here that you sounded happy." He slid his right arm around her, drawing her closer.

Fear struck as swift as the memory of her step-father roughly pulling her against him. She shoved against his chest, pushing away.

The arm released her. The hand followed her backward motions, gently cradling her face.

"I'm not going to hurt you. I only wanted to bring you closer." Donny's soft voice whispered in her ears.

It was Donny, not her stepfather. In the dark, she'd panicked.

"I'm sorry. I know. I…" Tears trickled from her eyes. Will I ever feel safe with a man?

"Shh… I've figured out some man did something to you." His hand drew only her face closer to him. "I promise. I will never hurt you."

"I know. In the dark…I…" She swallowed the shame she felt for thinking this gentle man would hurt her.

"You don't have to apologize. If I ever get my hands on the man who hurt you, he won't hurt another person."

The vengeance in his voice made her shudder. She wished her stepfather was still alive just to see him squirm under Donny's wrath.

She placed a hand over his mouth. "Shhh…I don't want you gettin' into trouble over me."

He kissed her fingers and breathed against them. "You're worth it."

Callie's heart raced. From the kiss, the words, and the man's sincerity. "I wish I believed that," she whispered and dropped her hand to her lap.

Hands grasped her head. "When you believe

that, you can face the demons that keep you up at night."

"What do you mean?" She knew what he meant but wondered if she'd said something in her sleep.

"I hear you moaning and tossing most of the night. Mac—" He stopped. "Please tell me your name. I want to say your name, not one you gave yourself to hide from who you are."

She bit her bottom lip and struggled with him knowing her real name. Donny's words said he believed in her, and he had shown in so many ways that he cared for her. She let out a sigh and hoped she didn't put him in danger. "Callie. Callie is my name."

"Callie."

The way he said it sounded like a pretty bird trilling in the early morning. Her belly fluttered at the sound.

"Callie, let me help you slay your demons."

Chapter Fourteen

Donny's heart pumped with excitement. He'd
won her trust. For her to tell him her name, even if
it was only her first name, was a victory to him. Especially after she'd pulled away from his embrace
earlier. He also meant every word of his promise to
hurt the person who hurt her and to help her believe
in herself and chase away her bad memories.

"My demons may be too deep for anyone to
slay."

The sorrow in her voice made his heart ache.
No one should feel that alone and that down-trod-
den.

"You never know until you let someone help."
He still held her head in his hands. She hadn't
pulled away. Her face was only inches from his.
He'd never wanted to kiss a woman as badly as he
wanted to taste Callie's lips. But he didn't want her

pulling away when he'd achieved a step forward. "Tell me what you dream about that makes you restless."

She shook her head. "I can't go back."

"I'm here. You can trust me." He knew she'd made one huge step toward trusting him already.

"It'll be morning soon. I need to get some sleep." She put her hands over his, removing them from her face. "Good-night."

He drew his right hand, with hers still clinging to it toward his face and kissed the back of her hand. "Good-night."

Her hand slipped from his. Rustling sounds and then silence told him she'd revealed all she would tonight. One thing Clay always accused him of was his persistence. He'd find out everything there was to know about Callie. *Callie*. The name fit the image he had of her in his mind.

He wiggled the toes on his left foot. This dang foot had to heal quickly. He needed to be able to take care of her when they headed to Sumpter. The protectiveness and emotions she brought out in him made him finally feel like a man and not a boy. Nothing he'd done or anything Clay or anyone had said to this point in his life had made him feel this happy. Gaining Callie's trust little by little and gaining her acceptance made his heart soar. He wanted her to trust him and know he would care for her always.

"Will you come here before you go see Swifty?" Donny asked when he heard Callie dressing in the morning.

She blew out air like a bored horse. "No. I'll be close to the tunnel at the laundry. It will waste time coming here before I meet Swifty."

"But you'll come straight here after you talk to him?" He couldn't go with her, but he wanted to be involved in all the actions she took on his behalf.

She didn't answer.

"You'll come tell me how Jasper is and whether you'll be meeting Iris or not?" He was insistent he knew where she was at all times. That was the only way he could help if something went wrong.

"Yes, I'll come tell you what Swifty learns about Jasper."

The air wafted by him. She was leaving.

"Don't worry about me so much. I've been takin' care of myself for three years. I don't like havin' someone worryin' about me."

The curtain swished and he was alone.

Donny smiled. Callie was a stubborn little thing.

The doc entered. Donny had become accustomed to the morning routine. The doc checked his bandages, fed him breakfast, and left. But he always placed something in Donny's hands to keep him busy.

Donny finished eating the soup he'd had for every meal since waking up. Handing the bowl back to the doc, he asked, "Do you know Swifty?"

Dishes rattled but the man didn't answer.

He reached out, found slick cloth, and grabbed a fistful. "Doc, do you know a man named Swifty?"

The hands he'd felt checking his injuries, pried his fingers free of the clothing. "No. I not know man."

"Do you know a soiled dove named Iris? She works for Bentine." He had to discover what he could about the people Callie was dealing with.

"She come once. Ask opium."

"For her?" He'd heard of soiled doves drinking. He figured it was to wash away the memories of the men they'd bedded.

"No. She smoke in den with women like herself. This for Mr. Bentine." The dishes rattled. He'd picked up the tray to leave.

"Does Mr. Bentine come into the tunnels?" He had to keep the man here long enough to answer his questions.

"No. Him stay out tunnels. Only send bad men."

"What about Iris? Has she ever seen C-Mac here? At your place." He'd nearly slipped and said Callie instead of Mac. Telling someone her secret after she'd trusted him with it would lose her trust. He couldn't have that.

"Missy Mac not here when Iris here. Missy Mac live with Wus."

"And Iris knows this?" He couldn't have Iris finding Callie. They would need to find another place to wait for Clay.

"Everyone use tunnel know Mac work and live with Mr. Wu."

Air fluttered over his bare chest. The man was gone. And so was his chance to ask any more questions.

Callie told Yi of the possible new plan to get a dress.

"No trust that kind woman," Yi said, wrinkling her face in distaste.

"If Swifty says Jasper is not doing well, I'll have to trust her." Callie was having even more misgivings about Iris after talking with Donny and now Yi. The only good that came of Donny pressing her for information last night was he knew her name and he seemed to genuinely care what happened to her.

"Moony eyes." Yi elbowed Callie. "You like your man." Yi's eyes glistened with tears. "Yi happy for you."

Callie was happy on the inside, but she wasn't about to get moony over a man who couldn't see her and asked too many questions. "He's not my man, and I'm not moony over him."

Yi giggled. "You say no, but eyes say yes."

Callie humphed and scrubbed the sheet harder on the wash board.

She worked hard until noon. Yi sat in her usual chair and placed a bowl of rice on Callie's chair.

"You can eat my rice. I have to meet Swifty and tell Donny what I learn. I'll be back as soon as I can." She didn't wait for an acknowledgement from Yi. Callie ducked out of the laundry and trotted down the tunnel to the gambling hall.

She listened at the escape door. There wasn't a sound on the other side. She crouched, pushed the door up, and moved through the opening into the hall. The murmur of voices stalled her feet. How many were in there? Would they know who she was and follow?

Her heart landed in her throat as she stood against the wall listening and trying to decide if the risk was worth getting the news about Jasper, a man she didn't even know.

Donny cared about the man. And he cared about her. Her mind conjured up the way he had caressed her lips and kissed her fingers the night before. No one since her pa had shown her such tenderness. She squeezed her eyes shut, sent out a prayer to a God she'd stopped believing in the night her stepfather crawled into her bed, and cautiously moved into the doorway to locate Swifty.

# Chapter Fifteen

Callie slipped to the side of the door and scanned the room. Three men played a game of cards at the table closest to the outside door. Swifty and another man stood at the heavy wood bar. Swifty was facing the door she stood in. He glanced her way and with the hand dangling by his leg, he motioned for her to go back in the tunnel.

She didn't have to be told twice to hide. One step put her into the door way, and several quick back steps slid her into darkness. She waited in the darkness for Swifty to come to her. The time ticked by slowly. Her stomach rumbled. Her mind conjured up all kinds of bad things happening to her if Swifty left her standing here too long.

Shuffling steps echoed in the silence. It had to be Swifty. She waited until the smell she associated with him, stained her nostrils. It was Swifty.

"Over here," she whispered.

He moved closer. His body was silhouetted by the light shining down the tunnel from the gambling hall.

"What did you find out?" she whispered when he stopped five feet from her.

"The big Negro in jail is healing. He's carryin' on about losing a blind boy. The doctor and the sheriff think he's crazy." Swifty rubbed a hand across his whiskers.

The rasping sound echoed in the dark as Callie worked on what to do about Jasper worryin'.

"Can you talk to the Negro? Or get a note to him?" The best thing to do would be to get the note to the man telling him Donny was doin' fine.

"I could talk to him if I get throwed in jail for the night."

"You don't mind goin' to jail?" She didn't want to ever set foot in a jail.

"They feed a man pretty good and the beds are better than the ground." Swifty scratched his head.

"Then tell Jasper. That's the Negro's name. Tell him Donny is bein' tended to and he's sendin' a telegraph to their boss." She peered through the darkness at the man. "Can you remember to tell him that if you get liquored up?"

"I won't get all liquored up. Just enough to make a nuisance and get hauled in." He put a hand on her shoulder. "Don't worry. I don't forget good people who do good things."

She knew he was referring to her help. "I remember friends as well. Thank you, Swifty."

"You need to be careful. Bentine's men killed a man named Hubert. Said he stole something but they couldn't find it. Their tearin' up the town looking for whatever it was, but they'll keep lookin' for you if Bentine says so."

"Thanks." Callie felt the watch in her pocket. She had a good idea she knew what the men were looking for.

"Swifty, what you doin' in that tunnel so long?" called a man.

"Get! He's one of Bentine's men." Swifty pressed himself against the wall and stuck out his foot.

The man spotted Callie. "Hey! You're—" He tripped over Swifty's foot.

Callie didn't stick around to see if the man got up. She bolted for the escape door. Ducking down, she ran through the door, and heard it whap the man on the head when he chased behind. Then another whap when the bottom of the door rotated and hit his shins.

She giggled but kept moving at a rapid pace in case the man figured out how the door worked and came running after her. Fearing the man might be behind her, she scrambled up and down the maze of tunnels before stopping outside Mr. Cai's. She waited until her breathing was normal before walking through the main room.

Whisking the curtain aside, she peered at Donny. His forehead was wrinkled. His hands held a piece of wood that he appeared to be polishing.

The frown faded and a smile curved his lips.

"What did Swifty learn?" he asked, setting the round wood to the side.

"Jasper is healing, but they think he's crazy because he's tellin' them there's a lost blind boy." She sat on the side of his cot. "I've a feelin' you're the lost blind boy." She teased.

He frowned and his mouth formed a disapproving line. "He still thinks of me as a boy. I turned twenty-two three months ago. They probably do think he's crazy. Anyone who found a blind boy wandering around would report it to the police."

"Swifty is going to get put in jail tonight and tell Jasper your bein' tended, and we've telegraphed for Clay." She smiled at the relief that smoothed his face.

"He didn't mind going to jail?"

"He said it would give him a good bed and a meal." She didn't add he still felt beholden to her for her kind deeds. Or the fact she had Bentine's watch and he'd killed a man looking for it.

Donny's hand found hers. He held it gently. "Then you don't have to meet Iris tonight." He fiddled with her fingers. "Is there anywhere else in these tunnels we can stay until I can walk out of here?"

"Why?" The only places she could think of were small depressions in the walls of the tunnels.

"I don't like that Iris has been here—"

"When?" she interrupted. If the woman had come looking for her today, then she could be a threat. Why would Iris come early other than to lure her out to Bentine?

"The doctor said she comes once in a while for opium for Mr. Bentine. She could show up while we're here." He stopped fiddling with her fingers and held her hand snugly. "I don't like the idea of Iris telling her boss where to find you."

"We have nowhere else to go. All the spaces large enough for us to sleep are used. There are small indentions along some of the tunnels, but we'd be found easier there and you'd have to be alone. That makes you more vulnerable." She'd grown fond of Donny's presence at night. While he said Callie wasn't sleeping well because he heard her reactions to her bad dreams, she was sleeping more since having Donny nearby.

"When I can walk and buy you a nice dress, we'll move to a hotel until Clay gets here."

It was a wonderful idea. She'd never been in a hotel, but she couldn't risk someone recognizing her. She'd let him keep that thought. But it wouldn't happen.

"I have to get back to work."

"Come straight here. You don't want to run into Iris if she's walking the tunnels looking for you."

The concern in his voice and the grip on her hand sent a tendril of heat from their touch, up her arm and straight to her heart. That warmth eased open the crack in the hard shell around her heart a little farther. This man was slowly making her believe there could be good in a male.

"I will." She gave his hand a squeeze and eased her hand away. At the curtain, she glanced at Donny. He sat a moment, smiled, and picked up the wood he was polishing.

Some of the worry was lifted from Donny when Callie said Jasper was in good health. He hoped her friend Swifty could get in the jail and let Jasper know he was well. He smiled. He'd first met Jasper when the man started working at the blind school as the janitor. Donny had been there a year as a student and had talked the superintendent into letting him teach the others how to make brooms. Jasper had helped Donny by gathering the materials and putting them in the room. Jasper even helped set up the foot pulleys and stations. They'd worked together even before Clay came along. Clay, being an adult, was put in the cottage with Jasper. The two got along well. Then Clay had talked the superintendent into having Donny teach him braille and in return, Clay helped Donny with the classes. They became friends. There was fifteen years difference in their ages and Clay had become like a father to him. And Jasper had become a second father. The two men had taught Donny a lot about life and how family treats one another.

He couldn't wait for the two men to meet Callie and tell him what they thought of her. He'd made up his mind she wasn't leaving Sumpter. Donny knew there were going to be lots of trials with his blindness. Mainly, she may not want to be married to a blind man. So far, she hadn't treated him different or made too much of his inability to do things. And he'd witnessed how well Clay's marriage worked. If two people loved one another they could handle any rough patches. With that sentiment lodged in his heart, he planned to claim her heart and ask Callie to marry him.

What he knew of her so far, it would be a battle. She retreated from physical contact and balked from telling him anything about herself, but he had faith she'd see he wasn't a burden. She was already allowing him to hold her hand. And she'd told him her real name, Callie. He smiled. That name fit her much better than Mac. Now, to get Callie to reveal her last name and why she believed she'd killed a man.

# Chapter Sixteen

Callie finished at the laundry for the day. She ducked out before Mr. Wu arrived to deliver the laundry. It still ate at her that she couldn't deliver for him. He was in more danger going up on the streets to deliver the laundry than she would be. She only had Bentine's men looking for her. Mr. Wu had most of the male population of Pendleton. But he'd insisted she was to stay hidden.

Heeding Donny's words, she took the shortest route to the kitchen to get their dinner and then straight to Mr. Cai's. She didn't want to run into Iris. Though…if the woman really did want her out of town, getting a dress now would get them all out of here quicker.

She stopped down the tunnel from where she'd met the woman the day before. I could hide in the shadows and see if she comes alone. She'd never seen any men other than the Chinese, and some of the whites who worked in businesses above the tunnels, down here. Would Bentine's thugs come with Iris? She doubted it.

A whiff of the soup she carried on the tray snapped her from her reveries. She needed to get the soup to Donny before it cooled off or he'd wonder what she was doing. He had a sense of everything she did and thought. It unnerved her, but at the same time made her feel closer to him than anyone else she'd had in her life.

Callie spun about and headed to Mr. Cai's and the room she now called home.

Donny heard Callie and the doctor speaking moments before a soft breeze fluttered across his skin and the scent of lye entered the room.

His stomach growled.

"Sounds like I brought your dinner just in time."

Her soft voice lifted his spirits and put a smile on his face.

"I had a notion it should be about time for you to be here. How was your day?" He held up his hands for the bowl of soup. The fish flavored broth and vegetables were getting old, but he refused to complain. He could be much worse off than having soup for every meal and being taken care of by a fine doctor and a beautiful woman.

"How was my day?" She laughed and placed the bowl in his hands. "Just like every day for the last year. I scrubbed bedding and clothing on a washboard all day. When I wasn't doing that I was rinsing and hanging the things to dry."

"I agree, not exciting. But it sounds better than my day of lyin' here wishing I could get up and walk around. Even washing clothes would be nice." He meant that. If he could hobble to the laundry and sit, he could scrub clothes and help out.

"You could scrub clothes?" she asked.

Her voice came from where he'd decided there was a chair. Her voice was about even with his head.

"I can do anything once I'm shown where things are. I'm not stupid. I just can't see." He knew she wasn't putting him down, but he had to make her realize, he wasn't that much different from any other man. He just didn't have the ability to see.

"I wasn't sayin' you were stupid!"

Her embarrassed tone made his chest ache.

"I didn't mean you thought I was stupid. I just…Damn, if I could get on my feet I'd show you I'm just like anyone else." The soup wasn't settling in his belly. He felt lower than a worm having made her feel bad.

"Well, it will be a couple more weeks before Mr. Cai will let you on your feet."

He heard her slurping the soup. She must not be too upset. He continued to drink the broth from his soup. She tapped his right hand with the wooden sticks they used to eat. He held the bowl with one hand and took the sticks, using them to scoop the meat and vegetables into his mouth.

"The soup is filling but what I wouldn't give

for a nice piece of roasted beef," he said, lowering the empty bowl to his lap.

"When I get the dress to deliver the telegraph, I'll bring you back some food." Callie took the bowl from him.

Dishes thunked on the tray.

"I don't want you doing anything to get you caught."

He heard an intake of breath.

"What did I say to upset you?"

"Nothin'." Callie stared at the man. Sometimes his comments made her feel like he knew everything about her.

"I said something. I heard you inhale like you saw a spider or something."

She latched onto that. "I did see a spider. Startled me was all." Callie picked up the tray of dirty dishes. "I'm going to return the dishes."

"You aren't thinking about seeing Iris, are you?"

His accusation stung. That was exactly what she'd planned to do while delivering the dishes.

"I won't talk to her. Just see if she's alone and has a dress." She nudged the curtain aside with her shoulder.

"That's not a good idea." He raised up and winced. "Don't go there alone. Take the doc or someone."

"I'll be fine. I won't even let her see me. I just want to see if she was setting a trap or not."

"Don't go." He didn't plead or order. He'd merely made a statement.

She stared at his concerned face. "I'll be fine. Don't worry." Callie slipped out of the room and into the tunnel. Donny's worry flickered a spark in her heart. But she also wondered if he knew something she didn't. Something she should be worried about. There wasn't any way he could know anything. He spent every day and night in that bed, hidden from everyone.

Callie hurried down the tunnel to the kitchen where she dropped the dishes into the wash tub by the stove and hurried down the tunnel to where she'd found Iris the night before. She slipped into a dark indention along the tunnel wall where she could huddle in the far corner and watch for Iris.

She didn't have long to wait. Sitting. Waiting. She thought about giving the woman Bentine's watch. It would get rid of one of the reasons Bentine might be looking for her. She could make a deal. She'd give his watch back if he forgot about her. The idea sounded good. But the stories she'd heard about Bentine didn't give her hope it would work.

Iris appeared from the tunnel leading to Mr. Bentine's gambling hall. She didn't have anything in her hands. Her head pivoted on her neck as her gaze searched down the tunnels leading to hers. Her skirt swished, and her steps clicked lightly on the dirt floor as she strode down one tunnel a short distance, pacing by Callie's hiding place.

*Should I say something and discover why she doesn't have a dress?* She thought on that a moment and decided it best to just remain hidden and see what happens. Ten minutes passed with Iris pacing ten steps down each of the tunnels intersecting with the one she'd arrived through.

The man, Mort, who'd hauled Callie off the street and into the saloon, stalked down the tunnel.

"What's keepin' you? The boss is lookin' for you."

Iris spun around. "Go away. I'm waiting for that girl Raymond wants so bad."

The man scanned the tunnels. His gaze stalled on the shadow where she hid.

Does he see me? Sweat beaded her brow and her hands clenched. She couldn't take off now, he wasn't that far away. He'd catch her before she could duck down a side tunnel.

"Go on, get. You'll ruin everything." Iris shoved on the man's chest.

His gaze landed on Iris. "You know you find that girl, you'll no longer be the boss's favorite."

Iris's painted lips sneered. "I'm not getting her for him. I'm getting her to go away."

"He won't stop until he has her. Just like poor Geraldine. He was obsessed with her. Got rid of her man and made her indebted to him."

"And then dumped her when I came along." Iris glared at Mort. "I won't be dumped for some miniature woman with a porcelain face."

Shivers ran down Callie's back. The way Iris talked, she didn't think the woman would bring her a dress, but she would find a way to make Callie go away, permanently. Huddled in the shadow, Callie wished both of them would leave so she could return to Donny.

"Come on, Iris. The boss will break his walking stick over my head if I don't bring you back." Mort picked Iris up, flung her over his shoulder, and hauled her down the tunnel like a sack of potatoes.

Iris pounded on his back with her fists and called him names Callie hadn't even heard the muleskinners use.

The minute the two were out of sight, Callie jumped from her hiding spot and ran back to Mr. Cai's. She didn't stop to catch her breath this time, she burst into the back room, and sat on the cot beside Donny, grasping his hand.

"You're shaking. And your hand is like ice." Donny rose up and wrapped his arms around her trembling body. "What happened?"

She clung to his strong body. Pressed her cheek against his chest and absorbed the warmth and life in him. Her arms embraced him, and she splayed her fingers across his bare back above the bandage on his ribs.

For several minutes she clung to him, allowing his embrace to melt away her fear. Slowly, she eased back and peered into his unseeing eyes.

His arms released her as his hands cradled her face. "I was worried when you took so long to return. Did she try to harm you?"

Callie shook her head, swallowed the lump in her throat, and spoke. "I hid in the shadows. She arrived without a dress. She paced back and forth, waiting for me to show. One of Bentine's men came looking for her. She—she told him she planned to get rid of me." Callie took a deep breath. "Like she meant more than send me to another town."

Donny pulled her back into his arms. His chin rested on her head.

Wrapped in his arms, knowing his concern, she felt safe and cared for. Something she hadn't realized she missed. Tears trickled down her cheeks. She mourned the loss of her father's love and the safety she'd had before his death and her mother married her stepfather.

He kissed the top of her head. "You aren't alone anymore. You have me. You can depend on me. Together we'll get out of here and you'll have a new life."

"I don't want to be alone. But I can't drag you into my troubles. You have enough of your own." She talked to his chest. The warmth of his skin and the slight tickle from the spattering of light colored hair on his chest reassured her Donny would keep her safe. He cared enough about her to make sure she left Pendleton alive. Her biggest fear was knowing she would have to leave him. She couldn't have her past ruining his future.

"You aren't dragging me anywhere I don't want to go." Donny leaned back, drawing her small body onto his. "Let me hold you while you sleep." He kissed the top of her head again.

She wanted to relax in his arms, feel comforted all night, but she couldn't shake the image of her stepfather looming over her bed and then covering her.

Callie squirmed and pushed on his chest with her hands. His arms immediately released her.

"I'll never hurt you," he whispered.

She peered down at his sincere face. "I know. I need time."

"I'm right here when the time is right." He smiled, put a hand on her cheek, and glided his thumb over her nose and across her lips.

She put a hand over his on her cheek, leaned into it, and then stood. "Go to sleep."

Callie watched Donny as she undressed down to her long johns. Her body heated. Even though those eyes staring up at the ceiling couldn't see her, she knew his ears were listening to her every move. Slipping into her bed roll, her mind replayed the comfort she'd experienced in his arms, the kiss he placed on her head, and the soft way he said he would never hurt her. *Have I found a man I can trust to not hurt me?* Her stomach fluttered. Donny's smiling face floated in her mind as she drifted off to sleep.

But the comfort didn't last long. She dreamed of her stepfather. His large form looming over her, his fetid breath, squeezing hands…Then blood. So much blood. "No! No! No!"

# Chapter Seventeen

Donny woke to scared whimpers.

Callie's fearful cries of "No, no, no!" shoved him into action. Donny rolled off the bed and onto the hard dirt floor.

He pulled his body the short distance across the floor. Feeling the bedding, he found Callie's shoulder and gently shook her. "Callie? Callie, you're safe. I'm here."

Her arms circled his neck, and she clung to him like a scared child.

"Shhh… I'm here. Nothing bad will happen." He ignored the ache in his side and leg as he scooted his body closer, easing it up off the cold floor and onto her bedding.

"Nothing can hurt you." He smoothed her silky hair and held her close. "I'm here. You're safe."

Her arms gradually relaxed.

He crooked an arm under his head, listening to her soft breathing. He rubbed up and down her arm with his free hand. The minute she came fully awake her body stiffened.

The arm he rubbed released from around his neck. By her motions, she was establishing they were on the floor.

"How did you get out of bed?" she whispered.

"Your whimpering woke me. Then you started crying, 'no, no.'" He traced his fingers over her face. "What scared you?"

Her face muscles tightened.

"Don't keep it inside. I know it had to do with a man."

She started to protest.

"Shh… I can tell by the way you pull back from my touch that a man treated you badly." He'd pondered all the scenarios he could while sitting alone in the dark the last week, and he'd come to the conclusion a man forced himself on her. He'd heard enough, eavesdropping on the Halsey conversations, to know the only way to win the heart of someone who'd been so terribly wronged was patience and steady caring. "Is that who you're running from?"

Her hand still around his neck moved through the hair at his nape. She cleared her throat, but didn't say anything.

He traced her face with his fingers. Her features were small, like a child's. How could anyone want to hurt such a fine-boned, young woman?

"You don't have to tell me who if that makes it

easier. But Rachel, she's a doctor married to Clay, says it's good for a person to talk about what's eating them up inside. She says half a person's health problems are just needing to talk and not so much what she can fix as a doctor." He missed the whole Halsey clan. He hadn't realized how much he'd become a part of the family until now.

"You know a woman doctor?"

She wasn't answering his questions, but at least she was talking to him. "Yes. Clay's wife. All the Halsey brothers have wives that have, or had, men's jobs at one time. Gil's wife Darcy was a marshal when he met her. Her brother, Jeremy, and I became good friends when I moved to Sumpter. He recently married a girl he met in Alaska. And Zeke is married to Maeve. They're Pinkerton agents."

"Really? Pinkertons?"

He didn't like the fear he heard in her voice. "They only go after the people they are sent to find." He slid his hand to the back of her head, holding her against his chest. It was clear she feared the law. Why? If a man had assaulted her, he should be the one looking over his shoulder.

"And Ethan's wife, Aileen, she was a miner. Her son, Colin, inherited land in England. He recently returned from there with a wife. And Hank's wife, Kelda, was a logger when he met her."

"That's a lot of people."

The awe in her voice reminded him of the first meal he'd eaten with the entire family. "It can feel a bit overwhelming at first, but I'm considered family. I'm glad I tripped over Clay that day at the blind school and we became friends. He even moved my mother and sister to Sumpter. Ma is a teacher and my sister is going to a teaching college to become a teacher." He was proud of how his family had overcome his drunken father's abuse and were living happily.

"Tell me about your mother and sister." Her fingers stopped playing with his hair. Her head snuggled into his chest.

He smiled. She was getting comfortable.

"Ma and Dara lived in a boardinghouse in Salem while I was at the blind school. I'd visit them on Sunday and take them the extra money I made selling brooms to help them make ends meet. Back then Ma wasn't teaching school. Dara was still small and needed her."

Callie yawned.

"I need to stop boring you and let you sleep," Donny said, pushing hair back away from her face.

"No, I like hearing about your family."

Her sleepy, slurred words said she needed sleep.

"I can tell you more tomorrow night. You're safe now. Sleep"

He brushed his thumb back and forth across her cheek. Her breathing slowed, took on an even rhythm, and she was asleep.

*In his arms.*

He pulled her closer and snuggled deeper onto the small pad. Waking in the morning with her in his arms was going to be the best day of his life.

It would be interesting to see if she remained in

his arms when she woke or if she bolted.

Callie woke with a stiff neck, but she was warmer than she'd ever been since sleeping in the tunnel. She tried to move and realized she was wrapped tightly in a blanket. She opened her eyes but the room was dark. She sniffed. Donny was close. She moved her arms and realized he slept next to her. By the hardness under them, they were on the floor.

Before panicking, she reached back in her memory. She'd had a dream, and he'd flopped onto the floor to soothe her.

I must have fallen asleep, and he couldn't get back in bed without help.

She started to squirm out from under the blanket and his body holding it down. The coolness of the wall above the blanket stalled her movements. He was warm. Her mind warred with her body. She should get up and help him back into bed. Put distance between them. But the heat his body emitted welcomed her. She'd slept fitfully in the tunnel from fear and the cold. Tonight, she had warmth and a strong body to protect her. She'd be stupid to wake him and make him move.

Callie closed her eyes and snuggled against Donny's warm body. His arms wrapped around her, pulling her close. She started to push away, but his hands remained clasped at her lower back. He never touched her in her woman areas. His touch was always light, soothing, sweet.

Closing her eyes, she immediately fell asleep.

Donny woke and moaned. The ground was cold and hard. He'd sheltered Callie the best he could. Especially after she'd awakened and snuggled closer. He could tell by her shivers, she was cold. He wanted to keep her warm.

But his rib ached from the position he slept in and his leg throbbed. While throwing himself on the floor brought them closer, it had been a stupid thing to do for his injuries.

Callie twisted in his arms and sat. "You need to get back on that bed."

He smelled kerosene, heard a match light, and sulfur stung his nostrils.

"Now I can see," Callie said. "I need to fix the bed. Scoot over onto my bedroll more."

Her hands helped maneuver him to his back, onto something warm and slightly softer than where he'd laid moments before.

"This is cold down here. How do you sleep?" he asked, listening to her moving about the room.

"I curl up. It's better than being out where I don't sleep for fear someone will stumble over me." Wood scooted across rock. "There."

"Can you sit up?" Her voice came from above his head as her hands slipped under his shoulders.

He sat, wincing as his rib protested.

"Which do you think would be easier, scoot across on your backside or try to stand and use me to hold your weight off your leg?"

He'd prefer to stand. He was tired of lying and sitting, but he didn't want to fall on Callie if he lost his balance.

"I'll scoot."

He pushed with his good leg. She directed his back the direction he needed to go. The side of the bed bumped his back.

"Can you lift yourself onto the bed?"

The question held her misgivings.

"Yes. Go get breakfast while I do." He didn't want her to see the pain getting into bed was going to put on his rib.

"I'm not dressed."

He heard rustling and knew the length of her pant leg that she pulled on and the size of the shirt she'd donned. While she slept and before he fell asleep he'd measured her against himself and had a pretty good image of her size in his mind. Callie was a tiny thing, but her courage and spunk had taken root in his heart. He grew fonder of her each day.

"I'm headed out. If it pains you too much wait until I come back." The curtain swished.

Donny waited until her scent faded. He'd discovered while holding her, she had a faint floral scent under the biting lye scent. He placed his hands on the cot edge. Just that effort stung his rib, but he ignored it, and pulled his body up using his good leg to push up as well. He sat on the side of the bed. It felt good to not be lying flat and not be reclining against blankets. Straightening his back, his rib twinged, but not bad. His good leg was bent, his broken leg stuck out in the middle of the room.

He remained upright and moving his joints until Callie returned.

"It's good to see you sitting up." She set the tray down. "Does anything hurt worse?" She stood to his right.

He held out a hand. Her small one settled in his palm. "You never told me what scared you so bad last night." Her hand tugged, but he kept hold. "I won't press you for details, just know you can talk to me." He held her hand to his lips, kissed the rough back, and said, "I care about you."

Her hand trembled. "Thank you," she whispered.

"For what?" He didn't know what he'd done, but he felt ten feet tall from her whispered words.

"For caring. I haven't had that in a while." Her hand disappeared. "You goin' to sit up while you eat today?"

"Yes." He held his hands up for the bowl. The weight settled in his palms.

He ate, wondering what she was thinking. Did Callie regret her dreams and his coming to her rescue? Or did the incident bring them closer? Time would be the answer to his questions.

# Chapter Eighteen

Callie went to work every morning hoping today would be the day a dress would come in that she could borrow to send the telegraph. Each night she'd return to Donny, tell him no dress, listen to his stories of his life, and help him exercise to become stronger and ready to walk when the telegraph did get sent.

The weight of the watch in her pocket was as heavy as her conscience. She had no right to keep the watch. However, knowing the man who had it before her was killed, she was determined to stick to her plan of pretending to find the watch at the telegraph office and give it to the clerk.

Two weeks passed. Mr. Cai said Donny could try to walk with a crutch today. Callie was excited. If his leg endured the bit of pressure, she could take him on short walks in the tunnels.

She stepped into the laundry and couldn't miss Yi's glowing face. Her eyes were shining and a smile spread across her small face.

"Today good!" she exclaimed and waved her hand to a pile of laundry.

On the top was a dress that looked small enough for Callie. "Mrs. Nelding brought in laundry?" She walked over to the dress and held it up. The bosom of the dress was too large, but the length was perfect. She could wear a shawl to cover the abundance of fabric in the bodice.

"I'll change now and send the telegraph. Then we can launder the dress."

Yi nodded. "Dwee, dwee."

Callie stepped behind the small partition in the room she and Yi used to change behind when Callie lived with the Wu family. Without the proper undergarments, she had to be naked under the dress. Her one-piece union suit would show at the neckline and short sleeves on the dress. She stripped down to her socks and slipped the dress on.

Buttoning up the front of the bodice reminded her of times she'd put behind her. While dressing like a boy gave her lots of liberties dressing like a woman didn't, she missed feeling pretty.

She stepped out from behind the partition.

Yi smiled and clapped her hands. "Missy Mac very pretty!"

Callie held a foot out. "I can't wear my boots with this."

Yi scurried across to the trunk that held the Wu's clothing. She dug to the bottom and came up with a pair of leather kid slippers. "Father say mother wear these when first come to America."

Callie hugged Yi. "Xia xia. These will be perfect." She sat and pulled the shoes on. "I'll also need a shawl." She grabbed the excess fabric on the front of the dress.

Yi giggled and rummaged through another pile of laundry. She sniffed and wrinkled her nose. "Too much flower, but work."

She accepted the shawl from Yi and agreed. The garment smelled like a bordello. Callie glanced at the pile where Yi found the shawl. That's where it came from. One of the bordellos. She waved it in the air trying to force some of the smell away.

"You ready?" Yi asked, the laughter had vanished from her face. Her eyes peered into Callie's.

"Yes. Donny's boss needs to know what has happened to him. And we need to get out of here." She dug into her trouser pocket for the message and the money Donny told her to take all those weeks ago. She wondered why, if the boss and people Donny talked about so much really cared for him, why hadn't they come looking for Donny and Jasper?

Her fingers skimmed the watch. Gathering it into her hand, she shoved it into the hidden pocket in the side seam of the skirt, along with the message and the money.

"Do you think it will matter I don't have a bonnet?" Callie asked, touching her hair. She'd braided it like every morning and it hung down her back.

Yi stepped behind her, wound the braid round

her head, tucked the end under and placed pins to hold it on.

"Xia xia," Callie said and hugged the woman.

"Go." Yi waved her out of the laundry.

Callie wanted to stop by and tell Donny she was headed to the telegraph office, but she didn't want him to fear Iris had arrived at his room by the smell of the shawl.

She hurried down the tunnels and used the entrance two blocks away from the telegraph office. Out on the sidewalk it was hard to remember to act normal and not slink in the shadows or duck down an alley. She'd spent the last three years avoiding people. It took all her courage to smile back when a woman smiled or a man tipped his hat.

The telegraph office was just ahead. A man wearing a badge had his hand on the shoulder of another man. They walked toward her. She could see they were deep in discussion.

"We've looked everywhere. He couldn't have vanished unless he's dead." The tall man without a hat said.

The man wearing a badge tipped his hat to her. "We'll find him. We found Jasper."

Callie turned abruptly and followed the two. They had to be looking for Donny.

The sheriff continued. "But I think Jasper was kicked in the head. I've never questioned his sanity but his story about a drunk saying Donny's fine is hard to believe."

"Mister?" It took every ounce of pluck she had to tap the sheriff on the shoulder. She'd been hiding in fear of the law for so long, getting his attention felt like betrayal to herself.

Both men turned.

"Ma'am," the sheriff said.

"I overheard your conversation." She fought hard to keep her eyes on the sheriff and not let her gaze drop to his feet. "Are you lookin' for Donny Kimball?"

The man next to the sheriff, stepped forward. "Yes! Do you know where he is?"

The man wasn't a threat, he was excited. But her instincts sent her feet backward.

"Don't leave." The sheriff made a grab for her arm.

She turned to run, but he was quicker. His arm circled her waist and her feet left the ground.

"Don't hurt me!" she pleaded.

"Calm down. We don't want to hurt you." The sheriff set her feet back on the ground. "We only want to find Donny. Do you know where he is?"

Callie peered at the two men. They had to be brothers. Donny said the Halseys would help her. She hadn't told him the full story about her step-father. But he'd said no matter what she did, if he believed in her they would.

She swallowed the lump of fear in her throat. "Are you Halseys?"

"I'm Gil and this is Clay," the sheriff said, patting the other man on the arm.

"Donny said he works for you." She nodded to the taller of the two.

"He does. I've been trying to find him ever

since he and Jasper didn't return."

"Jasper's not crazy," she said. "Donny was worried the law would think Jasper crazy when we heard he was saying he lost a blind boy. I sent a friend to the jail to tell Jasper Donny was fine and bein' taken care of."

"That clears up what Jasper has been telling us ever since we put him in the hotel." Gil said. "But where is Donny?"

"I saw the men beat up Jasper and Donny. I couldn't get to Jasper, but I pulled Donny down into the tunnels. He's been tended by a Chinese healer." She spotted one of Mr. Bentine's men walking down the street.

Gil looked over his shoulder toward the man. "You have a problem with him?" he asked.

"He can't see me." She started to walk away.

"You haven't told us where to find Donny." Gil stepped in front of her.

"There's a gambling hall under the Temple Hotel. I'll bring Donny there in two hours." She turned her back just as Mr. Bentine's man walked up on them.

"Take us to him." Clay said, reaching out toward her.

"I can't. Your type isn't allowed in the tunnels." She glanced at Bentine's thug and headed the opposite direction. She ducked down an alley and looked back. The Halsey brothers were having a heated discussion. She needed to hurry back to the laundry, get out of these clothes, and get Donny to the gambling hall.

Callie strode quickly down the sidewalk, the stairs, and into the tunnel and Wu's laundry.

She rushed through the door before stopping.

Yi looked up from the washtub. "What go wrong?" She wiped her hands on her apron and hurried across the room.

"Nothing. I didn't send the telegraph. I didn't have to. I overheard two men talking and one was Donny's boss. They were here looking for Donny." She tossed the shawl on the pile of clothing and hurried behind the partition wishing she could keep the dress. Walking into the gambling hall with Donny dressed as Mac would put her at risk even with a sheriff on her side. She dug the money, note, and watch out of the skirt pocket. Her gut clenched. Now she'd have to find another way to get rid of the watch. She shoved it all into a trouser pocket.

She walked out from behind the partition, tossed the dress on the pile where it came from, and handed Yi her mother's shoes. "Xia xia." She hugged her friend. "I don't know if I'll see you again before we head to Donny's home."

Yi sniffed. "Missy Mac like sister."

"I feel the same about you. One of these days, I'll come back and visit to meet your husband." Tears burned the back of Callie's eyes. Yi had become family. Callie's heart ached knowing she'd probably never see Yi again.

"I will look for you."

Callie stepped away. "I hate leaving you with all this work, but Donny's friends are here and it's my chance to get away." She waved her arms.

"Thank you for everything."

"Go! No one want Mr. Bentine get you." Yi waved toward the door.

"I'll remember you always." Callie ducked out the door and ran through the tunnels to Mr. Cai's.

She entered the back room out of breath.

"What happened?" Donny sat up, his hand outstretched, reaching for her.

She grasped his hand.

He sniffed. "Why do you smell like a soiled dove?"

"You know what they smell like?" she teased.

His cheeks brightened to a red the color of the stormy sunset. "I've been in a saloon a time or two when one approached us."

"It's because I had to use a shawl from a pile of laundry from a bordello to cover the top of the dress I borrowed."

His hands ran up her arms, over her shoulders, and tugged on the collar of her shirt. "Those are the same clothes you always wear. Did you send the telegraph?" His tone brightened.

"I went but didn't have to send the telegraph." Her cheeks hurt she was smiling so hard.

Donny frowned. "You had a dress, you went, but you didn't send the telegraph? Did one of Mr. Bentine's men see you?"

"Yes and no." She didn't know why she was so happy to give Donny the news. She knew how much it meant to him to get back with Jasper and the Halsey family. But it also meant she'd have to say good-bye to him in a few days.

"Well, which is it?" he asked, sliding a hand up to cup the side of her face. He smiled. "Why's there a big grin on your face?"

"I didn't send the telegraph because I heard two men talking as I walked by them. One had a sheriff's star. They said Jasper and Donny."

"A sheriff badge? Gil? Was Clay with him? Is that who you saw?" his voice rose with excitement.

"Yes, I did. Took all I had in me to tap Gil on the shoulder and then talk to them. While we were talking one of Mr. Bentine's men walked by."

"Where are they? Gil and Clay?" He stretched a hand out as if he thought they might be in the room.

"I told them we'd meet 'em at the gambling hall in a couple hours. Well, little over an hour now." She stared at the bandage peeking out from his unbuttoned long johns. Mr. Cai had put a smaller, thinner bandage about his body. But they'd have to deal with the splint on his leg.

"We have to get you dressed." She leaned close, buttoning his underdrawers. Her mind flashed back to the day she'd found him and how her hands shook unbuttoning this garment so Mr. Cai could doctor Donny. They'd spent enough time together now, she felt comfortable helping him. Touching him.

"I can do that. Find my shirt and trousers."

Donny's hands replaced hers. Sadness wrapped around her heart. Donny made out fine without her in his life before she dragged him down here. He'd get along just fine when she left him in Sumpter.

He finished buttoning and held out his hand

for his shirt. She handed it to him, close enough his hand touched the fabric.

"Here, you shouldn't move your arms too much." She placed his hands in the armholes and slid the garment up his arms, settling it on his shoulders. "Do you want the vest?"

"No. You can leave it here. One less time I have to strain my ribs. I'll just take my jacket."

Donny buttoned the shirt. She picked up the vest and put it on over her flannel shirt. The garment hung on her like a gunny sack on a scarecrow, but it smelled like Donny.

She started feeding his splinted leg through the left trouser leg.

"I don't know if this is going to work. Those sticks, Mr. Cai used to splint your leg, make your leg too big for the pant leg." She sat back and pondered what to do.

"Take the knife from the sheath in my left boot and slice the pant leg from the knee on down." Donny put his good leg in the other pant leg.

Callie pulled his boots from the corner where she'd dropped them three weeks ago and discovered there was a knife in a sheath inside his left boot. "Why didn't you use this when those men were beating you up?" She held the eight inch knife up. The blade was thick and wide. A menacing weapon.

"I didn't know where Jasper was and didn't want to accidently cut him." Donny held his pants by the waistband. "Go ahead and slit the pant leg."

She knelt at his left foot, held the pant leg away from his leg, inserted the blade, and let the sharp edge glide down the fabric, barely making a sound.

The pant leg flapped open, but Donny's leg slid through the top part. He stood on one leg to pull the garment over his backside and button it.

Callie put the knife back in the boot sheath. "You're only going to be able to wear the right boot."

"That's okay. The doc gave me a crutch this morning to start exercising." He stopped pulling on his boot and raised his face toward her. "Is he out there? I'd like to thank him and pay him."

"I'll see." She stood and ducked through the curtain. Mr. Cai was mixing powders.

"Donny would like to see you," she said.

Mr. Cai poured the powder into a small jar, twisted on the lid, and picked up a small cloth bag. He nodded and passed though the curtain.

Callie followed.

"Doc, I'd like to thank you for your help. My friends have come to get me, so I'll be leaving to-day." Donny held out his hand.

Mr. Cai placed the bottle and bag in his hand. "Medicine. Bottle help sleep. Herbs to heal."

"Thank you. How much do I owe you?" Donny ran his hands over his jacket and pulled out a small leather wallet.

"Three dollar," Mr. Cai said.

"Here I'll help you," Callie put her hands on Donny's.

# Chapter Nineteen

"I don't need help." Donny pushed Callie's hands to the side. This was one of the times when he could prove to her he wasn't someone to be helped. His fingers felt the corners of the bills. The school had taught him to fold the corners on the bills so that he knew the currency by feeling how they were folded. He grasped a five dollar bill and handed it to the doctor. "This should cover food and everything."

"Xia Xia," said the doctor.

He frowned. It was the first time the man had spoken his language to Donny.

"He said thank you," Callie said close to his ear.

Donny smiled at the man. "I should be thanking you. From what C— oof!"

Callie elbowed him.

"From what Mac has said, I'm lucky you all didn't leave me out in the road to rot." He rubbed the spot on his side that smarted from the woman's tiny elbow.

"Go now. Take care Missy Mac, she special."

The scent he'd registered as the doc's faded and the curtain swished.

He reached out and bumped into Callie's hip. Slipping an arm around her waist, he pulled her closer. "You didn't have to hit me."

"No one knows my name. And if you keep slipping up, I'll have to leave you before Sumpter. I can't have you saying my name and getting both of us in trouble."

The desperation in her voice tugged at his heart. He'd made up his mind she was going to be his wife, but proving to her that she didn't have to hide was hard when he didn't even know what she was hiding from.

"Why are you sure someone hearing your name will bring us trouble?" He used his free hand to cradle her face.

"I'd rather slip away with you still being my friend than you know the truth and hate me."

"Callie, I would never hate you." He took this moment to do what he'd been dying to do for the last two weeks. She'd lain in his arms for a while each night as they talked about his life and a little about her life when her pa was still alive and how she'd survived the last three years on her own. But she'd never said why she was on her own.

He rubbed his thumb across her bottom lip,

lowered his face, and touched her lips with his. She didn't pull back or gasp with fright. He pressed a little more and tilted his head to fully capture her mouth. He'd dreamed of this moment for weeks. The kiss was more intoxicating than he'd imagined a kiss could be. The only problem with kissing her—he wanted more.

Donny used all the restraint he could muster and gently released her lips, kissing her cheeks and forehead.

Air whooshed out of Callie's mouth, and he heard her swallow.

"What was that for?" she asked in a soft, breathy voice.

"To show you I would never hate you." He kissed her forehead again when he really wanted to taste her lips. "We better get going. I'm not sure how fast I can move with the crutch."

She nodded and pulled out of his hands.

"Here." She grasped his hand and placed the wooden crutch against his palm.

He clutched the long wooden pole and used it to help him stand. Tucking the Y-shaped end under the arm on his left side, he held out his right hand. "You'll have to hold my hand and lead me until we get into the tunnel. I can use your footsteps to guide me there."

"What about your jacket? You should put it on, the tunnels are cold."

His right hand was shoved into a sleeve. He moved the crutch to his right hand and shoved his left hand into the other sleeve. Placing the crutch back under his left arm he held out his hand.

Callie wrapped her small hand around his.

"Do you have a jacket on?" he asked.

"Yes. Come on."

His head brushed fabric. The curtain over the doorway, he'd guess. The room they moved through held the smells he connected with the doctor. Herbs, medicine, and the cloying tobacco scent.

Callie turned him to his left. "We're in the tunnel now. It is five feet across. Do you want me to walk beside you or ahead of you?"

The thumping of feet and the jangle of harnesses above him made it hard for him to concentrate on Callie's footsteps. "Walk beside me. I didn't realize there would be so much noise from up above."

"The board walkways are above the tunnels. Metal grates let some light shine in. The grates also bring the street noises, the rain, and the snow down here." Callie nudged him to walk.

By the time they turned the first corner, he was becoming tired. Laying around the last few weeks had weakened him more than he thought possible. "I need to stop." He hated to admit he was tired, but he didn't want to collapse and have Callie try to carry or drag him.

"How much farther to the gambling hall?" He needed to know how long he had to conserve his energy.

"We're about half way." She stepped closer to him. "You can lean on me if you need to."

He placed his right arm around her shoulders and hugged her. "I'm too big for you to be holding up. But a hug gives me strength."

She leaned her head against his side. Her head fit under his arm like the crutch on the other side. He kissed the top of her head.

"You know, I'm the one who dragged you down the stairs, and then Yi and I dragged you to Mr. Cai's and put you on the bed. Don't underestimate the power of small women."

He heard the conviction in her words.

"Never. Gil's wife is a small woman. Not as small as you, but she has done some mighty things. Things you wouldn't expect most women to be able to do."

"I'd like to meet her someday."

He caught the melancholy tone to her words. It was as if she didn't believe she would. "If Gil is here helping Clay, it's a good chance Darcy is at Sumpter staying with Rachel waiting for us to come back."

"We best get goin'." Callie stepped away from him and grasped his hand.

She took a step, and he started hobbling alongside of her.

He wondered if they'd head for Sumpter right away. He hoped so. While he needed more time to convince Callie to stay with him, he also wanted her out of this town where she was wanted by a bordello owner.

Callie walked slowly alongside Donny as he lumbered along, trying to keep weight off his broken leg. She tried to keep her mind off the kiss and his words. He made it sound like he expected her to stay with him, perhaps even marry him. She was fond of him. And trusted him. Something that she'd had a hard time doing with anyone since her mother remarried. But she couldn't stay in his life. Not being wanted by the law.

She stopped at the get-a-way door before the gambling hall. How would Donny get through it? He would have to crawl while she held it up.

"Why are we stopping," Donny asked.

"There is a door that opens from top to bottom with a bar in the middle." She dropped his left boot that she'd been carrying and placed his hand on the door. She pushed the top, rocking the bottom to come up. "Do you understand how it works?"

He touched the bottom that she held up and slid his hand as far as he could along the door. "It's like a table top."

"The way I'm holding it, yes. I can hold it up, but you'll have to crawl under it." She touched his arm. "Do you still have enough strength to do that?"

He captured her hand. "My friends and your future are on the other side of the door. I could crawl the length of the tunnel if I had to."

She swallowed the lump of emotion in her throat. His conviction in his friends was a wonderful trait. His belief in her made her stomach knot. He'd never know what her future held. She wasn't sticking around long enough for her past to catch up to Donny and his friends.

"Want me to hold the crutch while you crawl?" she asked.

"No, I'll slide it along in front of me. I'll need

it to help me get up." Donny slowly lowered his body to the ground and started crawling forward.

She waited until Donny's upper body appeared past the end of the door and followed behind him. Bending at the waist, she picked up the boot and ducked under the door, dropping it in place when Donny's feet were clear.

"You can stop crawling and stand." She bent to help him.

"I can do this." He rolled to his side, then to a sitting position, and shoved the crutch into the ground between his legs. Using the crutch to pull his body up and pushing with his good leg, he stood.

Callie pushed the long forelock of his hair to the side. Sweat beaded his brow. "Want to rest?"

"How close are we?"

"About twenty feet. Listen."

If she could hear the murmuring voices she was pretty sure Donny could.

"I hear it. Voices, clinking of glass, and cards shuffling." He sniffed. "Liquor, cigars, unwashed bodies, and kerosene." He smiled. "I would know where I was headed even if you hadn't told me."

She smiled and took his hand. "When we get to the doorway, I can't hold your hand. I want them to think I'm a boy, though if any of Bentine's men are in there, I might have to just hightail it back down the tunnel."

He tugged on her hand. "Gil will keep the men from grabbing you. Don't run. If you do, I won't be able to find you for another month." He raised her hand to his lips and kissed it. "I'm hanging on to you. It doesn't matter if they think you're a boy or a woman. You aren't being taken from me by anyone."

"You don't want to say that. You don't know—"

"I know enough about you to fight for you. Come on."

She tried once to pull her hand from his, but he kept a firm enough grip she couldn't pull loose. He led her to the entrance of the gambling hall and hobbled through the door.

Callie counted about a dozen men scattered about the room at the tables. Her gaze landed on Gil and Clay. They were watching the door to the street.

"There's that Mac!" one of the men exclaimed.

Callie tried to pull loose from Donny but he held tight.

"Gil? Clay?" he called out.

The two responded before he'd called out the first name. Gil broke a path through the men with Clay on his heels.

"Good to see you, Donny," Gil said, standing between her and the room full of men.

Clay moved forward and Gil placed his hand on Donny's shoulder. The man hugged Donny.

The man who'd called out her name was standing in front of the three men protecting her.

"You don't need that boy. He's supposed to go see Mr. Bentine," the man said, as if he was taking a burden off of them.

"Mac won't be seeing Mr. Bentine. He's going

with us." Donny started to move forward.

The man put his hand out, smacking Donny in the chest. Donny brought the crutch up and smacked the man in the arm, knocking it away.

"Unless you want me to haul you to the sheriff in this town, I'd suggest you stand out of our way." Gil pulled a pistol from his holster and tapped Clay on the shoulder. "The door is to your left twenty feet."

Clay, with his hand on Donny's shoulder, headed for the door. Donny had her wrist in a tight grip. She clutched his boot with the knife to her chest. If things went bad, she had a weapon. One she knew how to use. While Clay moved with confidence, he wasn't walking as briskly as she'd witnessed when she saw the two on the street. She moved a step ahead of Donny to lead them to the door quicker.

Clay's hand found the latch before she could reach for it. He opened the door and the three of them, with Gil following, climbed the steps to the street.

"Where's your hotel? The sooner I'm off the street the less trouble I'll bring you." She tried again to tug her hand from Donny's hold, but he refused to let her go.

"We're a block over at the Bowman Hotel." Gil didn't stop, he pushed them down the street.

Callie knew where the Bowman was and helped guide the two men in front of her who walked as if they could see where they were going. Clay veered toward the edge of the boardwalk once, but the minute his foot stepped on the area where the runners were nailed to the boards underneath, he moved back to the middle of the walkway.

At the hotel, Gil hustled them toward the stairway.

Callie stopped. "You have to let Donny rest. This is the first time he's been on his feet since the beating." She wrapped an arm around Donny's right arm, hoping to help keep him on his feet.

"Sorry, Donny," Clay said, thumping Donny on the back.

Gil waved to an area in the corner of the lobby. "Take him over there."

She helped Donny. His breathing came in puffs. His weight bearing down on her was more than he'd ever allowed himself to put on her.

"Here's a chair." She turned him, and helped him lower into a padded chair.

He released a huge sigh. "I was getting tired, but I didn't want anyone to catch up with you."

She grasped his hand and squeezed. "You'd all be better off if I just skedaddled out of here."

His grip tightened on her hand. "I told you I'd get you out of this town. We have help now. You aren't taking off on your own."

Clay stood to the side of the chair listening. He waved his hand back and forth. "It sounds like there's a story about you two. Want to tell me?"

Callie scanned the lobby. Gil was talking to the person at the registration desk. She didn't like that a lawman was her savior at the moment. For all she knew, he'd connect her with a wanted poster he'd seen. If ever there was a time to be able to distance herself from Donny and the other two men, now was the time.

"Not much to tell," she tried to pull her hand from Donny's. For a guy who was too exhausted to walk another step, he had a locked grip on her hand.

# Chapter Twenty

Donny held onto Callie's hand. A tremor rippled through her that alerted him to the fact she was thinking of bolting. He gave a little tug, drawing her closer.

"I need to ask you something," he said, crooking a finger for her to draw closer. The floral scent he'd noticed on her before from the shawl she said she'd borrowed, told him she was leaning close.

"What name do you want me to call you?" he whispered. He could tell she wore a hat by the slight tapping of the brim on his head as she leaned down.

"Mac, for now," she whispered back.

He leaned back. "Mac is shy about telling how she saved me."

A soft growl made him smile.

"They can tell you aren't a boy just as easy as I could," he said.

Her hand jerked, trying to break his hold. "Let go. Two of Bentine's men are headed this way." Her voice held frustration.

"Where's Gil?" Donny didn't know the layout of the hotel and was afraid without Gil's sight there was no way to hide Callie.

"Why?" Clay asked.

"We need to hide Mac from the men she says are coming this way."

"Stay in the chair. Mac, take my arm." Clay's voice sounded confident.

Donny could sense Callie's hesitation. "Take his arm. He'll get you out of here."

He released her arm and heard the two of them walking to his left. Hurried footsteps approached. He slid the crutch out to trip whoever was hurrying his way.

"Where are Clay and your friend going?" Gil asked.

Donny smiled. He should have known Gil was keeping an eye on them.

"Mac is trying to get away from a couple of men she saw coming this way." Donny used the crutch to push to his feet. "We need to get her up to a room and out of sight as quick as possible."

"Why is she hiding?" Gil's suspicious nature rang in his question.

"I know the people looking for her right now work for a powerful man who runs a hotel, saloon, gaming hall, and bordello. He wants her in his bordello." He put a hand on Gil's shoulder. "She's running from something else, but she's not willing to tell me much about it. I do know it has something to do with her stepfather."

Gil moved forward and Donny walked alongside of him.

"Do you know where Clay is taking Mac?" He hoped his boss could keep the flighty woman with him.

"He's headed to the back stairway." Gil stopped. "Put your hand on the rail. We're on the second floor."

Donny slowly climbed the stairs. It was an ordeal, placing his good foot on the stair above and using that leg to lift his body up while balancing with the crutch. Sweat dripped into his eyes and his right leg was quivering when his hand wrapped around the end of the handrail.

"You'll be sleeping for a week when we get you settled in a bed," Gil said, placing Donny's hand on his shoulder. "I paid for another room down the hall from ours. You can stay in there."

He nodded and noticed Gil didn't say he and Mac, which was how it would be. "Where's Jasper?"

"He's in the room Clay and I are staying in. We can move him into your room if you'd like the company."

"No. I'll have Mac in my room."

Gil stopped. "It's not proper you having a girl in your room."

"She's the one who's been looking after me ever since she pulled me out of the street. And I need to keep her off the streets until we leave here.

She's going with us. I'm getting her out of here before she ends up working for Mr. Bentine. Or worse, she ends up in jail for killing him."

Donny knew from the things Callie had told him, there was no way she'd work in a bordello. And if Bentine tried to make her, she'd make sure he never touched her. There was only one way she could do that. He didn't like to think of Callie as a killer, but he'd heard the wrath in her voice when she said she'd never be a victim to a man.

"I don't like the thought of her taking care of you if she's got a mind for killing people." Gil's tone was the one he used when dealing with thieves and murderers.

"She won't hurt me. I'm not a threat to her. I won't take her against her will." He smiled. "She's going to come to me when she's ready."

Gil chuckled and started walking again. "I see you've set your heart on this girl."

"Yes, but don't tell her that. She'd bolt quicker than if she saw Bentine's men." Donny heard voices.

"Sounds like Clay is having a time keeping your friend in the room." Gil stopped and Donny heard a door swish open.

Callie stared at the man standing in front of the door like a statue. She'd tried once to get by him and had to retreat or panic from his arms wrapped around her. It didn't help the Negro reclined on a bed watched the whole thing.

The door opened. Donny hobbled in with Gil behind him.

"Looks like you're standing guard like you do to keep your kids in line," Gil said, slapping Clay on the back.

"She's almost as small as Frankie." Clay relaxed his stance.

"Donny, you are a sight for sore eyes, boy," the Negro said, swinging his legs off the bed and walking toward Donny.

Callie wanted to move to Donny's side but feared the large man patting him on the back.

"Yes sir, when that drunk tol' me you was fine, I thanked the Lord for answerin' my prayers." He ruffled Donny's hair.

"That was Mac's idea," Donny said, holding out a hand.

She knew he wanted her to come to him. The urge to stand her ground was overruled by the tiredness she saw on his face and heard in his voice. He should be in a bed, resting his ribs and his leg.

Callie slid between the other three and put her hand in his. "You should be in bed." She scanned the room. "Which one do I put him in?"

"I paid for a room down the hall for him," Gil said, reaching for the door. "I'll show you where it is and you can get him settled."

"Can you stay on your feet, well foot, a little longer?" she asked Donny.

"Knowing I can lie down soon, I can make it." He held onto her hand.

She led him out of the room and down three doors to the one where Gil stood.

Entering the room she was amazed at the size

of the two beds in the room and the flower partition in the corner.

"There's two beds," she said. "Which side of the room do you want?" She peered into Donny's tired face. His brow furrowed.

"I want the bed closest to the door."

She thought that a funny request but led him to the bed, closest to the door. With all his exertion today, he was smelling more like Swifty, minus the liquor.

"Do you happened to have clean clothes for Donny?" she asked Gil, dropping the boot with the knife on the floor at the end of the bed and grasping the boot on Donny's right foot.

"We do." He walked to Donny's side. "Want me to help you to the water closet and fix you up with a bath? And I'll get a doctor up here to put a cast on your foot instead of those sticks."

"That all sounds good. In about an hour. I just need to rest right now." Donny lifted his broken leg onto the bed and lay back, slowly pulling his right leg up on the mattress.

"I'll be back in an hour." Gil stared at Callie, making her uncomfortable. "We still need to hear about how Donny ended up in the tunnels." He pivoted and disappeared out the door.

Callie stared at the door. He'd been studying her face. Did he recognize me? He certainly doesn't trust me.

"Ignore him. He distrusts everyone, especially when it involves family members." Donny patted the mattress next to him. "Come here."

She thought about refusing him, but he was so tired, she knew he'd fall asleep within minutes of her sitting on the bed.

Donny wrapped an arm around her waist when she sat and pulled her down beside him.

"Promise me you won't be gone when I wake up." His eye brows nearly touched above his nose as he made a stern face.

She shrugged. "Where would I go?" The only person she trusted was in this room. There wasn't anywhere for her to go.

"Nowhere. Callie, as long as you stay in this room with me, no one will know where you are. You're safe. No looking over your shoulder, no skulking in alleys. Stay with me. Here. In this room." His hand rubbed up and down her side.

The gentleness and comfort she experienced from his touch made her nod. "I'll stay in this room, but I don't think the Halseys will like it."

"I told Gil you were staying with me. He wasn't happy, but he won't make a stink. I'm a man and can make my own choices." Donny kissed the top of her head. "Stay here until I fall asleep. Then you can lie down on the bed and take a nap." His words slurred and his arm slipped lower until it rested on the bed.

He was worn out from walking the tunnel and then climbing stairs to this room.

His chest rose and fell in a steady rhythm under her hand. She glanced up, peering at his unshaven face and long hair. He gave off a musky, sweaty scent. One she'd grown used to. She'd only wanted to borrow the razor from Ting Lee once a week. It was coming up on time to borrow the shave things from him again. What would Donny look like cleaned up? She'd yet to see the real Donny Kimball. Only the bloody and bruised version and now the dirty, tired version. What would he be like when he was healthy, clean, and fully rested?

"I'll never know," she said quietly and stood. She padded across the thick rug and pulled the curtain back to peer down into the street. Her gaze landed on two men, pacing up and down the boardwalk across the street. She dropped the curtain and backed away from the window.

This was the safest place for her until they left the town. She ran her hand over the watch in her pocket. How do I get this to Bentine? She stared at the curtain, her mind flicking through scenarios. I should have dropped it out of my pocket when we were on the street.

She moved the curtain enough to peek at the men watching the hotel. If she could get this out to the men…

*Chapter Twenty-one*

The sound of knuckles rapping on the door pulled Callie from a dream of running through a maze of laundry.

"Just a minute." She sat on the edge of the bed and rubbed her eyes.

"It's probably Gil," Donny said from the other bed.

"Yeah." She padded across the room and un-locked the door.

"Donny awake? I'll take him for a bath. The doctor will be here in an hour to give him a new cast and check him over." Gil strode into the room. His gaze flickered to the rumpled bed where she'd napped, and her boots on the floor beside it.

"I'm awake and ready for a bath. Haven't had one since before I left home." Donny swung his legs over the edge of the bed and sat up.

"Make sure he doesn't do anything to harm his ribs," she said, watching Gil hand the crutch to Donny.

"You have busted ribs too?" Gil stared at Donny. "Why didn't you say something when we were rushing you along the street?"

"Getting C-Mac out of sight was more important than my discomfort." Donny didn't move when Gil started to walk. "Mac, you'll be here when I get back?"

"Yes." She would. Seeing Bentine's men outside the hotel, she knew there wasn't any way she'd set foot outside. At least not until she'd had a day to think on it. But she did have a plan to get the watch out of her possession.

The smile he bestowed on her made her belly flutter.

"I'll be a different man when you see me."

"You'll smell better, that's for sure," she teased.

He wrinkled his nose. "You still smell like that shawl."

She frowned. She didn't want him thinking she was a soiled dove because she smelled like one. "Go take your bath."

The two left the room. The minute the door closed, she rushed across the room and locked it. She didn't know how long Donny would take to get clean, but she wasn't leaving the door unlocked. If only she had something to do other than worry and watch the men watching the hotel.

Donny sat in a deep tub of hot water. As a boy

he didn't cotton to baths but as a grown up, he'd relished them for easing sore muscles and making a body feel clean and healthy. He'd dunked the leg with the splint in the water. Might as well since the doc would be putting on a new cast made out of cloth and plaster.

He scrubbed his hair. The length was longer than he usually wore it.

The door opened, swirling cold air into the room. "That you, Gil?" he asked.

"Yeah, brought you some clothes."

Donny dunked his head under the water, rinsing his hair. He bobbed up and swiped the water from his face. "Did you get the things for Mac?"

"Yeah. Figured she's about Darcy's size, though a mite shorter."

"Thank you. I know you don't trust her, but she saved my life and she has a good heart." Donny gripped the sides of the porcelain tub to shove to his feet.

A hand grabbed his arm. "Watch your step getting out of there. I can't believe you put that con-traption in the water."

"I wanted to get completely clean. Besides, it will come off soon." A rough towel pushed against his chest. He grabbed it and started drying off.

He heard Gil pacing.

"Why are you pacing? Need to get back to Darcy and the family?" Donny finished drying and found the chair he'd sat on to undress.

"No. It's Mac. She acts like someone hiding from the law and has some kind of grudge."

He didn't like the accusation in Gil's voice. "I told you she isn't going to kill me. She's got a good heart."

"Yet you said she'd kill this Bentine if she got the chance."

"No, I said she'd kill him if he forced himself on her." Donny held out his hand. A soft clean pair of drawers touched his palm. He worked his hand around the garment. "Where's the legs on this?"

"I bought a new pair but cut the legs off above the knees. Make it easier for you to be decent while the doctor puts the cast on."

Donny struggled getting the drawers over the splinted leg but liked that he was covered in the major area. He pulled on the undershirt. It smelled good. He'd become rank lyin' in that bed in the tunnel for so long. A soft garment dropped in his lap. Feeling the dimensions and buttons, he smiled. "What color is this shirt?" He slid his arms into the sleeves.

"Blue. I'll keep the pants until you get the cast on your leg."

The Y-end of the crutch bumped his hand.

"I have to walk down the hall in just my drawers?" he questioned Gil.

"Mac is in the tub at the other end of the hall. Clay's watching for people in the hall." Gil grasped his right arm and hauled him to his feet.

"Funny. How's Clay going to know who's coming until they get close enough he can hear them?" Donny knew his boss had honed his hearing since becoming blind but he wasn't ready to risk exposing himself to some lady.

"He's at the top of the stairs." Gil urged him toward the door.

"What if someone comes out of a room?"

"I'll see that. Come on. Your room is only a few doors down the hall."

Air wafted around his wet head as Gil opened the door. Donny couldn't do anything other than hobble as fast as he could to his room.

His knuckles smacked the door frame as they hurried through the doorway. Three steps and he found the bed, turned, and sat.

"There. No one saw you." Gil took the crutch.

Donny scooted back on the bed, propping his back against the headboard. "Hey!" His injured foot was raised.

"You're getting the bed all wet. I tucked a blanket under that soggy splint." Gil moved away from the bed. "The doctor should be here any time."

The clink of a watch cover dropping into place told Donny Gil checked his pocket watch.

A knock on the door pivoted Donny's head toward the sound.

Gil's steps and the click of the door knob turning revealed Gil answering the door.

"I'm Dr. Gordon, you requested my services?" The man's voice was high-pitched and young sounding.

"Yes. I'm Gil Halsey. This is the patient, Donny Kimball."

Steps drew near the bed. "Doc, pleased to meet you." Donny held out his hand.

Gil made a sound deep in his throat and said, "He's blind. He doesn't have a disease."

"I'm sorry." A soft, pudgy hand weakly grasped Donny's hand.

"I have a broken leg. The Chinese doctor splinted it," Donny said, pointing to his left leg.

"When did this happen?" Dr. Gordon asked. The sound of a buckle unfastening and medicinal aromas proved the man opened his doctor bag.

"About three weeks ago." Donny ran a hand over his side. "I had a bad rib. That seems to have healed."

"I'll be the judge of that. I'll take care of this leg first." He made a disgusted sound. "Why is this all wet?"

"I took a bath." Donny smiled.

He could tell by the silence and Gil's snicker the doctor wasn't impressed.

Callie sunk into the clean water sprinkled with the bath salts. She'd found the luxury wrapped in the package Gil handed her before leading her down the hall to the small room with a bath tub and running water.

She inhaled the scent of lavender and dunked her head into the water. Lathering up the soap, she washed her hair and then her body. It was wonderful to know the dirt mucking up the water was hers and not someone else's.

When Gil first arrived at the room with the package, she'd balked at taking it. He'd insisted it was all Donny's idea and if she didn't want to upset

Donny she should take the package and have a bath.

Once in the locked room, she'd opened the package and found two sets of undergarments, two dresses, and a night dress. Along with a hair brush, a tooth brush, and two wooden hair combs. And the bath salts on the top. The last time she'd had this many female fripperies in her possession had been before she ran away. On the bottom of the package was a pair of soft leather shoes. How Gil managed to get clothing and shoes that would fit, stumped her.

She completely rinsed and stepped out of the tub, draping a large, rough towel around her body. The last year living in the tunnels she'd thought nothing of the comforts she'd missed. Today, she was relishing in the small things she'd taken for granted before that awful night.

The undergarments felt foreign after so many months wearing men's undergarments. She readjusted the ties several times and finally left them. Even though the dresses were identical other than color, and knowing Donny wouldn't see the color, she favored the blue. With the dress on, she wiggled into her shoes and giggled at the lightness of them. The boots she'd been wearing had made her feet feel like ten-pound weights. She skipped in place a couple of times and grinned so hard her cheeks hurt.

There was a small mirror on the wall. She brushed her hair and pulled it up at the sides with the wooden combs. The woman staring back at her looked nothing like the scared girl who'd fled her home three years ago. She never wanted to be that girl again.

Callie refolded the brown paper over the extra new clothes and wadded the dirty clothes into a ball. Picking it all up, she moved to the door, opened it, and peered up and down the hall.

Clay stood beside the door to the room she and Donny shared. She walked up to him.

The man sniffed and smiled. "Lavender. I've always like the cleanliness of that scent."

Her cheeks heated. How did he know he was talking to her and not some woman walking by? "You can thank your brother for the scent." She stopped in front of the door. "Can I go in?"

"The doctor is still in there. And it wasn't Gil's idea for the bath salts. It was Donny's."

She stared at the man. "How do you know that?"

"Gil wasn't happy Donny asked him to get those things for you."

"But he did. Why? Gil could have just as easily said he did and let it go." She needed to understand Gil. He was the person she feared most right now. Bentine didn't know where she was, but Gil was a lawman. One who could have seen a wanted poster with her picture.

"Because Gil is a man of honor. He doesn't just wear the badge. He practices justice in all he does." Clay leaned against the wall. "So tell me about you. How did you come to be in the tunnels with the Chinese?"

She snorted. "I'm not tellin' you. I haven't told Donny everything. And I trust him."

Clay's smile drooped and the crinkles around his eyes disappeared. "You don't trust me?"

The hang dog expression on his face made her laugh. "You'll find I trust very few people."

"Then Donny should feel honored you trust him." The sincerity in his voice drew her gaze to his face.

"When did you come to Pendleton looking for Donny and Jasper?" she asked, curious as to when the man became worried.

"I waited an extra two days from when they should have returned. Thinking the wagon may have broken or they had to go around a landslide on a road. When they were five days late, I telegraphed the man in charge of the company where they were picking up supplies. He said they never arrived. I had a meeting with Ethan, Hank, and Gil. We decided Gil and I would come look for them."

He peered at her, and she would never have known he couldn't see the way his gaze seemed to linger on her. "I don't understand why Donny didn't send me a telegraph right away."

She'd wondered when this question would come up. She'd rather answer it for Clay than Gil. But knew she needed to address this with both men at the same time.

"When the doctor leaves, I'll explain it to you and Gil." She wanted to be sitting by Donny's side, holding his hand for fortitude.

# Chapter Twenty-two

"Thanks, doc," Donny said, leaning back against the pillow Gil placed between his back and the headboard. He was wore out from the bath and the doctor's prodding. Donny closed his eyes and listened. The door opened and closed as the doctor left the room. Gil and Clay spoke with the doctor in the hallway. The door reopened and the scent of lavender entered the room along with the swish of skirts.

He couldn't stop his lips from curving into a smile. This impression—lavender and feminine clothes—was how he'd thought of Callie from the moment he'd discovered she was a girl. He patted the bed next to him. "Come sit. I want to see what you look like in a dress."

The swish of skirts drew near. The bed bounced as she sat beside his hip.

"Did you have a nice bath?" he asked, finding her hand.

"Yes. Thank you for the clothes, the toiletries, and the lovely shoes." She leaned forward and kissed his clean-shaven cheek.

That she initiated the intimate touch made his pulse race. But he knew better than to do any more than smile. Gil and Clay could walk through the door at any minute.

He moved his hand up her arm. Thin cotton covered her arm. "What color is the dress?"

"Blue."

The smile in her voice made his heart sing.

He continued moving his hand up to her shoulder. The sleeves were a little bit puffy here. Then up to find a prim lace collar. He wanted to run his hand down her side to feel her shape but refrained. Perhaps later.

A soft knock on the door made Callie pull back.

"No. You're fine. Stay." He held her hand. "Come in."

The cadence of boots and softer-soled shoes told him Gil and Clay approached. A chair scraped the floor and creaked.

"Mac told Clay she'd tell us both why you never telegraphed letting us know where you were," Gil said.

Callie sucked in air and stiffened. Donny stroked the back of her hand with his thumb, trying to ease her fears.

By the level of Gil's voice from where Donny sat, Gil was on a chair. Clay was probably propped on a chair as well.

Donny cleared his throat. "The day Mac checked on Jasper at the jail, the owner of a saloon, gaming hall, and bordello, discovered Mac was a girl. She's been hiding from him since, and we didn't want to chance his men catching her."

Callie gripped Donny's hand, but her gaze was on the lawman. Gil's eyes narrowed and his forehead furrowed as Donny talked. Her conscience warred with her fear of the man. She could give the watch to Gil and he could give it to the sheriff or even Bentine. But would he think she stole it rather than found it? The stern set to his face told her he'd think she stole it.

"That doesn't make sense. What difference does it make if he discovered she was a girl? He can't force her to work in the bordello." Gil wasn't asking the question of Donny. His stare was leveled on her.

She gulped. Donny's firm grip and his thumb stroking the back of her hand gave her the courage to peer back at Gil. "That's true. But it seems every time Mr. Bentine decides he wants a woman in his bordello, things happen to where she has no choice but to go to work for him."

Gil shook his head.

"I don't understand?" said Clay. "Why does he want you? You obviously don't want to be there."

"Stories I've heard about how several of the women in his bordello came to be there aren't nice." She glared at Gil. "Or lawful. One woman's husband was killed, but his murderer has yet to be found. Rumors say it was Mr. Bentine. She had a time paying off her husband's debts. Mr. Bentine stepped in to take care of her financial troubles, only then she was beholdin' to him and he made her his personal woman. Until he found someone new and now this woman is working like all the others. And there's the two girls that he put in the bordello because their father lost everything at Bentine's gambling hall. Some say it was rigged because Bentine had been admiring the two young ladies the week before at a social function and the father had never gambled before." She stopped, letting what she had to say sink in.

"That still doesn't explain why it took you so long to try and contact us?" Gil's gaze flickered to Donny's thumb stroking her hand and back up to her face.

"Bentine sent men down into the tunnels looking for Mac. They were looking for Mac dressed in boys clothes." Donny said. "She had to wait to go up on the street until a dress came into the laundry that fit her."

Gil stared at Donny, and Clay's grin grew larger.

Callie wanted to get closer to Donny, soak in his warmth and confidence. He nodded his head for her to continue the story.

"That was today. A dress arrived that wasn't too long and make people take notice of me." She stared at Gil. "I was headed to the telegraph office when I overheard you and Clay talkin'. When you said Jasper and Donny's names I figured you had to be lookin' for them."

"I figured as much," Clay said. "But I thought you were a soiled dove because of the flowery scent you gave off."

Her cheeks heated. "The dress was too large in the top. I grabbed the first shawl I found. The pile was from a bordello."

"Are the women you stole the clothing from going to be looking for them and you?" Gil asked.

"No! I didn't steal them. I borrowed. After I left you two, I went to the laundry, changed back into my clothes, and left the garments to be laundered." She tugged her hand from Donny's and glared at Gil, crossing her arms. How dare the man accuse her of stealing? No matter how hungry or desperate she'd been since leaving home, she'd never once stole anything. And he'd think she stole the watch if she asked for help getting it back to Bentine.

"I think you hit a sore spot," Clay said. He rubbed his hands on his thighs. "We talked to the doctor. He said we can take Donny home as long as he rides in a wagon."

Callie's heart raced. She could get out of Pendleton tomorrow. Put distance between her and Mr. Bentine and everything nasty she'd encountered in this town.

Clay continued, "We did find the wagon when we arrived. Someone took it and the team to the livery. The liveryman was getting ready to sell it and the horses. Took a while to prove they belonged to us."

Donny found her hand, clasping it again.

"Jasper is ready to get home. How about you Donny?" Clay asked.

"I am. We're taking Mac with us. She needs to get away from Mr. Bentine. Nothing better than a four-man guard to get her out of here." Donny squeezed her hand.

Callie couldn't shake her uneasiness as Gil watched the whole thing and didn't say a word.

"We're going to go down and get dinner. We'll bring a tray up for the two of you." Clay stood and headed to the door.

Gil stood slower. He motioned for Callie to follow him to the door.

Reluctantly, she released Donny's hand and followed him out into the hall.

"I don't understand why you were hiding in the tunnels in the first place, and Bentine can't make a woman do something she doesn't want to do. All you have to do is let the lawman in the town know and he'd help you." He motioned with his head toward the room and Donny. "But that young man believes in you and I believe in his good sense. If you do anything to hurt him… I'll find you."

His intense glare bore into her as if he could seek answers.

Callie crossed her arms and stared back. "I don't plan on hurtin' anyone."

He pivoted and followed his brother down the hall.

Callie steadied her shaking hands and slipped back into the room. She closed the door and stood with her back against it wondering if traveling with the Halseys, Jasper, and Donny was a good idea. She didn't plan on any trouble, but lately, it seemed to dog her good intentions.

Donny waited patiently for Callie to return. He'd heard Gil's voice, low and stern. What was he saying to Callie? Would his suspicious nature send her away?

The door closed. Lavender invaded the room once more.

"Come sit by me," he said, patting the bed beside him. She didn't say anything, but her reluctance hung like a fog in the room. "What did Gil say to you?"

The chair scraped the floor. Her scent grew closer.

He reached out and found her sitting on a chair by the head of the bed. "Why are you sitting there?"

"It seems safer." Her voice faltered as if unsure of the words she wanted to say.

"Safer? You know I won't hurt you." He frowned. What had Gil said to her to make her think he'd hurt her.

"I know. I don't want to hurt you. I'm sorry you have been dragged into my troubles."

The sincerity in her words and vulnerability in her tone made his chest ache.

"You could never hurt me." He held out his hand, palm up. He needed the connection with her. Needed to remind her they were strong together.

She placed her hand in his. He pressed their palms together and laced their fingers.

"I-you…" A huge sigh stirred the air between them. "You're the first person in a very long time that I feel safe with and trust."

He waited as the silence thickened. His mouth wanted to tell her she was safe and he did trust her, but his mind told him to wait, give her time to decide what she wanted to tell him.

She cleared her throat. "Gil told me not to hurt you. I think he meant not physically, but then he's been glaring at me most of the time so I'm not sure."

"I'll tell him—"

She placed a finger on his lips. "You don't need to tell him anything." Her hand dropped to the collar of his shirt. Her narrow fingers played with the collar. "He doesn't trust me because he thinks he's seen me before." Another deep sigh. "He probably saw my picture on a wanted poster."

Donny felt his chin drop and his mouth open. He quickly shut his mouth and waited for his brain to quit spinning before asking, "Why would you be on a wanted poster?"

Her fingers stopped fiddling with his collar. Her hand, tugged slightly in his, but he kept ahold.

"I said I ran away from home. That was three years ago. When I was seventeen. My ma remarried when I was fifteen. On my sixteenth birthday, my stepfather started putting his hands on me when Ma wasn't lookin' and tellin' me he was goin' to visit my bed."

Donny tugged her toward him. To his surprise she slipped off the chair and settled on the bed next to him. "Go on."

"I stayed awake as long as I could each night. I spent a year fearing he'd come to my bed. The night of my seventeenth birthday, he cornered me. His hands…" she hiccupped.

"Shhh… You don't have to tell me this." He rubbed a hand up and down her arm. He wanted to pull her into his arms, but his mind had already jumped ahead to what he knew happened. Knowing this about her past, he understood her fear of being touched.

She sniffed. "I do. I don't want you hurt because of my actions. My mother called out and he left me. But I could tell by his eyes he'd come to my bed that night."

He heard her swallow.

"I took a butcher knife from the kitchen and put it under the mattress of my bed with the handle sticking out so it would be easy to grab." Her hand grabbed his forearm. "I didn't plan to use it, only frighten him. He came into my room. I'd been layin' awake waitin' and listenin'." Her fingers tightened on his arm. "He didn't give me time to do anything before he was in my bed and grabbin' me, shovin' his leg between mine." Her voice grew hard, distant. "I wasn't going to let him ruin my life. He'd already ruined Ma's by marryin' her and comin' after me."

Donny squeezed her hand. His heart ached as his mind soared to anger.

"He weighed over twice my weight and once he was on top of me, I could barely breathe let alone call out. But I managed to get my hand on the knife handle. I pulled it out and shoved it into his side. He rolled off and landed on the floor. I dropped the knife and scooted across the bed, climbing out the other side. I dressed, threw some clothes in a small satchel, and lit out of there."

Donny's mind was spinning. What this small woman went through and how she'd survived on her own was a testament to her strength. "Why didn't you tell your ma?"

# Chapter Twenty-three

Callie wiped at the tears trickling down her cheeks and stared at the man calmly asking a question after she'd just told him she'd killed a man. His free hand rested on top of her hand that clutched his arm.

"Ma would have said I started it. She'd been tellin' me to stay clear of her husband. Like I wanted him to ruin my life." She couldn't hide the disappointment and bitterness she harbored toward her mother.

"But to run away. Don't you have a relative you could have lived with?" Donny's questions didn't sound like accusations. His tone was quiet, low, and caring.

"My pa died when I was thirteen. He lost most of his family to cholera and Ma didn't have any family either. Pa taught me to hunt and train horses. I thought I could do that and make a living, but everyone I approached about that kind of work just laughed and told me to keep going. Even when I dressed like a boy no one took me serious."

"How did you survive? Three years is a long time." He grasped her hand.

His grip and thumb moving back and forth soothed the ache in her heart. His presence had filled the emptiness her heart had endured since her father's death.

"I'd get small jobs that fed me or gave me a roof, until I'd feel like too many people were watching me as if they knew, and I'd move on. I thought Pendleton was large enough I could get a job as a boy and not be bothered, but one night while I was sleeping under the steps of one of the hotels a drunk stumbled across me. He thought I was a boy until he knocked my hat off." She squeezed her eyes shut. "I kicked him like I'd seen a soiled dove do to a man who was trying to make her go with him. The man dropped to his knees, and I ran into the nearest steps to the tunnels. Yi found me."

She didn't flinch when Donny's arm wrapped around her, drawing her against his chest.

"Stay with me. I promise to keep you safe," he whispered and kissed the top of her head.

Callie rested her head on his chest and inhaled his clean male scent. He did make her feel safe. She could get used to being held in his arms and having a safe place to live. Snuggling deep into his embrace, she wanted it to last. But it couldn't. Not with her a murderer and his friend a marshal.

A soft knock sent her to her feet. She crossed the room and opened the door. Good as his word, Clay stood in front of the door holding a tray laden with food.

"Here, let me help with that." She took the tray. "Want to visit while we eat?" she asked, needing the extra distraction. She didn't want her mind to wander back to the safety of Donny's arms.

"If you don't mind. I'm still curious about you and what it's like in the tunnels." Clay entered, closed the door, and stopped in the middle of the room. "You moved the chair."

She marveled at his memory of where the chair was in the room. "Let me set the tray down, and I'll get the chair for you." She placed the tray on the table by the bed and set a chair in front of Clay. He put his hands on the back, walked around, and sat.

Donny swung his legs over the edge of the bed and sat up. "I'll eat here," he said.

Callie picked up one of the plates and rested it on Donny's lap.

"What did Clay bring us?" he asked.

"Roast, potatoes, beans, and a roll," she said, placing a fork in his right hand.

"Where are they?"

She stared at him. "On the plate."

Clay and Donny laughed at the same time.

"He means where on the plate is each food," Clay said.

"Oh. The roast is on the left side, the—"

Donny raised the hand with the fork stopping her. "Where are they on the plate like the numbers on a clock?"

"Meat at nine, potatoes at six, beans at three, and the roll is at twelve." She watched Donny find the roast with his fork and feel along the edges discovering the meat's size and shape.

"If you're going to be around the two of us, you'll learn to give us details a bit differently than you would most people," Clay said.

Her stomach clenched. She would be traveling with them to Sumpter. *Unless I leave them before.* After telling Donny the truth about why she ran away, she'd fallen even more vulnerable to the safety he gave her. If she stayed with him too long, she may not want to leave. If he married a person wanted by the law it could ruin his life.

Donny stopped cutting his meat and raised his face. His eyes appeared to be staring at her. "Why aren't you eating?" he asked.

She stared back at him. "How do you know I'm not eating?"

"I don't hear utensils clanking or you chewing."

"Are you saying I chew loudly?" she joked.

He grinned. "Like an old cow chewing her cud."

"Just for that I'll eat your dessert," she threatened.

Clay chuckled.

"I don't think so. I know where the tray is sitting." Donny reached his right hand toward the table.

Callie snatched up the tray before he could

touch it. "You're sure you know where it is?" she teased.

Donny grinned. "I take back my remark about chewing like a cow."

"Then you may have dessert." She placed the tray back on the table and picked up the plate. She took the chair next to the bed and started eating.

Contemplating how easy it was for her to talk to and joke with Donny, she listened to Clay and Donny talk about other Halsey family members and the business Clay owned.

Donny listened to Clay and responded when necessary, but his mind was still taking in everything Callie told him. If her stepfather wasn't already dead, he would have killed the man himself. She hadn't said if the man had entered her, but he'd damaged her heart and her trust. Donny's heart ached for the small girl attacked by a large man. He admired her courage to strike out on her own, and suffered her disappointment to be told she couldn't do the jobs she knew how to do.

"You and Jasper were missed," Clay said. "Jasper's organization and your skilled hands put us behind on our orders."

"We didn't ask those men to pull us off the wagon and beat us up." The anger he'd felt upon waking from the beating returned.

"You may have been pulled off the wagon, but you leaped into the fighting," Callie said.

"You what?" Clay asked.

When Callie had called him a fool for going to Jasper's rescue, he'd felt stung. "When I realized the men had pulled Jasper off the wagon and were beating on him, I had to defend him."

"How many men were beating up on them?" Clay asked.

"Six," Callie responded.

He'd never been told the number. When they had him on the ground kicking him, he'd felt several different boots.

Clay whistled. "No wonder the two of you look like you do. Mac, could you give Gil a description of the men? I'd like to make sure they are punished for beating up two men who were just going about their business."

Donny didn't need eyes to feel the tension in the air. Callie didn't want to go near the law. And he was in a tough spot. He believed her story and knew it was self-defense. He needed someone to look at the posters in Gil's office and see if the law was looking for Callie. Jeremy was his first thought, but then again, Jasper might be the best person. He knew about injustice.

"I don't remember their faces. I was lookin' at Donny and not the men beating on him." Her clipped, unemotional delivery told him she wouldn't give details of the men even if she did know them. She didn't need bad seeds, Bentine, and the law after her.

"That's too bad. This town could use more law enforcement. Beating up innocent people just because they are different shouldn't be tolerated." Clay's tone revealed he was on a mission. "We already have Jasper's descriptions of the men who beat on him. I was hoping Mac could look them over and say if she agreed."

"Clay, Pendleton isn't your town to worry about cleaning up," Donny said.

"I may not live here, but I do business here. I want my employees safe when they come to town on my errands." Clay's soft-soled shoes paced back and forth.

The chair by the bed creaked. "Is he a politician?" Callie whispered near Donny's ear.

Donny smiled. "He takes slights to anyone personal."

Clay stopped pacing. "I need to go see the head of the law in this town."

The door latch clicked, a breeze wafted by, and the door closed with a thud.

Silence.

Clay had left the room.

"My, he gets riled up about justice," Callie said.

Donny held out his hand. When her small palm met his, he drew her near the bed. "If he knew your story, he'd fight for you." He held her hand up to his lips and kissed the back of it. "I'll fight for you."

# Chapter Twenty-four

Callie's heart raced. She believed he'd fight for her. He'd proven he wasn't afraid of a fight when he'd jumped in to defend his friend. But she couldn't ask him to ruin his life for her.

She picked up his empty plate and gently tugged her hand from his. "Looks like you're ready for dessert." She placed the smaller plate with apple pie into his upturned palms.

He sniffed. "Smells like apple pie."

"That's what it is." She picked up her plate and dug into the sweet treat. This meal was the first normal meal she'd had since ducking into the tunnels a year ago. While her mouth enjoyed every bite, her stomach was gurgling and getting reacquainted with the heavier food.

They ate in silence, which was fine with her. She didn't have much to say after spilling she'd killed someone.

Donny held out his plate. She took it and placed it on the tray. If she didn't fear being seen, she would have used the excuse of delivering the tray to the kitchen to put space between her and the man relaxing on the bed. A smile curved his soft lips and crinkled the skin at the corner of his eyes.

Callie picked up the tray, clanking the dishes. She'd place it out in the hall. Perhaps Gil would see it and take it down to the kitchen.

"Where are you going?" Donny asked, his right hand extending toward her. His fingers touched her skirt and his hand raised, cupping her elbow. "Even dressed like you are it isn't safe for you to wander around."

"I know. I'm just placing the tray out in the hall." Her elbow warmed from his gentle touch. *What is happening to me? His touch makes me feel lighter, happier.*

She stepped away, opened the door, and placed the tray to the side in the hall. Standing, she glanced toward the stairs. Two men stepped off the stairs into the hallway. She ducked into the room and closed the door clicking the lock.

One of the men had been Mr. Bentine. What was he doing in this hotel? He'd stared at her long enough that night in his office he would recognize her no matter what she was wearing.

"What's wrong?" Donny pushed back to a sitting position on the edge of the bed.

She stared at him. How did he know something was wrong from six feet away?

"Come here." He opened his arms.

Ignoring the nagging in her head that she should keep her distance, she walked between his legs and into his welcoming embrace. She folded her arms across her chest and leaned against him, pressing her head to his shoulder.

His strong arms circled her, holding her, making her feel safe.

They remained this way for several minutes.

Donny kissed her temple and pressed her closer. "What did you see out in the hall?"

She'd hoped he'd forget, but she should have known better. He picked up on everything and dug to find the truth.

"Mr. Bentine and another man came up the stairs," she said, snuggling her face into the curve of his neck.

Donny's body stiffened. "Did he see you?"

"No. I ducked back in before they looked down the hall." She sighed heavily. "I hope we can leave here tomorrow. I don't like hiding or putting you in danger."

"I'm not the one in danger." He tipped her face up toward his. "I meant it when I said I won't let anything happen to you." His lips lowered to hers.

The gentle brushing of their lips sent a shimmer of joy racing through her body. The sensation was more exhilarating than anything she'd ever experienced. His hand remained under her chin as he deepened the kiss. His lips pressed a bit harder. They moved under hers, pressing, caressing, and pulsing happiness through her veins.

Her body pressed closer to his, her arms un-folded, sliding up around his neck. She didn't want him to stop kissing her. She'd never felt this alive and worthy before.

Donny had only kissed a few women. Most were curious about a blind man. Never had he ap-proached a kiss with so much caring and love for a woman. The heightened emotions and his yearning body battled with his good sense. He knew from her past he had to take things slow. From her inexperi-enced kisses, he knew her stepfather had not tried to woo the young girl. Only forced himself on her.

Shoving the anger he felt toward the man from his mind, Donny eased out of the kiss. When Cal-lie slipped her arms around his neck and pressed against him, his body sprang to life. He didn't want to scare her if she discovered his need for her.

She moaned, her lips following his retreat.

He smiled and held her head away from him. "I want nothing more than to continue kissing you, but we need to take things slow." He kissed her fore-head and rested his forehead against hers. "Callie, I have never kissed another and felt as peaceful and as heated."

She drew her head back. "You've kissed other women?"

Her innocent question made him chuckle.

"A few. Most were curious about kissing a blind boy and then a man. But I was just as curious about kissing as they were." He pulled her lips to his and kissed her again. Not as long or as deep. He couldn't do that again and stay sane. "But you are the only person I want to kiss for the rest of my life."

She inhaled and drew her head back. What was she thinking?

"What's wrong?" he asked, keeping his hand on her face so he could bring her lips back to his if he needed to remind her how good it felt.

"What you said. The forever part. I-can't."

"Can't what?" He stroked her cheek with his thumb. Her face wasn't warm and supple. Her facial muscles had tightened, her body in his hand become rigid and felt ready to bolt.

"I can't ruin your life." The words came out as a sad whisper.

"How could you ruin my life? You bring joy to me. I want to feel that joy every day." He hadn't come out and asked her to marry him. He wanted to wait until she was out of danger and not feeling beholden to him for keeping her safe.

"What if Gil discovers my past and takes me away? I don't want your friends and family to treat you poorly because of me." She placed a hand on his face. "You are special. Don't plan your life around me. I'll only bring you pain."

She believed her words. He heard it in the heartfelt plea. But he believed his life would not be whole without her in it.

"How about we just go day by day. You agree to allow me to have my feelings and I'll let you have yours." He turned his head and kissed the palm of her hand.

Her body trembled and she sighed.

"I want to agree, but my head says by allowing myself to enjoy your kisses, I'll be setting us both up for pain."

"But sometimes isn't the pain you experience after a happy event better than not having had the moment at all?" He wasn't sure what he was saying. He just had to show her she could have pleasure. To allow herself to be open to happiness. He knew it would be a rocky road, but he planned to claim her heart and make her his wife.

Callie stared at the man talking like a traveling salesman. Telling her what she wanted to hear. But he said it with such sincerity, she wanted to believe him. Trust him. His kisses, gentle touch, and sincerity in his words pried open the armor around her heart more. She wanted to believe there was a man who'd put her first and would never hurt her or leave her. But did she dare hope Donny was that man?

"Give us a chance," he whispered and claimed her lips again.

She melted into him, savoring the kiss and the delicious sensations warming her body. Never had she dreamed that kissing a man could be so thrilling and dangerous.

He drew back. "I'll take that response as a yes, you'll stick around."

The humor in his voice made her smile.

A yawn built and she couldn't hide it.

"We need to get some sleep. We head for Sumpter tomorrow." Donny released her.

"Yes, it's been a busy day." She stepped away

from him and immediately missed the comfort of his arms.

He stood. "I need to use the privy. Do you?"

"I don't want to set foot out of this room." Her face heated. "I'll use the commode behind the screen. Do you want to do that?" She wasn't sure how she'd help him relieve himself. That had been Mr. Cai's job when they were in the tunnel.

Donny grabbed the crutch leaning against the end of the bed and hobbled to the door. "Point me to Gil and Clay's room," he said, opening the door.

She turned him to his right. "Keep your hand on the wall. They are the third door down." Even knowing it wasn't safe to stick her head out into the hall, she couldn't close the door until Donny had stopped at the right room and knocked.

Gil answered.

She closed and locked the door and hurried to the screened off area in the corner of the room. She used the chamber pot in the commode behind the screen. Water in the pitcher on the washstand was luke warm. She washed up, trying to decide if she should get into her nightgown before Donny came back.

Glancing at the door that would need to be unlocked when he returned and not knowing if he would be alone or with Gil, she decided to wait to put her nightgown on until Donny returned. She laid out the garment and pulled the combs from her hair.

A soft knock on the door sent her across the room.

# Chapter Twenty-five

Donny waited by the door. Gil had wanted to come back to the room with him, but he'd made it down the hall to Gil's room and wasn't worried he'd knock on the wrong room on the way back.

The lock clicked and the door opened. The scent of lavender filled his nostrils and he smiled.

He hobbled into the room, stopping by his bed.

"I see you found the right room," Callie said, lingering near his bed as he set the crutch against the end where he could find it easily.

"Yes." He held out his hands. She placed her hands in his. "Are you ready for bed?" He ran a hand up her arm. Cotton. She was still dressed.

"No, I waited. I wasn't sure if Gil would return with you and didn't want him to see me in my nightdress."

He smiled. "He wanted to come, but I told him

there wasn't any need. I thought you might have changed and didn't want him to see you."

She giggled.

"What's funny?" he asked.

"It's funny how we have the same thoughts." She slipped her hands from his. "I'll get ready now. You can undress while I change."

"Are you going somewhere?" He'd detected a strange hitch to her voice.

"Just behind the screen, in the corner." Her footsteps faded to the far side of the room.

The rustle of clothing sent images into his head that heated his body. To distract himself, Donny stood, slid out of his trousers, pulled off his socks, and stuffed them into the pocket of his trousers. He took off his shirt, placing the shirt and trousers at the end of the bed where he could find them. He'd lost track of his boots, but Callie would give them to him in the morning.

Even though Callie had seen him nearly naked while helping the Chinese doctor, he didn't want to upset her when she came back around the screen. Lifting the covers on the bed, he slid under them and reclined on the pillow.

The rustling stopped. Soft padded footsteps grew louder. Clothing rustled, there was a click, and the creak of the other bed.

"Good night," he said, wishing she were sleeping in his arms.

"Good night."

Donny listened to her movements and then her soft breathing.

The conversation he and Gil had had while Donny used the commode in Gil's room still rankled.

"What's Mac's last name?" Gil had asked.

"I don't know." He'd felt sheepish not knowing the last name of the woman he'd decided was going to be his wife. But she hadn't told him, and knowing her past and fear of being arrested, he doubted she'd ever tell him.

"You don't know her last name? I bet Mac isn't even her first name." Gil's voice raised. "It isn't is it? I can tell by the expression on your face."

"Gil, I don't know why you're so worried about a little mite of a woman," Clay said.

"Because I know a small woman can be just as harmful to a man as a full-sized one. Remember, I'm married to a small spit-fire." Gil's voice softened as he talked about Darcy.

"I bet when you met there were things about her you kept quiet. Things that might bring her harm," Donny had countered. He knew the story. How Darcy had pretended to be a young man, much like Callie. And he knew that Gil had kept her secret.

"This is different. Darcy's secret was to keep her safe. Mac is running from something." Gil stated.

"So was Darcy," Clay said.

Donny smiled. Clay would stick up for him and Callie. He'd struggled with Rachel's parents being against him.

"What about this Bentine? I still don't believe

he is after her just because he wants her in his bordello. One woman isn't worth his time and effort to forcefully bring her into his business. Besides if he has met her, he'd know she'd cause trouble."

Donny agreed. It didn't make sense, but it seemed the bordello owner took pleasure in procuring belligerent women. "I don't understand. I only know the stories I heard from the Chinese doctor. He had no reason to lie to me. He cares about C-Mac." Damn, he'd slipped again.

"See there! You did it again, what is her real name?" Gil jumped on his slip of her name.

"I promised I wouldn't tell you or anyone. It's taken me time to build her trust. I won't do anything to jeopardize it." Donny would lie to Gil rather than lose the trust he'd gained from Callie.

"Trust. That goes two ways. Do you trust her?" Gil's tone had softened.

"Yes. She could have left me out on the street, but she didn't. She lost her job because of me." Donny had felt bad when she'd said she could no longer go up on the streets because she'd tried to learn information about Jasper for him.

"Has she trusted you enough to tell you why she was hiding in the tunnels?" Gil pushed.

"Yes." Donny walked to the door. He was tired of being interrogated. "Night Jasper. Night Clay." He put his hand on the door knob.

"But you won't tell us." Gil said, beside him.

"No. That's how I keep her trust. If it was something to worry about, I'd tell you. It isn't." Donny had stepped out into the hall and ran his crutch along the wall on the left.

"You know I think of you as family and you can trust me," Gil said from behind him.

"I know. But it's not my business to tell." Donny knew the man wasn't through digging into Callie's past. He'd have to make sure Gil wasn't left alone with Callie to hound her on the trip to Sumpter.

Callie pried her eyes open. Faint light shone through the window. Morning was coming. She stretched. That was the first night in a long time that she'd slept deeply. The soft bed and feeling secure had a lot to do with it. Glancing across the room, she watched the steady rise and fall of Donny's chest.

Memories of his embrace and kisses last night heated her cheeks and body. She would have never believed a kiss could make a person feel so wanted. After what her stepfather did to her, she'd shut her mind to ever having a man care for her. But the blind man she'd dragged off the street was slowly opening her heart and her mind to the possibility that she could live a normal life. One with love and a family.

She rolled to her side.

"Are you awake?" Donny whispered.

A smile curved her lips. This time he didn't scare her. "Yes."

"Is it morning?" he asked, pushing his body to a sitting position.

"Almost. There's a soft glow in the window."

He smiled. Her breath caught at the sight. Was he happy it was morning or that the sun was shining?

"I've been hoping someone would come into my life who could show me what I've been missing."

She stared at him. "I don't understand. What do you mean?"

"Your description of the sun. 'A soft glow in the window'. That's an image I can imagine better than the 'sun is shining.'"

Her heart fluttered knowing her words brought him joy. "Don't the people around you tell you what is there?"

"Just the obvious. Watch out for that tree. There's a hole. That type of thing. No one describes things in a way that lets me feel my surroundings."

"I'll try to remember that." She swung her legs off the bed and stood. "Did Gil say how early of a start we'd make?" Callie picked up the clothing she'd draped on the end of the bed and headed for the screen. "I'm changing behind the screen if you want to get dressed."

He laughed. "I don't know why you go behind the screen. I can't see you."

"I know, but the way you seem to peer at me sometimes when you're listening it looks like you are watching." She ducked behind the screen and dressed. The sound of Donny getting dressed made her smile. He didn't do it quietly. His clothes rustled, he cursed under his breath, and then she heard something thump to the floor.

She rounded the end of the screen. The crutch had fallen from its perch by the bedside table. Donny moved his right foot back and forth across the floor, no doubt searching for the crutch.

"I'll get it." She picked up the crutch and handed it to him.

"Thank you. I didn't answer your question. Gil said he'd bring us breakfast and go get the wagon from the livery. We should be hearing from him soon. It's a good three-day ride by wagon to get to Sumpter." Donny clasped her hand when she handed him the crutch. He leaned toward her.

She knew what he was searching for. Callie smiled and placed her lips against his. A morning kiss seemed like the right thing to do after last night.

His arms wrapped around her, drawing her against his body. "Good morning," he whispered before kissing her again.

"Good morning," she returned, when he ended the kiss. "This is a nice way to start the day." As soon as the words fell from her lips she realized by saying this he would think she'd decided to stay with him. She hadn't. Not really. Though her heart which had just learned happiness was now aching with the knowledge she would be leaving him once he was back home.

"It is a very nice way to start the day." He hugged her close, then stepped away. "Where are my boots?"

"At the end of the bed." She retrieved the boots from where she'd put them when they'd arrived, handing him the one for the right foot.

"Thank you." His brow furrowed. "Do you think the left one will fit with this cast?" He settled onto the chair by his bed and pulled on his right boot.

"I don't think so. We can put a couple socks over it to keep your foot warm and protected." She dug into the brown paper wrapped package on the table. Gil had bought new clothes for Donny when he'd shopped for her. There was another pair of socks.

Callie walked over to the chair where Donny sat. "Here is another pair of socks. See if you can put on all three."

He grasped her hand holding the socks. "Thank you for helping me. It's been a long time since I've had someone other than Jasper guiding me. I like your scent and soft voice a whole lot better."

She smiled. "I haven't had anyone to worry about other than myself for so long it's nice to think about someone else."

Knuckles rapping on the door drew her away from Donny.

She opened the door.

Gil held a tray of food.

"Morning," he said, passing her and placing the tray on the table. "Eat up. I'll be back in thirty minutes." He nodded toward the door. "Lock that behind me. There's two shady looking men hanging out in the lobby. We'll take the back stairs and load up in the alley."

Callie's hands shook as she closed and locked the door. Did Mr. Bentine see her last night? Did he send his thugs to grab her?

"Gil will get us out of town without trouble," Donny said.

"I know." The words didn't sound convincing to her own ears. She gathered a plate for Donny and walked over to where he sat in the chair. "Eggs at two, bread at six, and bacon at nine."

Before she placed the plate in his hands, Donny reached out, wrapping an arm around her waist.

"No one is going to take you away from me."

She rested her head on top of his a moment then placed the plate in his hand and moved to the table. There was no response. Dread formed in the pit of her stomach. She didn't want Donny and his friends being hurt because of her.

*Chapter Twenty-six*

Donny ate his breakfast listening to Callie. He could tell Gil's comment about the men hanging around was bothering her. The utensils sounded like they slid around the plate rather than food being stabbed and eaten.

She took away his plate when he'd finished.

"Coffee?" she asked.

"Please."

When she brought over his cup, he held onto her hand holding the coffee. "Don't let the two men worry you. Gil is good at his job. He'll get us out of here."

"But he can't keep all of you safe."

"Don't you mean us safe?" He'd caught the fact she hadn't included herself. Was she planning to slip away?

"He doesn't want to keep me safe. He's only

doing this for you, not me. I can tell. He believes I'm trouble."

She slipped her hand out of his, leaving him with a mug of lukewarm coffee.

"You aren't trouble. You are a woman in trouble. We all want to help you. Don't think the rest of us won't be able to protect you."

She exhaled. "Two of you are healing from beatings and two of you are blind. I can see why Gil doesn't want me around. I have men after me. Men who would stop at nothing to hurt me and anyone else in the way."

"What's wrong with taking a chance that we can keep you safe?" He set the cup on the bedside table and waved an arm. "You don't have to hide behind boy's clothing or in a tunnel any more. Come with us and you won't have to worry about the past. I want you to only think of the future." He'd never wanted anything as much as he wanted this woman to trust he and his friends could keep her safe.

He heard the clink of a pocket watch being closed. "Do you have a pocket watch?" It was the first time he'd heard her look at a watch.

"How do you know?"

Her accusation tightened his gut. What was she doing with a watch? Had she taken Gil's? He didn't believe she would steal, but why else did she have a watch now? "I heard the clink of the lid closing. Is that your watch?"

"No. I found it on the ground the night Bentine discovered I was a girl."

He heard a catch in her voice. She wanted to tell him more. "Where on the ground?"

She sighed heavily. "I didn't tell you everything about that night. The drunk who knocked me down, he must have stolen this watch because it was on the ground beside me after he fell on me. The man who hauled me into Bentine told the other men to find the watch. They grabbed the drunk and pulled him into an alley."

The swish of her skirts back and forth told him she paced.

"I thought he was a drunk?" Donny asked.

"I thought that at first, but I think he was stumbling around because they'd beat him up so badly. I put the watch in my pocket and didn't look at it until I was back in the room with you. It has an inscription. Raymond Bentine, three numbers, and a small key is attached to the inside of the lid. I was trying to figure out how to get it back to Bentine without him knowing I had it. Then Swifty told me the man they were beating on that night was found dead."

Her voice shook.

Donny stood and hobbled to the middle of the room, gathering her into his arms.

"Bentine was already looking for you. Do you think he knows you have the watch?" Donny now understood Bentine's desire to find Callie.

"There are so many men looking for me, I'd say he's figured it out. I was going to drop the watch at the telegraph office. Then pick it up and hand it to the clerk. I planned to tell him I found it on the floor, but I never made it to the telegraph office." She snuggled into his arms. "We have to give him the watch back. He'll just send men after us if we don't." She leaned back. "I didn't want to say anything. I was afraid Gil would accuse me of stealing it. I don't want it, but I couldn't figure out how to get it back without Bentine's men grabbing me."

"I'll think of something. Give me the watch." Donny held out a hand.

"I don't want you to get beat up." She pulled out of his arms.

"I'll drop it in the hallway when we leave the hotel. Someone will find it and Bentine will have to tell his men to forget about you." Donny wiggled his fingers.

Callie stared at Donny's outstretched hand. She wanted to get rid of the watch, but what if Donny didn't drop it? Then he would have it in his possession if Bentine's men caught up to them.

"I'll drop it on our way out of here. If you can't get it done, I don't want it found on you. I didn't want to tell you and have them beat you to get you to talk." She had the watch in her skirt pocket. She'd just slip her hand in and drop the watch in the street as they pulled out of town. Preferably in front of Bentine's saloon.

"I don't like you holding onto it any longer than necessary." Donny took a step toward her.

A knock on the door halted his steps.

She opened the door.

"Ready?" Gil asked.

"I'll gather our clothes. You take Donny." She

hurried to the two paper-wrapped parcels holding their clothes and bent to retrieve Donny's left boot. She grabbed a lightweight shawl that had been in the bundle with the clothes and wrapped it around her shoulders.

"I'm not leaving this room without you beside me," Donny said, shaking off Gil's hand and waiting for her to step beside him.

Callie shook her head at Gil who was getting ready to say something. "My arms are full. Slip your right hand through my arm."

He reached out, felt her arm, and slipped his right hand through the crook of her arm. "Let's go," he said.

They barely fit through the door walking side by side but she managed to get them through.

"We're taking the back stairs Clay brought you up yesterday," Gil said, striding to the room he occupied with Jasper and Clay. The door opened and the two men stepped into the hallway, a satchel dangling from one of their hands.

"Mornin'," Jasper said, tipping his head.

"Good mornin'," she replied at the same time as Donny.

"Look like good weather to travel?" Clay asked.

"Sun is shining," Gil said as they stepped out a door into the growing daylight.

Callie looked down into the alley. A buckboard with two horses stood at the base of the stairs.

Callie moved down a step and waited for Donny. Going down proved to be more awkward for him. He placed the crutch on the step below and slowly stepped down with his good foot before lowering his cast foot to the step. Gil grabbed the items she had in her arms, allowing her to use both hands to help steady Donny.

At the bottom, Gil tossed the men's satchels along with their wrapped bundles into the wagon. Jasper led Clay to the back of the wagon. Clay turned his back to the wagon and hefted himself into the back, then scooted to a side.

Jasper reached out to Donny. "Back yerself up to the wagon."

Donny backed up and placed his hands on the wagon bed. Jasper put his hands under Donny's arms and helped lift him into the back.

"Scoot on over to the side." Gil said, reaching for Callie.

She ignored his outstretched hand and climbed into the back of the wagon, sitting next to Donny.

The wagon swayed as Jasper and Gil climbed up into the wagon seat.

Donny's hand moved up her arm to her head. "Think you should cover your head? Just to make it less easy to see your face?" he asked in a low voice.

"I have a shawl." She pulled it up over her head.

The wagon lurched. They moved out of the alley and onto the Main Street.

Callie slipped her hand into her skirt pocket and wrapped her fingers around the watch. The wagon lumbered by Bentine's saloon. She dangled her hand over the side and dropped the watch. A huge sigh expelled all the air in her lungs.

"You did it?" Donny asked quietly.

"Yes." The elation at having rid herself of the watch moved her to kiss his cheek.

He smiled and found her hand. They held hands as the wagon swayed and carried them out of Pendleton.

Freedom was a heady thing. She was out of the tunnels, the watch no longer burdened her conscience, and she had a caring man looking out for her. For the first time in three years she had a glimmer of a future beyond running and hiding. A future she'd thought had been snatched from her the night her stepfather entered her bedroom.

Callie let the shawl fall away from her head when she could no longer see Pendleton. She wasn't going to hide any more. Donny knew her past and didn't condemn her.

"Where are you originally from?" Clay asked as the wagon rumbled along a dirt road over a grass-covered hill.

Donny squeezed her hand.

"I'm from Kentucky." She didn't have to give the town.

"That's a long way away. Do you have any family here?" Clay asked.

"No." She could answer without elaborating.

"You traveled out here all by yourself?" Donny asked, surprise echoing in his voice.

"I had to get as far away as I could. I stopped when my money ran out." She stared out at the mountains to their left. They were majestic. She'd been drawn to them when she'd caught a ride with a muleskinner who crossed the mountains hauling supplies. Callie figured Donny didn't need to know her money ran out about Colorado. It took her nearly two years to make her way to Pendleton.

"You can't be very old. Why did you need to get away?" Clay asked.

"I just did." She wouldn't tell anyone else why she left home.

Donny squeezed her hand.

She knew he'd keep her secret.

# Chapter Twenty-seven

Donny knew Clay's questions were hard for Callie to answer. He was intrigued that she'd traveled clear from Kentucky by herself. When they were alone, he had a lot of questions for her. Right now he'd listen, hold her hand, and be thankful she was able to drop the watch. They didn't need Bentine's men following them.

Clay took the hint she wouldn't talk about her past anymore and fell silent. The jangle of the harness, creak of the wagon, rumble of the tires and clomp of the horses hooves on the packed dirt road was a welcome and comforting sound. The occasional trill of a bird added to the joy he felt riding along, holding Callie's hand.

Before long the sway of the wagon lulled him asleep. His head tipped sideways, landing on a narrow shoulder. Callie's small hand patted his cheek, and he fell asleep.

"Whoa!" Gil's voice penetrated Donny's slumber.

Donny raised his head. He had a kink in his neck. Rubbing the sore spot, he asked, "Where are we?"

"It's a small clearing with a crick," Callie replied. "We're stoppin' to stretch our legs and water the horses."

The tap of heels and the swaying of the wagon told him Callie was walking to the end of the wagon and the men were crawling off the wagon seat.

He held onto the side of the wagon, moving to the back. At the back, he dangled his legs over and slowly slid, landing with his good leg on the ground. "Can someone give me my crutch?" he asked.

The wooden stick pressed against his chest. The force and the scent told him who to thank. "Thank you, Jasper."

"Welcome," he said, his voice fading.

The jangle of harnesses meant Jasper was watering the horses.

"C-Mac?" he questioned, hoping to go for a stroll with her away from the rest.

"You're going to have to stop doing that," she whispered by his right side.

"I'm sorry." He grasped her hand with his. "Let's walk away from the others."

She led him a distance away from the rest and stopped.

"If you'd just tell them your real name it would be easier to not have to remember to call you Mac," he said, holding her hand.

"You know why I can't." Her voice didn't hold as much objection as usual.

"I don't see how something you did in Kentucky would get clear out here. No one would expect a seventeen-year-old girl to travel that far on her own. You don't have to tell us your last name. Callie is a common name for a woman." He leaned on the crutch and placed his left hand on her cheek. "It's a beautiful name for a beautiful woman."

She pressed her face into his hand. "You don't know I'm beautiful."

"I don't have to see you to know you are beautiful. You have a giving heart and care about others. That makes you beautiful to me." He leaned closer, hoping for a kiss.

Her head moved backwards away from his searching lips.

"Please don't kiss me when others can see."

He was confused. "But you kissed my cheek in the street in Pendleton."

"That was an impulse. I was so happy to be rid of the watch, I-I just did what felt right to show my happiness."

A smile curved his lips. "If that's the case, you can be happy and show me any time you want."

"They're hitchin' the horses back up. Come on." She tugged on his hand, leading him back to the wagon.

"Can we tell them to call you Callie?" he persisted as they neared the commotion of the hitching and voices.

"I guess."

She didn't sound convinced, but he'd run with her hollow acceptance.

"Everyone," Donny said, gaining the other men's attention. "You can call Callie by her real name. Mac was the one she used when pretending to be a boy."

"Pleased to meet you, Callie," Clay said in a playful tone.

"Miss Callie, good to hear you aren't goin' by a boy's name no more," Jasper added.

"Glad to see you've decided to trust us," Gil responded. "Load up. I want to be to Pilot Rock before dark."

Callie wasn't used to people using her real name. But it was another step out of hiding. She helped Donny into the wagon and crawled up to sit beside him. Before them loomed the Blue Mountains.

"Are we crossing the mountains?" she asked no one in particular.

"Yes. We'll stay at Pilot Rock at the base of the mountains, cross them tomorrow, and stay in Starkey the next night," Clay said.

Callie leaned her head against Donny's arm as the wagon lurched and moved forward. He had napped on her, it was her turn to nap on him. She breathed in the clean air. The refreshing scent cleared her lungs of the damp, earthy scent of the tunnels. She'd been sitting in the stairwell getting fresh air the day Donny fell, battered and bleeding, in the street.

Fresh air had meant freedom, and today, she was free. Setting out for a new life as herself and not the boy Mac.

Donny squeezed her hand. Did she dare dream of a future with this man?

Callie catnapped through the afternoon. Sleeping, visiting with Clay and Donny, and staring at the spectacular scenery. The pine-covered mountains grew closer as the day progressed. The grassy hills ended at a valley with a large rock formation. The rock was tall, rectangular, and imposing.

The town was small. She'd traveled through many towns like this one. Gil stopped the wagon at the livery stable. A tall, thin man walked out.

"Need to stable the horses for the night?" the livery man asked.

"Yes. And store the wagon," Gil said. He handed the reins to Jasper and climbed down from the wagon, following the tall man into the livery.

A moment later, Gil walked out and motioned for Jasper to park the wagon alongside the livery. Once the wagon was in place they all climbed out. Gil and Jasper unharnessed the team.

Callie grabbed the satchels, handing one to Clay and one to Donny. She gathered up the wrapped parcels and Donny's boot, wishing she had a satchel for her and Donny's things.

Glancing up and down the street, she didn't see a hotel.

"Where are we staying?" Callie asked. Many

nights she'd slept in the back of a wagon or in a corner of a livery, but she had put that past behind her and after having had a bed the night before hoped for one again tonight.

"The saloon has beds upstairs that they rent," Donny said.

Callie always avoided saloons. But with the four big men to guard her, she was more curious than scared.

"Have you slept here before?" she asked.

Gil took the satchel from Donny, and Jasper put a hand on Clay's shoulder, directing him down the street toward the saloon.

Donny held out his arm. She slipped her left hand through his crooked right arm. They sauntered up the street behind the other men. They passed a mercantile, a drug store, and a blacksmith. The other side of the street housed another general store, the post office, another blacksmith and the saloon.

"I have a time or two. On the way to Pendleton, Jasper and I slept under the wagon a mile or so from town." Donny stopped when she did. "What's the matter?" he asked.

Her feet had stalled at the door of the establishment. The other three men had entered the big wooden door.

"I've always stayed away from these places. It's hard to make myself enter a saloon." She inhaled and scolded herself for being scared.

"I'm with you. This is a small place, locals come here to get a drink and the bartender usually owns the place." Donny drew her forward.

She pushed on the door. It swung open easily. They stood inside a small, dark establishment that smelled of yeast, sour tobacco, and stale smoke. Two men sat at a table with mugs of beer. Another man stood behind a bar at the back of the room. Gil was talking to him while Jasper and Clay drank a beer.

Callie led Donny over to the bar and the men.

"We don't have rooms for women," the man said.

"A room is a room," Callie said.

Gil peered at her. "Upstairs is one big room with beds. They rent the beds. There isn't a room for you to have privacy."

Her cheeks heated thinking of Gil, Jasper, and whoever else was sleeping upstairs seeing her in her night clothes. "I'll stay in the wagon. I've slept in one before."

"No! You're not staying in the wagon." Donny stepped forward. "How many others are renting beds?" he asked.

"Three. They rode in about half an hour before you did." The saloon keeper ran a hand over his face. "You might check with the widow Jennings at the far end of town. She sometimes rents out rooms to families traveling through."

"That's what we'll do," Donny said, smiling.

"She won't have room for all of you. Just the lady," the saloon keeper added.

"I'll be fine," Callie said, even though she didn't like the idea of being by herself in a strange place.

"Gil, get beds for you three. I'll stay with Callie," Donny said, turning her back to the door.

"That's not a good idea," Gil said.

"I won't leave her alone." Donny only stopped at the door long enough for her to open it.

Outside in the street, Callie turned to Donny. "A widow isn't going to let you stay with me."

He crooked his arm. "She will if she thinks we're married."

# Chapter Twenty-eight

Callie stared at him. "We can't lie!"

"Do you want to stay with the widow by your-self?"

"No. But I don't think passing ourselves off as married is a good idea." She paused. Saying they were married would mean one bed. "I'm not ready—,"

"I won't do anything other than hold you like the night you had the bad dream." Donny started walking.

"Wrong way." She turned him. Her heart raced with the thrill of the slight they were about to do and with anticipation of sleeping in Donny's arms. While she fought the idea of taking the intimacy further than an embrace, she welcomed his nearness in a strange place, and as herself and not a runaway boy.

She found the house at the end of the road. They walked up the small dirt path to the swept porch.

Donny knocked.

"Just a minute!" called a female voice.

"What does the house look like?" Donny asked.

"It's a square, two-story farmhouse. Long, wide front porch with two chairs and a small table. It looks clean and inviting. Lacy curtains in the windows. New whitewash."

The door opened.

A tall, robust woman with gray hair wound into a bun on the top of her head peered out at them through small, round glasses.

"Mrs. Jenkins?" Donny asked.

"Yes?" The woman's gaze traveled over Donny and then to Callie.

"Ma'am, the saloon keeper said you might have a room for the night for my wife and me. I'm Donny Kimball. This is Callie."

Callie stepped forward at Donny's prompt. "Hello, Mrs. Jenkins."

"Oh, we can't have a young couple like yourselves staying above that saloon. Come in. Come in." She ushered them into a sitting room to the right of the entry. To the left, a staircase stepped up the wall to the second floor.

"My, you seem to be a bit fettered with a cast on your leg," Mrs. Jenkins said, making conversation.

"Yes, I can't wait to get this off." Donny said, leaving his arm around Callie's waist.

The woman smiled, her gaze bouncing between them. Then she frowned. "Where is your luggage?"

Callie's cheeks heated. "At the moment our clothes are in these bundles. Donny's accident left us having to purchase new clothes. We've yet to get a satchel."

"I see." Her small gray eyes studied them. "Where are you headed?"

"We're on our way back home to Sumpter. We're actually traveling with three other men. They're staying at the saloon," Donny answered. "Something sure smells good. Is there any chance our traveling companions could pay you for a meal tonight?"

Callie saw the woman mentally calculating either money or if she had enough food, or quite possibly both.

"Yes, I believe I have enough stew to feed five more people." Mrs. Jenkins waved a hand to the upholstered chair. "Mr. Kimball, why don't you stay in the chair while I take your wife upstairs to put your things in the room. When I get back down, I'll send my grandson to invite your friends to dinner."

"That's a wonderful idea, Mrs. Jenkins." Donny released Callie's waist.

She turned him toward the chair and waited until he'd hobbled the three steps, found it, and started to sit.

"I'll be right back," she said and motioned for Mrs. Jenkins to lead the way.

As Callie suspected, the woman started asking questions once they were up in the room away from

Donny.

"What happened to your husband?" Mrs. Jenkins closed the curtains across the window in the room.

"He was beaten in the streets of Pendleton." Callie's voice shook with anger. In her travels she'd never witnessed anything so vile.

"Why? What did he do?" The woman took a step toward the door.

"Came to the aid of his friend. That friend will be coming to dinner. He's a Negro." Callie watched the woman to see if she would refuse to feed them or Jasper.

"Heavens!" Mrs. Jenkins fanned her face with a handkerchief she'd pulled out of her bodice.

"Will it bother you having a Negro eat at your table?" Callie asked.

"I've never had one at my table." The woman's eyes widened. "He's civilized?"

Callie snorted. "More than the likes of the men who beat up him and Donny."

Mrs. Jenkins nodded her head. "I'll send my grandson right over to the saloon. What is a name of one of the men?"

"Gil and Clay Halsey. Either one will do to give a message to," Callie placed the bundles of clothing on the chair. "Would one of the mercantiles still be open? I'd like to get a satchel."

"Yes. Somers Mercantile stays open until seven." Mrs. Jenkins stepped into the hall. "Dinner will be in an hour."

"Thank you." Callie followed the woman down

the stairs and found Donny playing the string game, Cat's Cradle, with a boy of about eight. He'd make a good father. Her cheeks heated at the notion. The thought of making children with Donny didn't scare her.

"Ira, run on over to the saloon and ask for Mr. Halsey. Tell him he and his friends are invited to dine here tonight." Mrs. Jenkins waved her hands toward the door in a sweeping motion.

The boy grinned at Donny and skedaddled out the front door.

"That's a fine grandson you have there, Mrs. Jenkins," Donny said, standing.

"There's no need to stand, young man. You need to stay off that foot." Mrs. Jenkins slid a stool over by Donny and placed his cast leg on top.

"That's kind of you Mrs. Jenkins."

"You rest right there while your wife goes to the mercantile and I get dinner."

Donny dragged his foot off the stool and stood. "I'll escort my wife to the store."

Mrs. Jenkins stood in front of him. "There is no need to escort her in Pilot Rock. We're a small hospitable community." She tapped his shoulder. "Sit and relax. It will help you heal."

He hadn't heard a word from Callie. Had she already left the house?

"Where's my wife?" he asked, standing his ground. He shoved the crutch under his arm and made to push off. He didn't know how close the woman was, but she was going to have to move.

"I'm right here." Callie's small hand wrapped

around his free one.

"I'll be," said Mrs. Jenkins.

A slight puff of air near his face meant the woman was fanning her hand in front of him.

"You're blind. I didn't notice until you asked for your wife."

"Thank you for your concern Mrs. Jenkins, but I'll escort my wife to the store." Donny took a step forward and was rewarded with Callie slipping her arm around his and guiding him to the door. Her quick learning of how to help him navigate made him smile.

"Dinner's at six," she called after them.

"Door," Callie whispered.

He held his hand out, moved it up and down and found the knob. Once they were back out on the street, he kissed the top of her head. "Thank you."

"For what?" Callie asked.

"For allowing me to move about like a man with sight and not leading me like a child." He meant every word. He'd learned independence at an early age and could only have a woman in his life who didn't treat him like a child.

"I do not consider you a child."

The huskiness in her voice when she said it made his body heat. She thought of him as a man. The same way he thought of her as a woman. A woman who could make his nights less lonely and validate his days.

"Why are you going to a store?" he asked, remembering the reason they were walking down the street when they could be relaxing.

"I would like to get a satchel to put our clothes in. Carrying the two bundles and your boot is awkward. If they were all in a satchel I would only need one hand to carry them."

"I could carry them for you if they are in a satchel." He'd forgotten about the boot being added to her burden of the packages.

"I'm not getting a satchel for you to carry."

Her stubborn tone made him laugh.

"What's so funny?" she asked.

"You are as independent and stubborn as me. This should make for some rowdy times."

She laughed. "I think we've already had a few of those."

He thought back to some of their first conversations. "I agree."

"Three steps up," she said.

He tapped the bottom one with his toe until he found the height. Put his right foot and crutch on the step and pulled his body up. At the top they took three steps and a bell jingled as they walked through a doorway.

The scents of pickles, leather, kerosene, and cinnamon hung in the air.

"There are so many items in this store I'll have to hold your hand and lead you. There's no room to walk side by side," Callie said, slipping her hand down his arm and capturing his hand.

Donny didn't mind holding her hand. She moved slowly. Items tugged at his coat on his right side, and his hand on the crutch bumped things on the other side.

"Can I help you?" a male voice called out from somewhere behind them.

Callie stopped. "We're looking for a satchel."

Footsteps slapped the wood floor. They stopped a few feet to their right.

"I have this one, or these two."

Callie released Donny's hand. He faced the direction of the voice.

"That one is too big," Callie said. Her body brushed by his. "One of these will do. What do you think?" She placed a handle in his right hand.

Donny raised the satchel judging its weight and size. "Yes, this one will work."

"That'll be a dollar and twenty cents," the man said.

Callie slipped the bag from his hand. Donny pulled his pocket book out of his jacket pocket. He opened the coin flap and fingered the coins. He held out a silver dollar. The man took the coin. Donny put his fingers back into the coin section and felt for two dimes. He found them and held them out to the man.

"Thank you!" The man said. "Is there anything else I can help you with?"

"Callie, is there anything else you need?" Donny asked.

"No."

Donny turned to his right and used the items brushing his knuckles to keep him moving in a straight line.

"To your right," Callie said quietly.

He turned right when he didn't feel anything

bump his hand. Callie's hand wrapped around his arm, directing him to the door.

Pushing on the door, he called over his shoulder, "Thank you."

"Come again," replied the man.

Back on the street Callie giggled. "I don't think that man figured out you're blind. Does it make you feel like you're playing a joke on them when people don't realize it?"

"No, it makes me feel normal." He wasn't playing games with people. He wanted the world to treat him normal.

Her head bumped against his arm as they walked. "I'm sorry. I'll never know how you feel. I didn't say you were trying to fool people."

He stopped and kissed the top of her head. "I know. And I want you to understand. My blindness isn't a game. It's my life and makes me have to do some things differently but with someone like you guiding me, it's a lot easier."

She started walking.

Her silence dug into his skin like a tick. What was she thinking? Why did this conversation all of sudden make her quiet and withdrawn? He'd felt the wall go up between them right before she'd started walking. How do I crumble that wall and keep her from building it again?

"What are you doing walking around out here?" Gil asked.

Callie stopped.

Donny stood as close as he could without it feeling awkward. He wanted her to know he would always be there for her.

"We were buying a satchel for our things. Why were you in the marshal's office?" Callie asked.

Donny shifted even closer to Callie. That could be why she fell silent, she'd seen Gil coming out of the marshal's office.

"I was checking in. It's courtesy to let the lawman know when another is in his town." He slapped Donny on the back. "We got the message about joining you for dinner at the widow's."

"Are you headed there now?" Donny asked, hoping he wasn't so he could have a moment more with Callie.

"Will be after I round up Clay and Jasper." He hesitated. "Did you find two rooms at the widow's?"

Callie shuffled beside him.

"No. I told her we were husband and wife. I'm not letting Callie alone until I'm sure no one is following us." Donny put his arm around Callie's shoulders.

"You all right with this?" Gil asked.

"Of cour—" An elbow jabbed Donny in the stomach. "Oof!"

# Chapter Twenty-nine

"He's talking to me," Callie said. "I'd rather have Donny with me than down the hall." She didn't care for the narrowed stare Gil gave her, but she meant every word. Being dressed like a woman and using her real name made her feel vulnerable. Donny might be blind but he'd protect her with every ounce of his being. That was more than she could say for anyone else who had ever been in her life.

"I'll tell the others, so they don't slip up. But playing at husband and wife is a lot easier than the real thing." Gil sent her a blunt glare and slapped Donny on the back before pivoting and heading to the saloon.

"He's not happy with us," Callie said. She knew to sleep in the same bed with Donny when they weren't married was almost the same as working in a bordello. Only she wasn't asking for money and she wouldn't give him her body. This wouldn't be any different than the nights they slept in the same room at the tunnel.

"I don't care what Gil or anyone else thinks. Keeping you close is the only way I can make sure you're safe. I promised you I'd keep you safe and I've always kept my promises." Donny started walking.

Callie had no choice but to go with him since his arm was still draped over her shoulder. A woman sweeping in front of the post office watched them with a frown. The disapproval tingled the hair on Callie's arms.

She ducked from Donny's arm and slipped her hand through the crook of his elbow for the remaining distance to the widow's house.

Being a guest, yet a paying customer, Callie wasn't sure if they should knock or go in. She opted to knock.

"That was a quick trip," Mrs. Jenkins said, opening the door.

"We were lucky the store had what we needed," Callie said, leading Donny to the parlor. "Have a seat, I'll put the satchel in the room and be right back."

Donny slid his hand down her arm and grasped her fingers for a brief moment before he settled onto the chair.

Callie hurried up the stairs. In the room, she laid out her nightclothes, hair brush, and tooth brush. Then she opened Donny's bundle. There was an extra set of men's underdrawers with the legs cut off at the knees, a shirt, trousers, tooth powder, and toothbrush. She left the tooth brush and powder on the bureau next to her night things and placed his extra clothes in the satchel. Being careful to not put too many folds in her extra dress, she placed it and her extra under clothes in the satchel. Then she folded the brown paper that had wrapped her items and placed it on top, setting Donny's left boot on the paper in the satchel.

She put the satchel at the head of the bed where she planned to sleep. Knowing there was a knife in the boot, she planned to keep it in her possession until she was confident no one wished her harm.

Men's voices carried up the stairs. She recognized Jasper, Clay, and Gil.

Hurrying down the stairs, she also detected two other male voices. At the bottom of the stairs, she stopped and listened.

The conversation was on the possibility of William McKinley being re-elected as President.

Callie entered the parlor. Her feet froze to the threshold. Another man wearing a badge stood beside Gil. Donny stood beside this lawman. Clay was in a discussion with the other man and Jasper. It would be strange for her to stand with anyone other than Donny, but her feet refused to carry her toward the two men wearing badges.

A hand pushed on her back, propelling her into the room. She glanced over her shoulder. Mrs. Jenkins smiled at her. I should have known it was the pushy old bird.

"Dinner will be ready in ten minutes," Mrs. Jenkins said behind her.

"Callie, won't you join us?" Gil asked, his eyes daring her to join the group.

She walked swiftly to Donny, linking her arm with his. He patted her hand and smiled at her. The jitters in her body slowly turned to tremors. She couldn't control the fear clamoring up her spine.

Donny leaned down and whispered close to her ear. "What's wrong? You're shaking."

She didn't dare speak. Her fear could cause her voice to carry to the men watching them.

"Just let me hold onto you," she whispered.

"Always," he said and kissed the top of her head.

"Newlyweds!" Mrs. Jenkins gushed.

Callie's cheeks heated.

Donny chuckled.

Gil glared.

"Callie, you've joined us?" Clay asked, heading their direction with Jasper's hand on his shoulder.

"Y-yes," she managed.

"It's a good thing you two decided to stay here. The beds and the atmosphere above the saloon isn't a good place for a young woman." Clay stopped next to her and smiled.

She smiled back even though he couldn't see it. "I'm glad we came here too. The room is pretty, and Mrs. Jenkins has been wonderful."

The widow smiled broadly. "I'm glad to have the company. It's been a long time since I've had this many men in my house." She glanced at the marshal. "Remember how my Theodore liked to have you men over for cards?" She sighed. "I miss those times."

"I don't know how you could miss us. We kept you moving all night bringing us food and drinks." The marshal shook his head.

"But you were all in good humor and having so much fun." Tears glistened in the woman's eyes. "I'll go put the food on the table."

Itching to get out of the room, Callie offered, "Would you like some help?"

Mrs. Jenkins peered at her a moment then nodded. "It would be nice to have some help. Thank you."

"I'll see you at the table," Callie told Donny and followed Mrs. Jenkins out of the room.

Donny reluctantly listened to Callie's and Mrs. Jenkins' feet tap out a cadence as they left the room. What had scared Callie when she entered the room? Was it because she was the only woman besides Mrs. Jenkins? Her quick offer to help didn't surprise him. Callie liked to stay busy and she liked to help. But it also got her out of the room.

"What do you think, Donny?" Clay asked.

"What? What do I think about what?"

A hand slapped Donny on the back. "Callie leaves the room and you can't concentrate on the conversation?" Clay's good-natured ribbing made him laugh.

"I thought that was supposed to happen when the woman was in the room with you," the man who'd been introduced as Mrs. Jenkins's son-in-law said. "She is a fine looking woman you have there, Donny."

Donny smiled. "I am a lucky man."

"Marshal Fulton, have you heard of a man by the name of Raymond Bentine?" Gil asked.

A marshal. That was why Callie was nervous. She didn't like being around lawmen. He should have thought of that when he was introduced to the two men. Donny was interested in the lawman's answer.

"He's got a lot of pull in Pendleton. I'd say half of his businesses are legal and half aren't. There are rumors about him that have the lawmen in the territory watching him. He's a slick one." The marshal's tone revealed he thought the man was as low as a gutter rat.

"Ever heard of him taking women into his bordello against their wishes?"

Gil was pushing into an area Donny didn't want Callie to hear.

"There's been rumors. Authorities haven't been able to get close to the women to ask them any questions. Bentine only allows them to service certain clientele."

"I know there were some of the women who used the tunnels under Pendleton to move around. Couldn't you contact the women you're looking for there?" Donny asked.

"You been down in the tunnels?" the marshal asked.

"Yes. Ca—" Donny stopped what he was going to say when Clay bumped his arm.

"Donny and Jasper were pulled off their wagon and beaten in the street. Jasper was picked up by the police. Donny managed to find refuge in the tunnels," Clay said.

Donny picked up on the fact he shouldn't mention Callie was living in the tunnels. It would bring up questions about their marriage.

"We were lucky to find both of them had been well taken care of," Clay added.

"Who took care of you?" the marshal asked.

Donny thought the marshal was talking to him, but he stalled to get what he wanted to say formed in his mind.

"Donny, he's asking you," Gil said.

"Oh. A Chinese healer wrapped my ribs, splinted my leg, and fed me a nasty-tasting tea that took away some of the pain." Donny didn't mention Callie. A hand on his shoulder squeezed slightly. He knew it was Clay's by the size and weight.

"Gentlemen, dinner is ready," said Mrs. Jenkins.

Donny hoped this topic didn't move to the table with them. While it was good to hear the law was watching Bentine and Callie's stories were well founded, he didn't want her to hear the discussion. It would only upset her more.

*Chapter Thirty*

Callie stood behind a chair. Mrs. Jenkins had insisted she sit to her left. Donny walked into the room behind Jasper. Callie smiled at the big man and he smiled back, leading Donny to her.

"Thank you, Jasper," Callie said, using her voice to tell Donny she was beside him.

Donny grasped the back of Callie's chair and held it for her as she sat. For not the first time, she wondered at how he'd been taught manners and how to do things when he couldn't see.

Once Donny was seated he leaned close. "Are you feeling better now?" he asked.

"A little," she whispered back. While helping Mrs. Jenkins in the kitchen, she'd learned that Marshal Fulton dined at Mrs. Jenkins house every night. She was paid by the town to feed the marshal, any deputies he had, and when there was someone in the jail, she provided the food for the prisoner. It had eased her fear knowing Gil hadn't brought the man here to see what she would do.

"Good." Donny brought her hand to his lips.

Her cheeks heated. Donny didn't realize everyone at the table was watching them. Mrs. Jenkins and Jasper grinned. Clay didn't know what was going on. The marshal and the other man smiled and ducked their heads as if afraid they were witnessing something they shouldn't. Gil stared at her.

She drew her hand from Donny's. "The food smells wonderful," she said.

The men all agreed.

"In this house we give thanks." Mrs. Jenkins bowed her head and prayed over the food.

Callie hadn't thanked God for anything since committing the sin of killing someone. She figured God wouldn't listen to anything a heathen like her had to say.

Donny murmured, "Amen."

She glanced over at him. He believed. Just another reason she couldn't be a part of his life.

Everyone started picking up dishes and scooping food as soon as Mrs. Jenkins finished the prayer.

Callie filled her plate and Donny's. "Peas at twelve. Chicken leg at three. Roll at six. Potatoes and gravy at nine," she said, adding each food to his plate.

"Thank you." He picked up his knife and fork and started eating.

Callie glanced down at the food on her plate. She hadn't eaten this much in years. The conversation lulled as everyone forked the delicious food into their mouths. She added some of the food from her plate to Donny's. Mrs. Jenkins patted her arm and smiled when she caught her moving potatoes.

"How much food did you put on my plate?" Donny asked her quietly when he'd slowed his eating.

"I added some from mine," she said, apologetically.

"I can't eat another bite. Mrs. Jenkins this was a fine meal," Donny said, reaching out and grasping the glass of water above his utensils.

"I'm glad you enjoyed it. I'm sure your wife is a good cook." Mrs. Jenkins glanced from Donny to Callie.

"I'm afraid Donny is getting much better food from you than I prepare." Callie's cheeks heated again. This time out of inadequacy.

"Surely, your mother taught you how to cook?" questioned Mrs. Jenkins.

Callie's skin crawled. She could feel all the men watching her. Gil to learn more; the others out of curiosity. "I'm afraid my ma couldn't get me to stay in the kitchen long enough to teach me how to cook."

"But a little mite of a girl as you, what would you be doing if not learning to be a wife?" The quizzical expression on the woman's face almost softened her reaction.

"I hunted with my pa and helped him train horses." She didn't look around the room. Donny's hand sought hers, giving her a fortifying squeeze.

"You hunted and trained horses?" the woman exclaimed. "What was your mother thinking letting you run about like a boy?"

"It was my doin'. I didn't cotton to housework. I was good at trackin' and trainin' a horse." She was proud of her abilities. Glancing around the table she could tell the men weren't believing her story. She didn't care. One of these days she'd wipe that smug smile off Gil's face when she brought home a deer for her family. *Her family*. The warmth of Donny's hand holding hers, gave her the belief she might have a chance at a family.

Mrs. Jenkins placed her cloth napkin on the table and stood. "I guess now's a good time to teach you what you'll need to know to keep that husband of yours happy. Come on. You can help me get dessert ready."

Callie didn't want to help get dessert. But the men sitting around the table looked like they would jump up and help if she didn't.

Donny squeezed her hand and quietly said, "Go on. You know I don't want you to change, but we are a lot for Mrs. Jenkins to tend to."

She'd never get used to him knowing what she was thinking.

"I do feel bad for her having to feed all of us." Callie released his hand and picked up their plates. She carried them into the kitchen. She was a little curious about the dessert and what was needed to tidy up after a meal.

Donny sat in a chair in the parlor. The men, all

but Mrs. Jenkins's son-in-law, had left the house. The son-in-law had a room upstairs with his son, Ira, the boy Donny had played Cat's Cradle with earlier. Callie was helping Mrs. Jenkins do the dishes. He smiled. When Callie had told him about being a tomboy, he hadn't realized she knew so little about cooking. He'd thought she'd meant when she was younger, before becoming a young lady.

The swish of skirts, short clip of women's heels, and a lavender scent told him Callie had entered the parlor.

"You're still down here?" Callie asked.

"Waiting for you." He stood. "And enjoying the quiet." He held out a hand.

Callie grasped it. "Yes, all those men talking at once was hard to keep up with."

They both walked out of the room and to the stairs.

"Good night, you two," Mrs. Jenkins called from down the hall.

"Good night," Donny replied, putting his crutch on the first step.

"I can fix up a room downstairs for you, Mr. Kimball," Mrs. Jenkins said only a short distance behind them.

"This is good for building my muscles back to where they were before the accident," he assured her, pulling himself up the step and placing his crutch on the next one.

"I'll wait until you're to the top before I turn out the lights." Mrs. Jenkins's clipped walk retreated.

"These stairs are narrow. Would you rather sleep downstairs?" Callie asked.

Donny released her hand and cupped her cheek. "I am sleeping in the same room as you. I won't leave you alone until we know Bentine has called off his men."

She leaned her head against his palm. "I feel safe when you're near."

"Good." He hated to move his hand, but he didn't want Mrs. Jenkins returning and insisting he remain on the bottom floor.

Callie's patience with his slow climb up the stairs warmed his heart. She would be good with children. Their children. They hadn't said any vows, and he didn't plan to make love to her until they had said their vows, but he already felt as if they'd been married for several years. Being together and dependent on one another for nearly a month had drawn them close in a short amount of time.

The long, flat surface of the second floor sent a wave of relief to his tired body.

"We're the first door to the right," Callie said, walking beside him slowly.

"I can't believe I made it up all those stairs at the hotel last night." Donny's right hand discovered the door. He found the knob and waited for Callie to enter ahead of him.

When they were both in the room, he shut the door firmly and stood facing the room. "Describe where things are, please."

"It's a small, but nice room. The quilt-covered bed is straight ahead. There's a small bedside table with a lamp to your right at the head of the bed. To your left is the foot of the bed and on that far corner is a wash stand and commode."

"Window?" he asked.

"Yes. Would you like me to open it for some fresh air?" Her skirts rustled. Her steps were muffled.

"There's a carpet on the floor?" he asked.

"A rug. Well, there are three of them. One on each side of the bed and one at the end."

"Good to know so I don't trip." Donny slid his feet until he touched the edge of the rug. Once he felt the obstacle, he raised his foot and stepped onto it.

"Did you want the window open?" Callie asked.

"Yes, it is a bit warm in here." He found the bed and sat. "If you need to use the commode, I'll remain facing the door."

"Thank you," she said embarrassed. "But you can still hear."

He laughed. "I could say I'd cover my ears, but we both know you'd still know I was here." He stood. "I can stand out in the hall."

"No. You've been on that foot too much tonight." Her small hand patted his shoulder. "I'll have to get over my shyness if you keep telling people we're married."

Her scent faded. The rustling of clothes kept his imagination busy.

"Would you like to use the commode?" she asked softly.

The night before he'd retreated to the room full of men to do his nightly duties. He didn't have that option tonight.

"I can step out into the hall, or go to the kitchen for a glass of milk."

"Are you still hungry? Why did you give me your food?" There were so many things about the women he wondered about.

"No. I'm full. It would just be an excuse to leave you alone. To do…you know."

The shyness in her voice made him smile. "I would like a glass of milk. Thank you."

The release of air in the quiet room told him she'd hoped for that answer.

"Is there a wash cloth on the wash stand?" he asked, figuring on getting himself all the way into bed before she came back.

"Yes. And I placed your toothbrush and the powder there too."

"That's thoughtful. I'll be in bed when you return."

She moved by him. Donny reached out, grasping her hand. He pulled her in front of him. "That conversation at dinner about you not being able to cook…" he started.

"I never—"

He placed his finger on her mouth. "I don't care. I'm blind, but I do what I want. You're a small woman, but if you want to hunt and train horses then that's what you should do. Life is too short to not do things you enjoy." He ran his hand around to her neck and up to the back of her head. "You've wasted the last three years running and hiding. It's time for you to do what you want. I only hope you allow me to be there to share your happiness." He kissed her. He'd been longing to all day.

She leaned into him as he deepened the kiss. Still hesitant he might do something to trigger a bad memory, he only held her by her head. He wanted her to take their intimacy as far as she was willing.

# Chapter Thirty-one

Callie's body melted against Donny. His hand cradled her head, keeping it where he could kiss her. The heat traveling through her body, swirled and centered in her lower regions. She didn't know why, but Donny's lips dancing with hers had her yearning to be held in his arms.

Maybe I need to show him. She slid her arms around his neck as the kiss continued. His free hand pressed against her back, holding her close. Safe, secure, loved.

The word bounced around in her head. Did he love her? Do I love him? She gently eased out of the kiss, releasing her hold around his neck.

"I should go get that milk," she said, stepping away from him and heading for the door.

"Did I do something to scare you?" Donny asked.

"No. Nothing. It's getting late."

Callie exited the room and slowly walked down the dark stairway. Mrs. Jenkins had been true to her word. She'd turned off every light in the house. The blackness made her journey to the kitchen take twice as long. Once there, she fumbled in the muted moonlight shining through the kitchen window to find a glass and pour the milk. She was pretty sure neither one of them would drink the milk. It was a pity to waste the white liquid. The idea of waste grew on her conscience. She poured the milk back in the pitcher, rinsed the cup, and filled the cup with water. If they didn't drink the water, she could use it to wash in the morning.

Retracing her steps, she quietly and cautiously climbed the steps to the first door on the right.

She drew in a deep breath, let it out, and opened the door. The light still burned. The lacy curtain fluttered in a soft breeze, and Donny was in bed under the covers. His bare shoulders and arms visible above the quilt.

"You were gone a long time," Donny said after the door clicked shut.

"It was pitch black. Mrs. Jenkins doesn't believe in leaving any lights on at night." She placed the glass of water on the table near Donny. "I brought back water. I couldn't stand the thought of a glass of milk going to waste if neither one of us drank it."

Donny chuckled. "Good thinking. I didn't use all the water in the pitcher."

"Thank you." She moved away from the bed

and over to the wash stand. Donny remained lying on his back on the bed. He couldn't see her, and she'd undressed in the same room with him before, but for some reason tonight she was shy and more aware of him as a man.

She unbuttoned her dress, slipping it over her hips and to the floor. Next was her chemise. She stood in the room bare from the waist up. Quickly, she grabbed her night dress, pulling it over her head and dropping it over her underskirt. She untied the underskirt, dropping it to the floor with her dress. Picking up the dress and skirt, she hung them on hooks on the wall beside the wash stand.

Glancing at Donny, she couldn't miss the smile on his face. He was listening to her every move. She shivered. Not of revulsion but of anticipation. Of what, she wasn't sure, but the sensation made her warm and recognize she was taking a step into womanhood.

She sat on a chair, untied her shoes, peeled off her stockings, and wiggled her toes. The shoes were a good fit but her toes were used to wearing boy's boots that gave her feet more room.

At the wash stand, she washed her face, brushed her teeth, and brushed her hair. She glanced around the room and couldn't think of anything else to do to prolong climbing into bed alongside Donny.

"I don't hear anything. Are you finished?" he asked.

"Yes." She stood beside the bed, staring down at him.

He flipped the covers back. "Then crawl in

here. It will be a long day tomorrow crossing the Blues."

Callie climbed into the bed keeping her body on the very edge of the mattress. "The light is on your side," she said.

Donny raised his hand, feeling the table, and then up the lamp.

She rolled over against him, reached to the light, and turned the wick down. "You're going to burn yourself or the house down."

The dark room, Donny's masculine scent and warm body under her, and her racing heart, froze her.

"You plan to sleep on me all night?" he asked softly.

"No." She flopped back to her side.

"You didn't have to get off. I was just going to wrap my arms around you and hold you if you'd planned to."

The humor in his voice eased a bit of the panic she'd felt at her actions.

"I'm not sure I can lay in your arms in the dark in a bed." A flash of the night her stepfather came to her bed, caused her body to tense.

"How about I start with just holding your hand?"

Donny's fingers fluttered against her arm. "Okay."

Donny's gentleness breached her defenses.

He laced his fingers with hers, meshing their palms, and skimmed his thumb back and forth in a caress.

Her body relaxed, her mind thought of the earlier kiss. The man sharing her bed would never do anything to intentionally hurt her. He cared about her.

She fell asleep peacefully, dreaming of the man holding her hand.

Donny woke. A cool breeze fluttered across his face and something warm pressed against his side. *Callie*. She was no longer arm's distance away. Her small body curled against him. He turned toward her, cupping her body and draping an arm across her. Everything about Callie made him happy. Her courage, her stubbornness, her empathy for others. He would do everything in his power to keep her with him. His heart wouldn't keep beating if he lost her. He fell back to sleep, happy she had sought his warmth.

Callie snuggled into the warmth. Light flickered across her face. Her lashes fluttered as she tried to open her eyelids. She'd forgotten how hard it was to rouse when having slept soundly all night.

Knuckles rapped on the door. "Breakfast will be ready in ten minutes."

Her body tensed from the sudden sounds.

"It's just Mrs. Jenkins," Donny's low, husky morning voice said in her ear.

The tension eased, until her mind grasped she was pressed against Donny with his arms wrapped around her.

"I woke up during the night, and you were

snuggled against me. I figured you were cold." He whispered in her ear.

The sensation of his warm breath on her neck, his body against her, and strong arms holding her, eased her tension. She didn't want to think about anything other than the security she felt in his arms.

He kissed her neck. "We need to get dressed and get breakfast. I'm sure Gil and the rest will be here early."

"I know." She wrapped her arms around the arm draped over her and hugged it. "I never dreamed after…that I'd ever want to be in a bed with a man." She released the arm and spun, facing Donny. "You are making it difficult for me to move on."

His brow furrowed. "Move on?"

"I can't stay with you. I won't bring my past into your life." The words lodged in her throat, making her swallow a couple times to say them. She didn't want to ever leave this man. But she cared enough—no, loved him and didn't want to bring him more pain by having the law drag her away from him.

"Stay with me. We can stand together if your past catches up to you." He grasped her head in his hands. "What you did was self-preservation. There isn't a jury that wouldn't agree. Don't keep running." He kissed her softly. "Please."

The armor around her heart melted completely. Tears trickled from her eyes. "I want to stay with you. But—"

He stopped her protest with another kiss.

"No buts." He released her. "Get dressed. We have a long day today."

Donny wasn't going to let any of her doubts be spoken. He would prove to her she could trust him and live a happy life with him. She wasn't going anywhere. Donny decided during the night, he wasn't going to give her time to run. As soon as they returned to Sumpter he would marry her. He'd set his heart on her.

Callie rolled out her side of the bed.

Donny sat up, reached to the end of the bed for his clothes and pulled them on, listening to the rustling of clothing behind him.

"Do you need to use the commode?" Callie asked almost in a whisper.

He smiled. She'd soon get over her shyness when they were married. "I'll use the privy outside after breakfast."

"Okay. I'm ready."

He heard the jingle of a buckle. "Is everything in the satchel?"

"Yes." Callie walked up beside him.

"We'll take it down with us." He used the crutch to stand and held out a hand to take the satchel.

"I'll carry it. You'll have a hard enough time navigating the stairs without it."

He laughed. "Yes, ma'am."

They left the room and headed down the stairs. Male voices filtered down the hall when they stepped off the last stair.

"Mrs. Jenkins must have invited everyone back

for breakfast," Callie said.

Donny agreed. He recognized Gil and Clay's voices.

Callie moved away from him for a few seconds.

"I set the satchel by the door," she said, returning to his side.

He nodded and they walked down the hall to the dining room. Walking through the doorway, the conversation stopped.

"Morning, sleepyheads," Clay said.

Donny felt Callie tense. He touched her arm. She took the motion to mean lead him to a chair. Which was fine by him.

"Good morning, everyone. Didn't expect to find you three here for breakfast," Donny said, following Callie's lead to the table.

She stopped. He felt the chair backs in front of him and held one for her, before taking the chair to her right.

"Mrs. Jenkins suggested we might as well come here for breakfast since we had to pick you two up anyway," Gil said.

Donny didn't detect any suspicion or ulterior motive to Gil's words. He smiled.

Callie dished food onto his plate. "Soft eggs at three. Ham at six. Potatoes at nine. And toast at twelve."

"Thank you." He picked up a knife and fork and started eating. He heard Callie stirring her food on her plate. "Eat," he said, leaning close and whispering.

The conversation started back up. Mrs. Jenkins's son-in-law carried most of the conversation. He was the local banker. From the way he talked about his customers, the people of Pilot Rock, he wouldn't have his job long. A banker needed to be trusted and gossiping about the people and how they spent their money wasn't a good practice.

Mrs. Jenkins poured them all a cup of coffee and took their plates. "Callie would you help me carry these plates in?" the woman asked.

"I guess."

He heard Callie's hesitance. Donny reached under the table and squeezed her hand.

She stood, dishes clanged, and her scent disappeared along with her soft footfalls.

"Are you two ready to go?" Gil asked.

"The satchel is by the front door." Donny sipped his coffee.

"I'll get it loaded," Jasper said.

"I need to get to work. It was nice meeting you all," the banker said. His footsteps clicked like a woman's step as he left the room.

"You two ready for a long day?" Gil asked.

Donny listened. "Do you mean me and Clay or me and Callie?"

"I guess I should have said you three," Gil said.

"We have the easy part. All we can do is sit in the wagon. I'd sure rather have a horse under me," Clay said.

"I agree," Donny said, even though he wasn't as good a horseman as Clay. Clay grew up riding horses. Donny didn't start until he moved to Sumpter.

"At least the road should be pretty good this time of year. It's had enough traffic since winter to have knocked some of the ruts down." Gil slid his chair back. "Let's go."

"What about Callie?" Donny wasn't leaving her behind.

"I'll get you two heading to the wagon and then get Callie," Gil said.

Donny would have rather gathered Callie himself, just to have a few more minutes alone with her.

# Chapter Thirty-two

Callie finished helping Mrs. Jenkins and ex-
cused herself to use the outdoor privy. The thought
of taking care of business without someone listening was a freeing thought. She entered the small
wooden structure and sat down. Birds trilled and
sang songs in the surrounding trees. Harnesses
jingled and the creak of leather caught her attention.
Walking to the privy she hadn't noticed horses or a
wagon. Why would the men have brought the wagon back here?

She finished and exited the little building.

Two men stood next to horses watching the
outhouse.

"Who are you?" she asked, glancing to the
house to see if anyone happened to be close by.

No one.

"We were sent to fetch you," the tallest of the

men said.

"Fetch me? I don't know who you are." Her heart pumped fast and her feet itched to run. They weren't wearing badges. Not lawmen. There was only one other person who wanted her. Her heart lodged in her throat.

"Mr. Bentine sent us." The smaller man started forward.

"Donny!" The strangled cry carried on the wind as she sprinted toward the house.

An arm wrapped around her middle and a hand slapped against her mouth.

Callie kicked, bit, and squirmed, trying to release the man's hold. She continued fighting against the man as he laughed and carried her toward one of the horses.

She didn't want to go to Bentine. She'd kill everyone who tried to touch her. That wouldn't be good for his business. She wanted the life Donny offered her. She continued to fight. His hand slipped off her mouth. "Help!" she screamed.

"Keep her quiet," the other man ordered.

"She's a hellcat for being so small." The man carrying her stopped at his horse. "Help me tie her up."

"I've got a better idea."

The man on a horse moved beside them. She barely noticed the butt of his gun before it struck her head. Pain ricocheted through her head before darkness swept her away.

"Did you hear that?" Donny asked.

"Yeah, it sounded like Callie," Clay said.

Donny turned toward the sound and started hobbling as fast as he could.

"Where you two goin'?" Jasper called out.

"Callie yelled."

"Help!" Callie's cry spiraled fear into Donny's gut. He couldn't move faster and couldn't see what was ahead of him.

Heavy footsteps ran past him. Jasper.

"No you's don't!" Jasper hollered.

A gun boomed. The acrid scent of discharged gun powder stopped Donny.

The cadence of hooves raced by.

"Callie!" Donny shouted.

Laughing carried on the air back to him.

"What's going on out here?" Gil asked.

"Where's Jasper?" Clay asked. "I heard a shot."

"I's right here. They only winged me." Jasper's voice rose from the ground.

"Jasper, did you see Callie?" Donny asked, wishing he had sight so he could ride out after them.

"Yeah, she was slumped over the tall man's lap. She looked like a rag doll." His voice broke on the last sentence.

"Damn! Gil we have to go after them." Donny turned around and headed back the direction of the wagon. "And not in a damn wagon. I want a horse."

"Calm down. We have a pretty good idea who has her." Gil grabbed his arms, halting his movements. "Tell me why the man wants her? The truth."

"We've been telling you the truth. You heard what Marshal Fulton said about Bentine." Donny tried to shake Gil's hands off him. All three men Donny travelled with had twenty to thirty pounds and several inches on him. He didn't have a chance at doing anything they didn't want him to, but he'd damn well try with Callie's life on the line. He'd promised he'd keep her safe. Lot of good I was. I couldn't even see the men to stop them.

"She's been too skittish for it to just be the man wants her in his bordello." Gil pushed for answers, but he let go of Donny's arms. "Jasper, get that arm looked at by Mrs. Jenkins. I'll round us up four horses."

Jasper's heavy footsteps headed to the house. Gil's lighter, quicker steps walked a short distance and stopped. His voice was low, but Donny made out words like—ask him. Truth. He was asking Clay to find out what he could.

"Come on, Donny. Let's go sit on the porch while we wait for Jasper and Gil." Clay's somber tone revealed he was as upset with the turn of events as Donny.

He followed Clay's steps, hobbling along with his crutch.

At the porch, Clay said, "There's a small step we can sit on."

"We can sit on the chairs on the right side of the porch," Donny suggested.

"How do you know there are chairs?"

"Callie described the house to me. She said there were two chairs and a small table to the right." Donny passed Clay and found the first chair. "Here."

Clay stopped beside him and felt the chair. "There it is. Did you find the other one?"

"Yes." Donny sat. "We have to find her before Bentine—" He couldn't say any more. To even think what Bentine had in store for Callie his anger bubbled hot.

"Gil will get us there in time." Clay said.

"But he thinks Callie is lying. She isn't. She dropped the watch Bentine wants."

"What watch?" Clay asked.

"The night Bentine discovered she was a girl, she'd been knocked down in the street in front of his saloon when Bentine's thugs were roughing up a man. When she fell in the street her hand landed on something. She picked it up and put it in her pocket. Then Bentine's man dragged her in the saloon after telling the other thugs to find the watch." Donny ran a hand over his face. "She didn't realize what she had until she was back in our room in the tunnels. She cleaned it up and saw it was a watch inscribed with Bentine's name and some numbers along with a key."

"That could be a combination to his safe and the key to the drawer inside," Clay said.

"How do you know that?"

"I happen to have a safe. It takes three numbers to turn the dial and then a key to get access to a special drawer inside."

"Callie was afraid to go to the street or even near Bentine after he said he wanted her in the bordello and had men looking for her. She planned to drop the watch in the street when she telegraphed you."

"But she discovered us and forgot about the watch," Clay added.

"Yes. So the plan was to drop it as we drove out of town in the wagon. She said she dropped it."

"You believe her?"

"Yes. She doesn't lie to me."

"But she does to others?" Clay questioned.

"Not lie. She just holds back some details." Donny liked the fact she trusted him enough to tell the truth, and trusted him when she was in trouble. I have to get to her.

"Either this Bentine is an arrogant son of a bitch or he hasn't found the watch and still thinks she has it," Clay said.

"Damn!" Donny stood. "He'll beat her to death like he did the man in the street if we don't stop him."

The sound of horses approaching stopped his tirade. He knew Clay would tell Gil everything, but he wasn't in the mood to tell the lawman anything the way he'd been suspicious of Callie from the start. He didn't want to get her back from Bentine to have Gil haul her to jail for murdering her step-father. A man, who in Donny's estimation, deserved what he got.

"I have horses and a person to take you two on to Sumpter," Gil said, dismounting.

Donny hobbled off the porch. "I'm not going to Sumpter. I'm going with you to get Callie. She's going to need me when you find her."

"With that leg of yours, we can't ride as fast as

we should to catch up." Gil's tone said he expected his orders to be followed.

"I will be there when you find Callie. You don't know her past. You don't know how that man forcing her…she needs me there." Donny didn't want to tell the men anything about Callie's past. It was her past to tell. But if they didn't take him with them, he'd find someone who would get him to Pendleton.

"Let him go. He has the most at stake," Clay said.

The door opened. "I's ready." Jasper's heavy footsteps crossed the porch.

Before Donny realized the big man was beside him, hands lifted him off the ground.

"Spread your legs, boy, if you plan to sit on a horse." Jasper's tone was clear. He wasn't going to let Gil leave Donny behind.

Donny spread his legs. The saddle seat met his backside, and he grasped the saddle horn.

"Only the right foot will fit in the stirrup." Jasper said, placing his foot in the stirrup. "What you gonna do with that stick?" he asked.

"I'll need it when I get off the horse." Donny felt the saddle. "Put it in the rifle scabbard."

"Here's the reins," Jasper said, pressing the leather straps into his hands.

Donny was grateful for Jasper's friendship. Jasper wouldn't let Gil pull anything over on Donny.

"Let's go." Gil said.

The tempo of four horses' hooves rat-a-tatted down the hard-pack street of Pilot Rock. Donny listened intently to the horses ahead of him. Two. It must be Gil and Clay. And then himself with Jasper bringing up the rear to make sure he and Clay didn't stray off.

It had taken them a day in the wagon to get to Pilot Rock from Pendleton. On horses they could stay at a steady trot and get there in half the time. He only hoped they arrived before Bentine hurt Callie.

# Chapter Thirty-three

Callie's head throbbed and her stomach churned. Why am I so sick? She tried to open her eyes, but the slight movement and trickle of light pierced her head with more pain. Her stomach reacted to the onslaught of pain. She rolled to her side, even though her head could shatter into jagged shards at any moment, and retched over the edge of the bed.

"The least you could have done was warned me!" shrieked a female voice.

The voice had a familiar quality to it, but the pain in her head trumped all rational thinking. Callie remained on her side, her head hanging over the side of the bed. The stench of her vomit only added to the roiling of her stomach. But staying in one place eased the throbbing.

"Dorothy, get in here!" the female voice ordered.

She heard a murmur and the smell grew stronger. Callie opened one eye long enough to see dark-colored hands cleaning up the mess she'd made.

"I'm sorry," she whispered and closed her eyes from the effort.

The smell faded. Something thunked on the floor under her head. Slitting open one eye, she spied a chamber pot. The next heave she'd try to hit the pot.

"Is she awake?"

The sound of the deep male voice sent fear spiraling down her spine.

*Bentine.*

"Barely. She just vomited all over the floor."

The disgust in the woman's voice sent more shivers through Callie's body.

The man growled. "Get me Dover!" he shouted.

Callie clenched her head from the sound.

"Did you find it on her?" he asked.

"No," the woman answered.

Bentine cursed.

Callie moaned. They hadn't found the watch in the street.

"Go get Doc Vincent." Bentine ordered.

"You know he doesn't—"

"Get him!" Bentine shouted.

The sickening floral scent that had hung in the room faded. Callie hoped she'd been left alone. Fear prickled the back of her neck. She wasn't alone.

Her head hurt too much to do anything other than remain where she was and hope Bentine would wait until she could see straight before badgering her for the whereabouts of the watch or putting her to work.

Donny dismounted without any help. Someone, most likely Gil, strode forcefully away from them. His boots clunked on a wooden walkway, fading to silence.

The jingle of harnesses, horses snorting, many feet thumping, and multiple voices told him they were back in Pendleton. He'd disliked this town when they arrived all those weeks ago and his dislike had grown. He feared they wouldn't get to Callie before Bentine beat her for the watch, took her to bed, or both.

"Where are we?" he asked.

"The courthouse. Gil's getting authority to go into Bentine's and find Callie," Clay said.

"Will he get some help or are we it?" Donny asked. He was ready to storm the bordello and find Callie, but it would be hard for Gil to keep track of two blind men and do his job.

"We's gonna find out soon. Here he come," said Jasper.

Gil's long strides hastened their direction.

"What did you find out?" Donny asked when the footsteps stopped.

"We're on our own, but I can use my badge here." Gil's tone revealed he was irritated with the local law.

"Bentine have the marshal in his pocket?" Clay asked.

"From his reluctance, I'd say so. We better move fast before he sends word to Bentine we're here for Callie." Gil's footsteps headed away from them.

Donny slipped his crutch under his arm as a large hand landed on his shoulder.

That hand had guided him the last ten years. He nodded at Jasper and took out as fast as he could with a crutch. It would have been nice if Gil had given them some direction.

"Any idea what he's going to do?" Donny asked.

"Knowing Gil, he's heading in through the front door and confronting Bentine," offered Clay.

"I don't think that's a good idea. He may have a badge and authority, but we can't help him fight his way out." Donny thought hard on what he knew of Pendleton. Mostly the underground.

"Callie has friends that will help get her out. Stop Gil and let's make a plan." Donny knew Gil didn't like to take orders from anyone, but it wasn't the woman Gil loved that was in harm. Donny stopped and turned to Jasper. "Go get Gil. Bring him back here. He has to listen to my plan."

Jasper's heavy footfalls hurried ahead.

"You sure your plan will work?" Clay asked.

"It will be less likely to harm Callie than Gil barging in and demanding her return."

Two sets of quick steps advanced on them.

"Jasper says you have a plan. What is it?" Gil

asked.

"Take me to the gambling hall where you and Clay waited for Callie to bring me." Donny hoped Swifty was there and would help him spread the word to the Chinese community that Callie was in trouble.

Firm hands grasped her shoulders, rolling her onto her back. She wanted to fight them, but her head still throbbed and her body refused to do anything she asked it.

"My God! How did she get this gash and indentation in her head?" The male voice was outraged.

"One of my men didn't understand my orders. He's no longer a problem."

Bentine's calm statement sent shivers up Callie's spine.

He'd killed the man who hit her with the rifle butt. That he cared was a bit reassuring, but if she couldn't produce the watch, she was pretty sure he'd have her dealt with as well. She had to get out of here. Would Donny figure out where she was? He'd never be able to find her.

"Can you hear me?" the doctor asked.

She tried to talk, but her mouth and vocal chords didn't respond. Nodding didn't happen either. The agony of opening her eyes churned her stomach. There were two identical men hovering over her. She closed her eyes quickly as a wave of nausea hit. She couldn't make her body roll to the side of the bed. The contents of her stomach erupted, spewing down her cheeks and chin.

"She has a concussion, if not worse," an enraged male voice said. The doctor rolled Callie to the side of the bed and wiped at her face with a wet rag. "If she is left on her back, she could drown in her vomit."

Tears burned the backs of Callie's eyes as her head continued to throb and her body ignored all her instructions to move.

Stale beer, smoke, and the sour tang of spittoons assaulted Donny's nose as he hobbled into the underground gambling hall. The whirl of a wheel was the backdrop for voices. The place sounded busy. The air was hot and suffocating.

"Now what?" Gil asked, putting Donny's hand on a chair back.

Donny sat and waited for the rest to settle. "Jasper, do you see Swifty, the man from the jail?"

"Don't see him. I could walk around."

"Not a good idea," said Gil. "There's a couple of men at the end of the bar looking like they'd like to start a fight with you."

"We need Swifty's help. Callie said he comes in here after hours and cleans up. That's how she contacted him to talk to Jasper." Donny didn't like the idea of sitting here waiting. Especially if there were men in here looking to pick a fight.

The click of a watch told him Gil had checked the time.

"We have about eight hours until things slow down around here."

The undertone in Gil's statement sparked Donny's decision.

"Take me to the door Callie and I came through the day you found me. I'll go into the tunnels and find the Chinese doctor. He'll help me get word out about Callie and come up with a plan."

"What about us?" Clay asked.

"I don't want you sitting in here waiting for me. Go book a room for the night. I'll figure out how to get to you when I have Callie." Donny stood.

Gil's hand landed on his shoulder. "I don't like sending you off by yourself."

"I know the people. They love Callie and will help. They are our only chance." Donny hoped the marshal hadn't told Bentine they were here looking for Callie. That would make finding her harder.

"Come on, then." Gil led him fifteen steps and stopped. "Put your hand out. That's the doorway."

"Thanks." Donny felt the threshold and started into the tunnel. The smells and dampness he remembered swirled around him. With his right hand on the wall, he hobbled along. His toe hit something that swung. He stuck a hand out before the door hit his face.

The swinging door.

He lowered to the ground. Crawling forward, he pushed the door with his head. The slab of wood bumped down his back, over his back side, and wedged against his legs. He rolled face up, grasped the door with his hands, and pulled his legs out of the way. Using his crutch, he stood and hobbled down the tunnel. He counted the steps and was off by two when his hand found another tunnel. Retracing the path Callie led him down on their way to the gambling hall, he made a left turn. He followed the fishy smell of the kitchen until the fish was replaced by the cloying scent of opium smoke. The low murmur of voices speaking Chinese told him he was headed the right direction.

"You not come back."

He knew the voice. "Doc, Mac needs your help. We had her to Pilot Rock and Bentine's men grabbed her. We need help getting her out of the bordello."

"Come."

A small arm wrapped around his right arm, leading him down the tunnel. They turned right and then right again. "Where are you taking me?" he asked.

"Missy Mac's friends."

# Chapter Thirty-four

"This girl is in a bad way."

The doctor's voice sounded far away.

"How bad is she?" Bentine's deep voice sent more shivers up her spine.

"She could die. I don't know how to help her other than to wait and see how the concussion and cracked skull affects her."

Bentine cursed.

If she could have shrunk into a ball, Callie would have. Bentine's anger filled the room. She could barely think let alone find a way out of here.

The door opened and closed.

"Go get Mort," Bentine ordered.

Someone left the room. She could hear Bentine breathing. He leaned close.

"If I find out you're pretending to keep from telling me where my watch is, I'll find anyone you care for and show you I don't tolerate thieves."

The door slammed.

Callie tried again to open her eyes, but the pressure in her head took over and she gave in to the relief of sleep.

"I need someone to get me close to the Bowman Hotel." Donny said. "My friends are there. I'll let them know about the plan." Donny held out his hand to the Chinese doctor.

"He not shake hands. He bow," said Yi Wu, Callie's friend, and the one risking her life to go into the bordello to find Callie.

Donny bowed. "Thank you. All of you." He spread his arms.

"Sing Lee take you tunnel door close hotel," said the doctor. "Him no speak English. On street, go right, cross two streets. Hotel right."

Donny nodded that he understood the directions. Someone grasped the cuff of his right sleeve and led him away from the group setting off to get Callie out of the bordello.

He hoped Yi didn't get caught. She said there were two Chinese women working in the bordello. They complained no one ever knew who was who. Adding in one more no one would be the wiser unless all three entered a room at the same time.

Fresh air filled his lungs moments before his escort led him up six steps. Sing Lee released his sleeve and disappeared.

The thunk of a door behind him meant Donny was alone on the street. He heard the sounds of wagons and horses in the street and felt the wood walkway under his feet. Someone brushed by him. He hoped there weren't too many people on the walkway.

Pivoting on his good foot, he turned to his right and hobbled down the walkway. He heard the movement of wagons in front of him moments before his crutch didn't hit the board walk and sunk six inches deeper and into soft dirt.

The first street he had to cross.

Donny cocked his head and listened. He didn't hear a wagon. Someone on a horse could easily navigate around him. He stepped off the boardwalk and hobbled across the street. No one yelled, and his crutch hit the boards on the other side. He shoved up onto the walkway and continued down the street. A sweet, yeasty scent caused his stomach to rumble. I must have passed a bakery. Counting the steps, he was ready for the next street before he heard the traffic passing in front of him.

He listened again, judging the best time to cross. A body bumped him and moved on by. Thinking it was safe, he dropped off the walkway and headed across the street.

The ground rumbled under his foot. Jangling of harnesses peeled in the air like a church bell.

"Get out of the way!" hollered a gruff voice.

Donny stood still not knowing which way to go. He'd never felt so vulnerable in his life. He'd put himself in several close calls but this… The rumble under his feet grew as well as the jangle of harnesses.

"Get out of there you fool!" shouted another man.

"Donny!" Gil's voice drew his attention.

Before he could respond, a body tackled him, throwing him backwards several feet before he landed on the ground with someone on top of him.

The body quickly disappeared and a hand grabbed his. "What were you doing in the middle of the street?" Gil asked.

"I was crossing it. I didn't hear a wagon coming and someone brushed by to walk across the street. I thought it was clear." Once on his feet, he assessed his ribs and leg. The ribs hurt a little and his leg was fine. Getting run over by a freight wagon would have hurt a hell-of-a-lot worse. He held out a hand. "Thanks."

"Don't do that again." Gil pulled him into an embrace. "You're welcome. Clay's been going crazy wondering where you were. He sent me out to look for you. I saw you standing in the street with that freight wagon heading for you…"

"Take me to Clay. I'll tell all of you what's happening." Donny had never been happier to have a hand on his shoulder guiding him. That was the first time he'd nearly been run over and he didn't like the feeling of vulnerability that still lingered in his mind.

In the hotel room, Gil explained his near miss which brought back a moment of the panic.

"Did you learn anything about Callie?" Clay asked.

"Not yet." Donny lowered onto the chair Gil

said was behind him. "Yi, a friend of Callie's is going into the bordello to look for her."

"Won't they know she shouldn't be there?" Gil asked.

"She said there are two Chinese women who work in the bordello and they complain no one can ever tell them apart. She's hoping that no one will realize there is an extra Chinese woman in the building." He hoped she was right. Callie would be furious to know he'd pulled her friend into helping and she could get hurt.

"When Yi finds Callie, she'll get her out and down into the tunnels. Then they will contact Swifty, and he'll let us know. We'll get her out at one of the tunnel exits." He hoped this plan went as smoothly as telling it did.

"Then we's to just sit here and wait?" Jasper asked.

The tension in his tone reflected Donny's impatience. "That's the only thing I know to do. Other than storm into the bordello and demand Bentine hand her over."

"That won't happen," added Gil. "I've been asking around some more about the man. He's been nastier than usual. That watch he thinks she has means a lot to him. Word is he kills anyone who stands between him and what he wants. "

Donny's chest squeezed with fear. "Then we have no choice but to get her away from him."

The restaurant was crowded and noisy. Donny hadn't wanted to come down to eat but Gil insisted sitting in the room wasn't good. It allowed too many thoughts to spill into one's mind.

Raised voices in the lobby drew Donny's attention.

"I need to see the Negro, Jasper!" a raised voice said.

"Sir, you're kind aren't allowed!" the clerk said, raising his voice.

"Gil, someone in the lobby is asking for Jasper." Donny said, nodding toward the sound.

"I'll go check it out." A chair scooted across the floor and long decisive strides thunked boot heels on the wood floor.

Donny tried to hear more, but the voices no longer shouted.

Gil's footsteps returned, along with a shuffling gait.

The scent of alcohol and sweat followed them to the table.

"Donny, this is Swifty. He has something to tell us." Gil's voice came from beside Donny.

"What is it Swifty? Did the Chinese get C-Mac out of the bordello?" His heart raced believing he'd be reunited with Callie soon.

"No. I seen Mort, Bentine's big man, carry her out and put her in a wagon."

"No!" Donny shot to his feet.

A hand pressed on his shoulder, forcing him back into the chair.

"Did you follow them?" Gil asked.

Donny tried to listen to Gil, but his mind was racing. She'd either denied Bentine what he wanted or tried to kill him and was killed in return. His heart shattered. He'd promised to protect her.

"Yeah, he hauled her over to a house on the edge of town and carried her in. There's an old lady that lives there. I think she's a healer of some sort."

Donny stood. If he didn't bury her she was still alive. "Take us there. Now."

"Sure. Sure." Swifty's stench faded.

"Come on," Donny said, hobbling along in Swifty's scented trail.

"What about the girl in the bordello?" Clay said.

"Swifty, wait up!" hollered Gil.

Donny stopped. *Damn*! He'd forgotten about Yi. "Someone has to go in there and tell her to get out."

"I'll go," Clay said.

"How are you going to be able to find her?" Gil asked.

"I'll ask for a Chinese girl and whoever they give me, I'll ask her to tell Yi, that's her name?"

"Yes." Donny's gut clenched thinking of the trouble Callie and possibly Yi were in.

"Have them tell Yi we've found Callie." Gil said.

"But say Mac. She won't know who Callie is," Donny pressed.

"I will. Jasper, lead me to Bentine's bordello. I'm sure they'll let you in as a blind man's aid." Clay said.

"Come on." Gil put his hand on Donny's shoulder and they started forward.

Donny caught a whiff of Swifty and knew they were following him.

They moved through the streets quicker than he thought the old man was capable of and himself with a crutch.

"There. That house is where I seen Mort take her," Swifty said.

"He was carrying her?" Gil asked.

"Yeah. She looked limp, like a rag doll."

The sorrow in Swifty's tone tightened the knot in Donny's gut.

"Then she can't walk on her own." Gil paced a few steps away and back. "You two stay here. Swifty, let Donny know if you see anyone coming. I'll go get a wagon. That way we can get her away from here without too much notice. If I carry her down the street word will get out."

"Just hurry," Donny said, wishing he could rush into the house and pull Callie into his arms and ask her what was wrong.

# Chapter Thirty-five

Callie heard a female voice. She tried once again to open her eyes. Pain radiated from behind her eyes and pulsed throughout her head. It wasn't worth the pain to try to see.

Her limbs were raised one by one. She didn't feel it so much as sensed it. Where am I? Who is this person? There wasn't the cloying perfume she'd noticed at the bordello. This place had herbal scents. Like Mr. Cai's, only without the overtone of opium smoke.

Something hard hit the wall and the room shook.

"Where is she?"

Donny's voice.

She wanted to call out but nothing happened.

"Get out of here. You have—" The woman's voice was cut off.

"You can't hold a woman against her will."
Gil's voice.

She'd know that stern authoritative voice anywhere. Callie tried again to open her eyes but the pain chased away her efforts.

"Callie? Callie?" Donny's voice hovered over her. His touch moved up and down her arm.

She wanted to open her eyes. See him. Tell him she was… she didn't know what she was.

"What's wrong with her?" he demanded. "Did you drug her?"

"No. She was like this when Mort brought her over."

"Why is there a bandage on her head?" Gil asked.

"One of Bentine's men hit her with a rifle butt. Doc Vincent thinks there's damage in her head."

The woman's monotone delivery kept Callie from panicking.

"No!" Donny's voice carried so much agony Callie wanted to reassure him, but the pain in her head pulled her into darkness again.

"We have to do something." Donny insisted. He wasn't giving up on Callie. She had too much spirit and fight to die easily.

"Let's get her out of here first. Once we have her, we'll make a decision." Gil took charge. "Stand back so I can pick her up."

Donny didn't want to leave her side, but with his broken leg, he couldn't carry her. He listened as Gil picked her up and headed to the door. Donny followed close behind.

"You'll be sorry when Bentine finds out!" the old woman shouted.

"Climb in the wagon. I'll put her head on your lap," Gil said.

Donny hobbled forward until he felt the wagon box. He backed up to it, pulled himself up and into the box. He kept backing up until his back was against the wagon seat. Within minutes the weight of Callie's head and shoulders filled his lap. "Do you have a blanket?" he asked.

"Yes."

Air wafted around him as the blanket settled. Donny grasped the edge and pulled it up to Callie's chin. Starting at her chin, he moved his hand up her face until his fingers grazed the cloth wrapped round her head. He cupped her face and skimmed his thumb back and forth across her lips, feeling the soft puffs of air from her nose as she breathed. She had to stay with him. He'd envisioned their future, and he didn't see a happy life ahead for him if she wasn't in it.

The wagon rumbled along the street.

"I'm parking in the alley behind the hotel. We'll wait to move her until we've made our next plan," Gil said.

"We should take her to the doctor." Donny wanted her well.

"If he already looked at her at Bentine's and didn't do anything other than bandage her head, I doubt there's much he'd know to do."

Donny hated the thoughts bouncing around in his head. If the doctor couldn't do anything, did they just wait and see what happened? Or was his reluctance to do anything because he knew she would die? Tears burned behind his eyes. He rubbed at them, forcing his pain to stay hidden.

The wagon stopped. "Stay here. I'm going to see if Clay and Jasper are back."

There was no place else he'd go. He wasn't leaving Callie's side. She'd been there when he needed help and she'd seeped into his heart. It would take an army to pry him away from her now.

The street sounds filtered into the alley. When would Bentine learn Callie was no longer at the woman's place? Would she go straight to him and tell him Callie'd been taken? Questions. So many and no answers. He had one question he planned to ask Callie as soon as she was awake. Would she marry him?

Three sets of footfalls descended the back stairs of the hotel.

"Clay found Yi and helped her out of the bordello." Gil's voice penetrated his concentration.

"Good. Callie would never forgive me if something happened to Yi." Donny continued to caress Callie's lips with his thumb.

"Gil says Callie has a head injury," Clay said. "I suggest we telegraph Rachel and ask her to meet us in Baker City. We'll take the train. It will be faster and smoother for Callie."

"I think that's the best way to get her the medical attention she needs," added Gil.

"Then let's go." Donny waved the arm not cradling Callie.

The wagon swayed as the three men climbed on.

Clay sat with his back against the seat, his shoulder touching Donny's. "Don't worry. Rachel will know what to do."

"I hope so." Donny wanted to hold Callie in his arms, but didn't want to do more harm.

They made a stop. Gil said to send the telegraph.

Donny remained in the wagon with Callie at the train station as Gil bought tickets.

"Come on. I bought tickets for a Pullman car. I asked for two spaces in the back of the train. We'll have to keep one bed made out the whole trip for Callie." Gil's voice came near Donny's head. "The train leaves in forty-five minutes. Why don't you stretch your legs, and I'll watch her."

Donny shook his head. "I'll stay with her. I can stretch my legs walking onto the train." He stroked Callie's soft hair and blocked out all the noises of the busy depot. This tiny woman had become his life while helping him heal. He wanted to give her a life full of love, family, and promise.

The wagon swayed.

"Donny, tell me her last name." Gil said. "If she doesn't make it we'll need to contact her family."

"I can't. I don't know her last name. She never told me." He stroked her cheek. "I know all her dark secrets, but she never told me her last name."

"What are her secrets?" Gil coached.

"I promised."

"Is she a thief?" Gil asked.

"No! I told you she is honest. I had fifty dollars in my pocket when she dragged me into the tunnels. The only money missing afterwards was the money I told her to take to pay for the telegraph. In all the excitement of finding you, she forgot to give it back to me until Pilot Rock."

He raised his head toward Gil. "Look at her. She's so tiny. She was only defending herself."

"Defending herself. Earlier you said something about killing. Did she kill someone?" Gil was persistent.

Donny had known Gil for ten years. The man never forgot he was a marshal. And now that they were taking Callie to Sumpter—the center of his family, he knew the man was going to want to know everything about the woman coming into their lives.

"Gil, I can vouch she isn't going to hurt anyone in your family." He had to make Gil see Callie wasn't a threat.

"What about you? You're family."

"She won't hurt me. But my heart…If she doesn't make it… I'll have nothing to look forward to."

Gil's hand landed on his shoulder and squeezed. "You know all of us will do whatever we can to help."

"Yeah. I appreciate that."

The clatter of metal on metal, the ear-splitting whistle, a whoosh of steam and screeching brakes signaled the train had pulled into the station.

"Come on. Let me take her from you. I'll hand her over to Jasper. He'll carry her onto the train."

Gil drew Donny's hands away from Callie, and she slowly rose off his lap. The wagon swayed and righted.

"Okay, slide to the back," Gil said.

Donny moved to the back of the wagon, dangled his feet over, and slid until his feet touched the ground. A hand on his shoulder guided him through the people on the station platform. Skirts brushed his pant legs, scents floral, musky, and unwashed swirled in the air. A shoulder bumped his moments before a child ran by, hooking on his crutch.

The crutch jerked on his arm, pulling him forward. He shot both hands in front of him to block his face from hitting the ground.

A hand grasped the collar of his jacket and kept him from landing on the ground.

"Sorry," said a young voice. The wooden crutch tapped his hand.

"When you're in a crowd you need to be more careful," Donny said, grasping the crutch and jamming it back under his arm.

"Yes, sir," said the small voice.

Donny smiled to show no hard feelings and continued forward. Was Jasper having to fight this crowd while carrying Callie? He hoped she wasn't being jostled and bumped.

"Steps two feet ahead," Gil said.

"Where's Jasper and Callie?" Donny asked.

"We's right behind you. Go on," replied Jasper. "I have her cradled in my arms like the sweet angel she is."

Tears burned behind Donny's eyes. Jasper had

become more like a father than a friend, and right now he welcomed the bond they'd created over the years. The man would make sure Callie came to no harm.

Donny reached out and found the railing to the steps.

"Stop!" The deep voice held authority.

Donny turned to the sound.

"Damn. Bentine," Gil said quietly.

"Where are you going with that woman?" Bentine boomed.

Donny stepped away from the railing and toward the voice.

"We are taking her to get medical care." Donny stopped when he registered the presence of the man an arm's length away.

"She has something that belongs to me."

Donny didn't flinch from his menacing tone. He took one more step toward the man. "Why do you think she has something that belongs to you?"

"An associate knocked her to the ground. When we searched him, he didn't have my property. She is the only other person who could have it."

Donny shook his head. "She tossed the watch into the street in front of your gambling hall when we left town yesterday. If you don't find it there, then someone else picked it up."

"Why should I believe a blind fool like you?" Bentine goaded.

"I might be blind, but I'm no fool. Go dig in the dirt and find your watch. If you or any of your men come near this woman again, I'll have you arrested for assault and kidnapping." Donny waved his hand. "Marshal Halsey, take a good look at this man. If you see him anywhere near this woman, I want him arrested."

"You think you can intimidate me with a marshal?" Rage made Bentine's words quiver.

"I also know two Pinkerton agents who might need to look into your business dealings. There's a rumor you force women to work for you and your gaming tables aren't fair."

The train whistle let out one long mournful wail.

"We need to board this train." Donny turned his back on the man.

"Come on, Jasper and Clay are in the train," Gil said quietly.

Donny grasped the railing, again. "Has he left?" he asked.

"He's standing where you left him. I'm proud of how you stood up to him." Gil slapped his back.

Donny smiled. He'd hopefully saved Callie from Bentine.

The railing shook under his hand. He needed to board quickly. If his memory was correct, the first step was the tallest. Using the crutch, he felt around until the wooden stick clanked on the metal step. Yep. The stick was higher than most stairs. He used the crutch and the railing to pull his body up onto the step. The next two were easy. He moved into the rail car, walked past the lavatories, and stood beside the first set of seats.

"Donny, sit in the seat to your right. We'll put

Callie with you while we get a porter to make this side up for sleeping," Gil said.

Donny patted the padded fuzzy seats and sat.

"Here she is," said Jasper, settling Callie's limp body in his lap.

The first thing he did was find her nose and feel for air. Still a soft steady puff. His breath whooshed out. He pushed the hair off her face and felt down her body, making sure she was in a comfortable position.

"Rachel will be able to help her," Clay said from across the aisle.

"I know. I just hope we get there soon enough." Donny didn't like the clenching fear that had settled in his gut. They had to get to Baker City in time for Rachel to save Callie.

"Have faith. If you and Callie are meant to be together, you'll both come through this stronger."

Donny had believed in Clay's positive attitude back when they first met. It was that quality that had made Donny see his life differently. Before, Donny had been bitter and only lived because he knew his father had wished him dead. Why else would he have thrown his only son against a wall? But after meeting Clay, he'd discovered life could be full of happiness and warm, caring people.

"I want to believe she'll be fine." He thought a minute. "Will Gil go back and arrest the man who did this to her?"

"If Callie wakes up and gives us the details, I'm pretty sure he'll do whatever he can to make the man pay."

Muffled footsteps approached.

"We'd like this one made into a bed. We have an injured young woman we're taking to Baker City for treatment," Gil said.

"I see," said a man's voice. Clanks, clunks, and the sound of sheets being lofted filled the area around them as voices grew in the front of the Pullman car.

"We should be pulling out soon," Gil said.

"How long to Baker City?" Donny hoped they arrived in time for Rachel to help Callie.

"We'll be there around midnight," said the voice of the porter.

"Will Rachel be there when we get there?" Donny knew the ride to Baker took half a day.

"She'll be there," Clay said calmly.

"Everything's ready," the porter said.

"Let me put her in the bed," Jasper said, near Donny's left side.

"Can I sit up there with her?" Donny asked. He'd not ridden in a Pullman car before.

"It's not easy to get in and out of with two working legs," Gil said. "Jasper, leave her close to the edge so Donny can stand and easily reach her."

"Yes, sir."

Callie rose out of Donny's lap.

After a few moments, Jasper's large hand, grasped Donny's arm, hauling him to his feet. "There. She's all settled. Move two steps to yer left and reach up."

"Excuse me," said a female voice toward the front of the car. "I'd like to use the facilities."

"Sorry, Ma'am." Gil's tone was softer than he used with Callie. "Boys step to your left and let the lady through."

Donny was already to the left and groping the sleeping area to find Callie. He touched her arm as the woman moved past. Her skirts dragged heavily against his cast.

"I can't stand here all night. I'll just climb in with Callie." He moved his hands to the right and found rungs like on a ladder.

"You can't climb up there with that cast." Gil's statement was punctuated by his hand landing on Donny's shoulder.

"I can't stand here in the aisle 'til midnight. That woman's skirt nearly took me out when she went by." Donny tugged against Gil's hand.

"Let him go. If he's up there it's one less person you have to keep tabs on," Clay offered.

"But he can't get his cast foot up the ladder," argued Gil.

"He don't need to."

Jasper's large hands grasped Donny under the arms and raised him. "Duck yore head."

Donny shoved his chin into his chest and felt for the edge of the sleeper with his hands. His backside scraped the edge of the compartment. He shoved with his hands to get his body in farther.

"Not too far. I's didn't put yore girl all the way over," Jasper said softly.

"I'm touching her leg." Donny slid himself all the way to the end of the sleeper. He moved his hand around to find the end of Callie's feet and pushed with his good foot to shove his back against the side of the railroad car. He had just settled next to Callie when the train lurched and the wheels started clacking.

# Chapter Thirty-six

"Come on, boy. Baker City is coming up soon."

Baker City? Donny ran a hand across his face. Jasper had been waking him up for ten years and he'd never said Baker City was coming up. He noticed the bed under him moving, the clack of train wheels registered, and he remembered why he was in a train.

He'd talked to Callie for hours. Holding her hand, telling her about the places he wanted to take her and the people he wanted her to meet. Reasons why she should wake up. He'd even argued with himself about telling Gil everything. Exhausted from the horse ride, discovering Callie unconscious, and his confrontation with Bentine, he'd fallen asleep.

He still held Callie's hand in his. He squeezed, reminding her he was there. A flutter in her hand started his heart pounding. Had she responded to his touch?

"Callie, Sweetheart. Stay with me. Rachel will look at you soon. She'll know what to do to wake you up." He brought her hand to his lips and kissed it. "I'll always be here for you."

"Come on. We want to be the first off the train," Gil's voice intruded.

Donny shuffled to the end of the bed, shoved his feet and legs out the opening, and wiggled to the edge.

"I's here." Jasper's large hands grasped him under the arms again. "Go ahead and drop, I'll keep ya on yore feet."

He had complete confidence in the big man. Jasper had hauled Donny out of half a dozen messes he'd gotten into.

Without a thought to not being caught, Donny dropped off the berth. True to his word, Jasper caught him and brought him down gently.

"Thanks." He slapped the man on the arm.

"You know you's like a son to me. Never have to ask me to help. I's always be there."

Donny hugged the man. "I know. I think of you like a father."

The big man released him. "Go stand next to Clay. I's get yore girl."

"I'm right here," Clay offered.

Donny hobbled forward until he bumped shoulders with Clay.

"Gil is talking to the porter, getting him to open this door first," Clay said. "How's Callie?"

"It felt like she tried to squeeze my hand this morning." He was going to hang onto that small tremor as a sign she was going to get better.

The train whistle echoed down the tracks as the pulse of the wheels slowed and the train stopped, throwing their bodies forward slightly.

"The porter is opening this door. Come on. I thought I saw Darcy. That mean's Rachel is here." Gil's voice started Donny and Clay walking toward him.

A hand on his chest stopped Donny.

"Take two steps and grab the railing with your right hand," Gil instructed.

Donny took the two steps, reached out, and encountered the railing. Using the railing as his guide he started down the steps. At the bottom small hands latched onto his arm moments before he was pulled to the side and hugged.

"We were all worried sick about you two."

He knew the small woman hugging him by her voice and her small, energetic body. "Hi, Darcy."

"Where's Rachel?" Clay asked.

"She's at Dr. Stanley's office. She said to bring the patient straight there. Oh!"

Clay's elbow nudged Donny. He didn't need eyes to know Gil had apprehended his wife and was most likely kissing her senseless. He'd discovered when a Halsey wife went silent it usually meant her husband was kissing her.

"We need to get this here girl to Rachel," Jasper said.

"Oh, my yes!" Darcy's voice was a bit high and

breathless.

"She is a girl. Who is she?"

"She's a young woman and her name is Callie. How far is the doctor's office?" Donny asked.

"Not far. Come along." Darcy linked her arm with his and started forward.

"How did Rachel convince Dr. Stanley to let her look at Callie?" Clay asked from what sounded like the other side of Darcy.

"Remember when Dr. Stanley had a patient in Sumpter and couldn't take care of him? Rachel helped out. She reminded Dr. Stanley of that and he reluctantly let us use his doctor's office," said Darcy.

How did Gil feel about his wife escorting two blind men down the street when he hadn't seen his wife in several weeks? If Callie were between him and Clay, he'd be proud she was his wife. He thought on that and decided that must be Gil's reaction.

"Here we are." Darcy slipped her arm from his.

Donny took a step forward and felt another hand locating the door knob just as he did.

"I'll let you hold the door this time," Clay's voice was laced with humor.

Donny pulled the door open and held it as Darcy, Clay, Gil, and finally Jasper carrying Callie walked through. He counted to five and followed.

"Who do we have?" Rachel asked.

Darcy's small hand on Donny's back propelled him forward.

"Donny, what can you tell me about this girl?"

Rachel's soft, soothing voice caused a knot of emotion to clog Donny's throat.

He swallowed twice and finally thought he could speak without making a fool of himself.

"Callie was struck in the head with a rifle. She saved my life when men jumped us in the middle of the street. She dragged me down into the tunnels under the city and found a Chinese doctor to fix my ribs and leg." He held out his hand and found Callie, cradled against Jasper. "She's not a girl. She's twenty and she's tough." He swallowed the lump creeping back up his throat. "Please help her. I'm going to ask her to marry me."

"Well then, we best get to it," Darcy grabbed his sleeve. "Gil take Donny and Clay down the street for some breakfast."

"Jasper bring Callie into the examination room, please," Rachel asked.

"I'm not going anywhere. Let me sit in the room. I promise to be quiet and stay out of the way." He wasn't going anywhere. Not while Callie wasn't awake.

"It's best you aren't in the room." Rachel tried to sway him.

"Come on." Clay tugged on his arm. "Let Rachel and Darcy get to work."

"I want to be here. In case…" He couldn't say, in case she didn't wake up. But he wanted to be with her if Rachel couldn't work a miracle.

Voices murmured for several seconds.

"You can stay, but you have to stay where we tell you," Darcy ordered.

"I will." Relieved they would let him stay he didn't care if they made him stand the whole time in a corner. He would be nearby if Callie woke, or if she needed comfort at the last. He wouldn't leave her alone.

Darcy wrapped her arm around his, leading him down a short hall. Stepping over a threshold an antiseptic wall slammed into his face. He sucked in the air but felt as if he hadn't inhaled. The stringent scent stung his nostrils, made his eyes water, and drenched him with doubt. Maybe it wasn't such a good idea to insist on being close by. What if he brought something into the room that caused her complications?

"Sit."

He followed Darcy's order and sat. The chair had a straight back and a hard, wooden seat.

"How long ago did this happen?" Rachel asked.

"Jasper said she was laying across a man's lap as they rode out of Pilot Rock. I'd guess yesterday morning." That had to be when the man struck her with the gun. Why she hadn't been fighting to get away from him. Anger burned in his gut. Once Callie was well, he'd make damn sure Gil found the man and set the law after him and Bentine.

The snick, snick of scissors and the tearing of cloth held his attention.

"My—" Darcy exclaimed before cutting off her words.

"What?" Donny's anger spiraled into fear. What could they have uncovered under the bandage?

"Nothing." Rachel said firmly. "Darcy, go in

the surgical room and bring back the instruments wrapped in a towel labeled head trauma."

Darcy's short, fast footfalls left the room.

"What did you find?" he asked.

"It appears as though a piece of her skull broke off when she was struck. I'll have to cut the scalp, see if I can repair the skull or pull the piece out and make sure the brain hasn't been ruptured or has edema."

He didn't know what edema was. He wanted to ask Rachel questions but had promised to keep quiet. A piece of her skull was loose. He'd heard enough to know injuries this bad to the head could cause all kinds of damage to a person. His heart clenched as anger roared from deep in his gut. His hands fisted. If he got his hands on the man who did this to her, Donny'd break his skull.

Darcy's footsteps entered the room.

"That's the right one," Rachel said. "Put it on the table and wash your hands."

Utensils clinked and clanked. A sweet scent permeated the stringent antiseptic scent.

"If she wakes up while I'm working on her, drip chloroform and put her to sleep," Rachel said.

"What else do you want me to do?" Darcy asked.

"Pray. You too, Donny. I'm a decent doctor, but I'm going to need some help on this one." Rachel's soft voice held confidence, but it also had the humility that Clay had fallen in love with.

"I haven't prayed in a long time," he said.

"Then I'd say this a good time to start again."

## Chapter Thirty-seven

Donny's backside was numb. He pulled out his watch and felt the hands. Rachel had been giving Darcy orders for three hours. Was that too long for her to be working on a head injury? Donny shifted in the chair and stretched both legs out in front of him.

"That's all we can do. Now we wait," Rachel said and metal clinked against metal.

"Will she be okay?" Donny asked.

"We won't know the extent of the damage until she wakes up." Rachel's voice sounded tired. "Darcy, bring in Gil or Jasper to carry Callie into the recovery room."

"When do you expect her to wake up?" He didn't like to hound her after working so intently for three hours but he needed a time frame. Something to cling to.

A hand rested on his shoulder. "It could be hours. Or it could be days. The brain is a sensitive part of the body." Rachel's soft voice answered. "You need to get something to eat. I'll sit with her until you get back."

He placed his hand on hers. "She'll wake up and be well?"

The moment of silence before she spoke started his guts churning all over again.

"The swelling should go down over time. I took the bone fragment out of her head to prevent it shifting and possibly injuring the brain. She'll have a small indention in her head but it's under her hair. We had to cut her hair around the injury." She took a deep breath. "I'll do more reading on head traumas, but I want you to know, she could have complications."

"Complications?" He knew all about complications from head injuries. Blindness.

"We won't know what those are until she wakes. But she could have difficulty speaking, walking, using her hands. The brain controls everything we do. When it gets injured it can cause difficulties."

"She could be blind?" Like me. How could they marry if they were both blind? She was a help to him as a wife with sight. He'd have to help her learn to live in a dark world.

"That's a possibility. From where the injury is located, not as likely as the other things I mentioned."

He wasn't sure if he was relieved she could

be crippled rather than blind or if that terrified him more.

Several footsteps stopped at the door.

"Here is everyone," Darcy said.

"Jasper, would you bring Callie into the next room for me?" Rachel walked away.

Donny stood. "Can I see her when you have her settled? Then I'll get something to eat."

"Yes. Sit tight a minute." Rachel's voice came from farther away.

A hand landed on his shoulder. "Don't worry, Rachel is always reading the latest medical information." Clay's pride in his wife showed.

"She said there could be complications." Donny's mind spun with all the things Rachel said.

"Callie will have you and all of us to help her heal," Clay said.

"You can come in now," Darcy slipped an arm around Donny's, leading him away from Clay.

She led him out of the antiseptic room, down a short hall and through a door. The antiseptic scent didn't curl his nostril hairs like in the other room, but it filled the area. Darcy stopped and took his hand, placing it on Callie's small hand.

"Thank you," Donny said and picked up Callie's hand. "Rachel patched you up. She says you'll wake up when you're ready. Don't keep me waiting too long to hear your voice." He leaned down and kissed the back of her hand. "I'm going to try and eat, but I'll be back before you miss me, I promise."

He released her hand, tucking it beside her under the covers. She was so small and frail. Why would a man strike her with a gun butt? Anger. That's what he needed to keep him fired up and not dropping into an abyss of self-pity and worry. He'd make sure Bentine and his man paid for what they did to Callie.

"Come on." Jasper's large hand fell on his shoulder. "I's been elected to take you to the restaurant."

The way Jasper said it made Donny smile. "That makes me feel special."

"I can't figure why these two think they want to spend time with their wives," Jasper added, moving Donny toward the door.

"Hey. We haven't seen them for several weeks looking for you two. Think you can stay out of trouble for an hour?" Gil said.

Jasper laughed, filling the room with his booming good humor.

"Come on, boy. We'll get you fed and back here before these two quit sparkin' they's ladies."

Donny knew Jasper had his best interest, but he really didn't want to leave the room or Callie. "Go somewhere close by. I'm not that hungry and don't want to be gone too long."

"Don't you worry. I's know the perfect place."

Stepping out onto the boardwalk, Donny inhaled the clean air. It would be hard returning to sit in that room, inhaling the stringent medical scents, but he'd do just about anything for Callie. His mind went to the things Rachel said could be complications.

Jasper turned him and a door opened. Jingling

a bell.

"Mornin' Jasper. You're lookin' a bit worse for wear," said a deep female voice.

"You miss me, Miss Gertrude?"

Donny heard the sweet way Jasper said the woman's name.

"Not a lick. Where you been?"

Jasper moved Donny forward and placed his hand on a chair back. Donny sat, intrigued by the conversation, his curiosity roused. He'd never known Jasper to sweet talk any woman. When had he met this one?

"Had a little trouble at Pendleton. Me and the boy." Jasper's voice rumbled straight across from Donny.

"I see the boy has a plastered leg." The woman stood next to Donny. "You know hanging out with this man goin' to get you in trouble."

"I'm finding that out, Ma'am," Donny said, smiling for the first time in two days.

The woman chortled and slapped his back. "What can I get you?"

"Eggs and potatoes," Donny said. He knew he needed to keep up his strength. He hadn't eaten much the day before, but he had a feeling his stomach wouldn't accept much until he knew Callie was awake and well.

"A big ole slice o' ham, two eggs, and yore biscuits," said Jasper.

"Didn't you eat with Clay and Gil?" Donny asked, surprised by the amount of food Jasper was ordering.

"I was savin' my appetite for Miss Gertrude's cookin'."

"You tell too many stories and your tongue's goin' to fall out." The woman's footsteps faded.

"How do you know Miss Gertrude?" Donny asked.

"Met her one of my trips to Baker City for Clay. She tole me about her restaurant and I's come here every time I's in town."

"Why don't you take her to dinner or for a walk?" Donny suggested.

"She wouldn't go with me." The uncertainty in the man's voice shocked Donny.

"From what I just heard between you two, I believe she would." It was the same kind of banter he and Callie shared. A bit of teasing, a bit of getting the other person riled up, and all in good fun just to keep the conversation going.

"Depends on what Clay says. He might send me back to Sumpter to watch over things while you're here." Jasper's tone sounded like he'd prefer to stay in Baker City.

Donny decided he'd say something to Clay.

"Here ya are, boys."

The smell of ham and fried eggs set his stomach growling. "Thank you, Ma'am. This smells delicious."

"Eggs at three, taters at nine," Jasper said, before his utensils started clanking his plate.

"Coffee?" Miss Gertrude asked.

"Please," they replied in unison.

"How's that food taste?" she asked.

"I didn't realize how hungry I was until I smelled the food. And it tastes better than it smells." Donny scooped another forkful of potatoes into his mouth.

"You make the best biscuits," Jasper said. "Donny, you want one?"

Donny held out his hand and a warm, biscuit filled his palm.

"I's buttered it already," said Jasper.

"So this is Donny." Miss Gertrude's voice came from beside Donny at the level that suggested she sat in a chair beside him.

Donny swallowed the bite of biscuit. "You know me?"

"You're all this big fool talks about." She patted Donny's arm. "It's good to meet you."

"This is the first I knew about you. When did you two meet?" He was happy to have the conversation on anything other than Callie.

"I met Jasper nearly a year ago, right?"

"Yes, Ma'am. I was walking across the street and this slow poke nearly got herself runned over by a wagon."

"It wasn't like that at all."

He heard the embarrassment in Miss Gertrude's voice.

"A year and he hasn't taken you to dinner or a ride in the country?" Donny asked.

"He just comes in here and eats and smiles."

"What's a matter with you?" Donny asked Jasper. "You have a nice woman who can cook, and even talks to you, and you haven't taken her to dinner or a ride?"

"I don't usually stay in town long enough to do either." Jasper's disappointment rang in his voice.

"I won't be going back to Sumpter until Callie is well enough to travel," Donny said to Jasper. That thought made the light and fluffy, buttery-tasting biscuit hit his stomach like a rock. "I need to get back to her." He grabbed the crutch he'd leaned against the table and shoved to his feet. "It was nice meeting you Miss Gertrude. I hope to visit with you again, but I need to get back to Callie."

"Who's Callie?" she asked.

"His girl," said Jasper. "Save my food. I's take him to Callie and come back and finish my meal."

"You don't have to take me back. I can find the way."

"I's coming." Jasper's large hand settled on his shoulder. They walked out the door, turned left, walked a block, turned right, and continued a couple more blocks.

He caught the stringent scent moments before Jasper's hand left his shoulder.

"Here you are. I's goin' back to finish my food."

"Thank you." Donny opened the door and walked in. He'd thought of teasing Jasper one last time about Miss Gertrude, but his heart was too heavy.

"That was fast," said Gil.

"Couldn't eat any more." Donny kept walking.

"To your right. Second door on the left," said Darcy.

"Thank you." Donny followed her directions and encountered a closed door. He opened it and walked through.

"We didn't expect you back so soon," said Rachel.

"Need to be here." He hobbled toward Rachel's voice.

"There's a chair at the head of the bed." Rachel grasped his arm, helping him turn and sit. "On your left is a small table. There's a pitcher of water, a glass, and a cloth. Try to get some water in her by soaking the cloth, dabbing it on her lips and trying to squeeze some water into her mouth. We don't want to choke her but she needs the liquid."

He touched the table and the contents. "Anything else I can do for her?"

"All we can do is wait. The swelling has to go down before she'll wake."

Two sets of footfalls moved toward the door. "I'll check in every hour or so and give you a break when you need it," Rachel said.

"Clay?" Donny questioned.

"Yes?"

"Let Jasper stay in Baker City a couple days. He's sweet on a lady and hasn't had the time to court her." Donny was happy his friend had found a woman to court.

"Really? I didn't know that. I'll see what I can do."

The door closed. Donny moved his hand along the edge of the bed until he found the bump of Callie's hand. He drew it out from under the covers and laced his fingers with hers.

"I'm here. When you wake up, I'll be the first face you see. Callie, sweetheart, no matter what, I will always be here for you." He kissed her hand and continued to hold it as he told her tales of his days in the blind school in Salem.

## *Chapter Thirty-eight*

Callie slowly rose from the black abyss. A familiar voice spoke softly. The pounding in her head had become tolerable. Since the blow to her head, she'd realized when the pain became severe, she fell asleep. Now, she wanted to remain awake, to reassure the soft voice telling her a story.

"I didn't want to like Clay when he offered to help me teach broom making in return for me teaching him to read braille, but he's a hard person not to like."

Donny. His voice sounded hoarse.

"Time to give you some more water." He released the hand she'd just realized he held.

Water splashed.

"Here you go. Rachel said to keep giving you liquids. I wish you'd wake up and drink this water. If you were awake I could hold you without fear of hurting you."

Something wet touched her dry lips. The wetness was welcome. She parted her lips slightly to get some water for her parched throat.

"That's it, Callie. Open, so I can give you the water." The jubilation in his words surprised her.

He placed the cloth between her lips. Water trickled across her tongue and down her throat. She swallowed and wished for more.

"More," she tried to say but the word didn't come out. Only the last half whispered around the cloth. "Ore."

The cloth moved. "Callie! Did you just say something?"

"Ore," she said a little louder.

"Water? More water?"

The wet cloth returned to her lips. She parted them and he squeezed more water.

"Can you open your eyes?" he asked.

She tried. The pain increased a bit, but slowly, her eyelids rose. She stared at a blurry, disheveled Donny.

His hand cupped her cheek. His thumb wandered over her face, skimming across her lashes.

He leaned down and kissed her.

"I have to tell Rachel. I'll be right back."

She watched him walk to the door without his crutch. She couldn't move her head to see if he still had a cast on his leg. How long had she been asleep?

Do I dare try to close my eyes? For fear she wouldn't be able to open them again, she willed her eyelids to remain up. *Where am I? How long have I been asleep?*

Donny returned with a woman.

"She's awake!" Donny exclaimed.

His excitement made her heart beat harder.

"It's good to see you awake. I'm Dr. Halsey, but you can call me Rachel. Any friend of Donny's is a friend of all the Halseys."

Callie nodded slightly and worked her lips into a smile. *Rachel.* Donny said she was Clay's wife. She tried to say hello, a garbled sound came out. Fear raced up her spine and landed with a heavy blow in her mind. *I can't speak!*

"What's the matter?" Donny edged up alongside of Rachel. His hand found Callie's and clung to it.

"Donny, go sit in the chair. I'm going to examine Callie." Rachel's voice held authority.

"What's wrong?" he asked again.

"That's what I'm going to find out. Go sit," she ordered. "If you don't sit, I'll have Clay take you out of here."

Donny released Callie's hand and moved out of her line of sight. Callie stared up at the doctor.

"Can you move your head?" Rachel asked.

Callie used every bit of energy she could to move her head from side to side.

"Good. I'm going to put pressure on your limbs to see how your reflexes react." Rachel tickled Callie's arm, and pushed on a point at her elbow. Callie's hand moved without her doing anything. Rachel did this on both arms, then moved to Callie's feet, tickling the bottoms making her toes wiggle. Rachel then lifted her legs at the knee and hit them, making her legs jerk.

"Your motor skills seem to be working. Does it hurt too much to follow my finger with your eyes?" Rachel asked, holding a finger in front of Callie's face.

Callie nodded. Simply trying to focus on Rachel's finger started Callie's head throbbing.

"I won't make you do that exercise until the headache is gone." She leaned down. "I'm going to find a chore for Donny to keep him occupied. While he's busy we'll evaluate your speech."

Grateful the woman understood she didn't want Donny to hear what might or might not come out of her mouth, tears trickled down her cheeks.

"Donny, Callie is ready to eat. Go out to the kitchen and have Clay dish up some broth and add a slice of the bread Kelda brought over this morning, please."

"She's going to be all right?" Donny asked.

"From my initial examination, she'll be just fine. She's been asleep for two weeks and is nothing but skin and bones. Go get her some food."

Two weeks! No wonder Donny no longer hobbled on a cast. He'd walked straight and swiftly out of the room.

"W-w-where am-m I-I?" she asked like a stuttering drunk.

"You're in my recovery room in the house Clay and I own in Sumpter." Rachel studied her. "When you were taking so long to become conscious and

Dr. Stanley in Baker City was getting tired of all of us traipsing in and out of his home and using his recovery room, we transported you to here." She pushed a strand of hair off Callie's forehead. "You're a lucky girl. Donny has barely left your side. I do believe he's smitten with you."

Callie turned her head. "H-h-he w-w-on't-t-t w-w-when h-h-he s-s-sees I-I-I c-c-can't t-t-talk."

Rachel smiled. "Donny is loyal. He's not going to run just because you're speech is different."

"I-I-I d-d-don't-t-t w-w-want l-l-loyalty. I-I-I w-w-want t-t-o b-b-be l-l-loved." Panic shook her to her heels. She'd never even voiced the need to be loved to herself, and here she'd just stuttered that statement to a stranger.

Rachel's smile grew. "Oh, I have no doubt you have Donny's love as well. It was love that had him riding from Pilot Rock to Pendleton to find you. Love that had him ask your friend Yi to look for you in the bordello."

"Y-Y-Yi i-i-in t-t-the b-b-bordello? S-s-she c-c-could-d-d h-h-have b-b-been h-h-hurt." She frowned.

"According to Donny all your friends in the tunnels stepped up to help find you. Turned out a drunk saw the man carrying you to an old woman's house where Gil and Donny broke in and took you away." Rachel put her hands under her back. "Let's sit you up a bit so you can eat the broth Donny is bringing back."

Callie was still rehashing what Rachel told her when Donny walked into the room carrying a tray.

He'd lost weight, but it was good to see him walking on both legs. Hunched over his crutch hobbling along, he had seemed more an old man than manly. Now, watching his confidence as he walked to the table by the bed and placed the tray on it, she saw him as the virile man who had jumped into a fight when he couldn't see his opponents.

This new Donny made her shy. And vulnerable. She wasn't the one in control any more.

"I have the broth and bread. Also a cup of water." Donny sat on the chair between the table and the bed. "Are you through examining her?" he asked, his hand seeking Callie's on the side of the bed.

"Yes. Callie's motor functions seem to be a bit sluggish but that is reasonable. Her speech however… When a person receives the kind of blow she did to the head, it can upset many things. In this case, it is her speech. She can talk, but you need to be patient and listen carefully. Over time this could improve."

Callie watched the woman walk to the door.

"I'll be in my office seeing patients if you need me." Rachel walked out the door.

Left alone with Donny, Callie didn't know what to say. She was pretty sure she loved him. But would he still want her when he discovered she wasn't the same person who'd dragged him into the tunnels.

"Callie, will it hurt you if I hold you a minute?"

His soft voice cracked her heart completely open. She did love this man.

"N-n-n-o."

"I've been wanting to hold you ever since we found you, but I was afraid I'd hurt you worse." He gathered her into his arms and pulled her onto his lap.

She rested her head on his shoulder and wrapped her arms around him. Holding him, feeling his solid body, and feeling his heart beating as fast as hers, bonded them.

Donny's heart soared as well as wept. He'd needed this contact with Callie ever since he'd heard about her injury. Holding her, knowing she would be well, his heart was full. He'd feared the worse sitting beside her day after day and night after night waiting for her to wake up. Rachel had said the longer she remained asleep the less likely the chance of her waking up.

But she was awake. Thin. Horribly thin. His fingers traced her sunken cheeks and could count her ribs.

"I should get you back in bed and feed you," he said into her ear.

"N-n-not-t-t y-y-yet." Her arms clung to him, her face nestled into his neck.

"I can hold you all day." He kissed her head, his lips meeting the bandage. "Callie, I love you and want you to be my wife."

Her body stiffened in his arms. She drew her head from his shoulder. "Y-y-you d-d-don't-t-t w-w-want a-a-a w-w-wife w-w-who c-c-can't-t-t t-t-talk."

He grasped her head in his hands, gently, careful not to touch her near the injured area. "I don't care if you can or can't talk. I love you. I want you by my side the rest of my life." He lowered his head and found her lips. They tasted salty. His thumbs encountered tears as he spread his fingers. "Don't cry. We're both better when we're together. We'll work on your speech together. I'll be here for you always. You can count on it." He kissed her again.

Her stomach rumbled. Donny drew out of the kiss. "Back to bed so you can eat." He lifted her, placing her on the bed. She weighed half of the feather weight she'd been before.

Once he had her settled and covered with the blankets, he set the tray on her lap. "Clay was going to let everyone know you woke up. But I'll tell them you need to rest so they don't come barging in to meet you."

"H-h-how m-m-many?" she asked.

Donny smiled. "There's the five Halsey brothers. You've met Gil and Clay and their wives Darcy and Rachel. No, I guess you didn't meet Darcy. She helped Rachel do the surgery."

"S-s-surgery?"

"When we arrived in Baker City, Rachel and Darcy met us. Rachel had to remove a piece of your skull that was loose and injuring your brain." He ran his hand up the side of the bed, her body, and onto the bandage on her head. "She said there will be a slight indention in your head and she had to cut your hair to get the piece out."

Callie's hand covered his then moved to explore the bandage. "I-I-I o-o-owe R-r-r-rachel-l-l f-f-for b-b-being a-a-alive?"

"Her and everyone who helped us find you."
He set her hand down on the tray. "Eat. You've
grown too thin. It's not healthy."

"H-h-how w-w-would y-y-you k-k-know?" she
asked.

"When I held you, I felt more bone than woman." He rubbed a hand up and down her arm.

"W-w-who e-e-else w-w-wants t-t-to m-m-
meet-t-t m-m-me?"

"Ethan and Aileen. Ethan is the oldest Halsey.
And Hank and Kelda. Kelda made the bread you're
eating. She's a good cook but would rather be out in
the woods cutting down trees."

"C-c-cutting t-t-trees?"

"Yeah, it's a long story, but she was brought up
with brothers. She helped with the logging and in
the camp kitchen. Hank met her when her family
contracted with him to log the Halsey land."

"Th-th-that's o-o-only f-f-four."

"Zeke and Maeve don't live around here all the
time. They have a place, and they stay when they
are in between assignments. They're Pinkertons."
He was proud of the fact the husband and wife duo
had stopped several bad things from happening and
jailed a number of outlaws.

"Jeremy and his wife, Clara, are here visiting.
He's been wanting to get in and see you. We've
been friends since Clay brought me here. He's
Darcy's brother." Donny had liked Jeremy the
minute the two were introduced. He'd made Donny
be self-sufficient when they did things together and

never treated him like he couldn't see. Other than to joke about what pretty women he wasn't able to see.

"I-I-I d-d-don't w-w-want t-t-to m-m-meet a-a-any o-o-of t-t-them. N-n-not w-w-while I-I-I t-t-talk l-l-like th-th-this."

# Chapter Thirty-nine

Callie knew Donny wouldn't make fun of her and the way she talked, but she feared what his friends might think. She wasn't prepared to have people she didn't know watch her and criticize her speech and wonder why Donny wanted her for a wife. His declaration of love and wanting to marry her had warmed her heart and made her feel she deserved a happy life with him. But did she dare believe he could overlook the way she talked? Or the fact she'd killed a man? Or that Bentine would hurt him if he found them?

"Callie? Why are you so quiet? I won't let anyone in here until you're ready." Donny's quiet voice seeped through her thoughts.

She dunked the bread she'd broke into pieces into the broth. "Y-y-you a-a-aren't h-h-here a-a-all th-th-the t-t-time."

His mouth spread into a mischievous grin. "I've been sleeping in this room and only leaving it to get food and relieve myself. I'm not leaving here until you do. I promised you no one would ever hurt you. I'm not leaving your side."

There he went saying something that sent happiness shooting through her body and melting her heart. "W-w-where? O-o-on th-th-the f-f-floor?"

"Ethan brought in a cot."

She looked around the room and noticed the cot on the other side of the bed. "I-I-I s-s-see i-i-it." Callie spooned a hunk of bread saturated in broth into her mouth and slowly swallowed. The first piece landing in her empty stomach took some time to be welcomed.

"You might as well get used to the fact I'm not leaving you. You dragged me down into that tunnel and now my heart won't let you go."

She enjoyed hearing Donny say he loved her, but it also made her uncomfortable. No one had told her she was worth loving since her father died.

A soft knock sounded on the door. It opened and Rachel walked in followed by a smaller woman.

Callie froze. She didn't want anyone gawking at her.

Donny stood. "Callie doesn't want to see anyone yet." He stood beside the bed, his back to her, his arms crossed.

"Darcy wanted to see for herself that our patient is awake," Rachel said.

Darcy. Gil's wife and the woman who helped Rachel. Callie leaned back a bit to get a look at the woman. She was only a few inches taller than Callie. She wore a print shirt, riding skirt, and boots.

Donny remained a wall between Callie and the women.

"Donny, we aren't Mr. Bentine. You may have kept him away from Callie and put a bit of fear in him, but you are no match against two Halsey women," Darcy said, approaching the bed.

Callie grabbed his shirt sleeve and tugged. "Wh-wh-what d-d-does sh-she-she m-m-mean?" When had Donny stood up to Mr. Bentine?

Donny turned to her, but it was Darcy who spoke. "Gil said Bentine tried to keep them from taking you on the train. Donny stood toe to toe with the man and told him to leave you alone or he'd see to it the man went to jail."

"R-r-really?" She peered into Donny's face. The stern set to his jaw and the way his hands clenched told her he had stood up to the man. "Th-th-the w-w-watch-ch-ch…"

"I told him to go dig around in the street in front of his gambling hall." Donny grasped her hand. "He isn't a threat to you anymore."

She gave two tugs on his sleeve. He sat on the side of the bed. "Th-th-thank-k-k y-y-you."

He squeezed her hand in reply.

Darcy stepped forward with her hand extended. "Hello, I'm Darcy Halsey. Gil's wife."

Callie withdrew her hand from Donny's and grasped the woman's hand.

"All these big Halsey men thought I was a handful. Sounds to me like Donny's going to have his hands full with you." She winked.

Callie liked this woman. She was full of spit and fire and not afraid to speak her mind.

"You're wearing one of my nightgowns. I've taken apart a couple of my old dresses and made them up for you. When you get out of that bed you can wear them until you have the strength to get more."

Callie stared at the woman. Darcy had helped with Callie's surgery and now she was giving her clothing? Callie was going to owe this family more than she could ever repay.

"Th-th-thank y-y-you," she stammered. "I-I-I d-d-don't kn-n-n-ow wh-wh-when I-I-I c-c-can r-r-rep-p-pay y-y-you."

"If you make Donny happy, that's all the re-payment we need." Darcy faced Rachel. "I have to go. Now that she's awake, I need to get back to my family. Gil will be happy to be relieved of the chil-dren." She smiled at Callie. "Looking forward to seeing you up and around. We're having a party for my brother Jeremy and his wife Clara next week. I hope you're able to attend."

The woman whisked out of the room like a fire was licking at her heels.

"What's the party for Jeremy and Clara?" Don-ny asked Rachel.

"They are permanently moving to Sumpter. The man they hired to run things is doing so well Clara agreed to move here and wants me to deliver the baby." Rachel's face glowed with excitement.

Callie had known from the first moment she

met Rachel she was a competent and knowledge-able doctor, but to have family moving to Sumpter so she could help with the birth of their baby, made Rachel even more special in Callie's eyes.

"I see you're eating the broth and bread. After having nothing in your stomach for the two weeks I'm afraid that's all you can have until your stomach gets used to food." Rachel picked up the tray.

"I-I-It's m-m-more th-th-than I-I-I h-h-had m-m-many t-t-times th-th-the l-l-last th-th-three y-y-years."

The startled expression on Rachel's face made Callie wish she could take her words back. No one had told the woman Callie had been living on her own for the last three years. What will she think of me now? Will she think I'm not a good enough wife for Donny?

And I'm not. I have to make him see, I can't marry him. I can't talk properly and my face is on a wanted poster. She sank deeper into the pillow and closed her eyes. I have to get out of here before someone discovers my past. Or Donny thinks I'll marry him. Her heart ached at the thought of leaving him. He was the first person in a long time to make her feel she could have a life other than running and hiding. She didn't want to think about it now. Too much thinking started her head throbbing. Sleep eased the pain. She drifted to sleep to evade the pain.

A tug on his sleeve pulled Donny away from the bed.

"She's sleeping," Rachel whispered. "Come

outside and talk with me. I don't want to disturb her."

"I told her I wouldn't leave her," Donny whispered back.

"We'll be just outside the door. No one will come in, and you can hear if she wakes up," Rachel persisted.

Donny followed the woman out of the room. He stopped at the door and listened. Once the door closed, he asked, "She'll wake up again, won't she?"

"Yes. Even though her body has been shut down the last two weeks, she is weak from lack of food and tired from her body healing." Rachel stood to his right. "What did she mean about this being more food than she's had in the last three years?"

Donny battled with himself. He'd promised not to tell her story to anyone but what if how she'd been living had something to do with healing her? And he wanted to make sure no one was looking for her. Give her a reason to stay and not move on. While he believed she cared about him, she'd yet to say she loved him and would stay with him as his wife.

"She's been running and hiding the last three years. Something bad happened to her. She believes she killed a man."

Rachel inhaled in shock. "She's too small to hurt anyone. Have you told Gil or Zeke so they can look into it?"

He listened to see if Rachel and any more reactions. He'd always known her to be fair and non-judgmental. He'd always found it easy to talk to her. But should he have told her so much about Callie? He'd promised not to tell anyone. His head argued he wanted to know more but his heart ached at what they might find. He didn't want to lose her.

"No. She hasn't told me her last name. She didn't even tell me her first name when we met. She did say she's from Kentucky." He knew it wasn't much information. It would be nearly impossible for someone to discover her past with that little of information.

"Send Zeke a letter and explain what you know and have him look into it. If she's cleared of killing someone, it would help her heal and make her more susceptible to your charms." Rachel bumped his arm. "Go watch over your lady. I'm taking the dishes to the kitchen and finding my family. I have a free afternoon and I plan to use it spending time with Clay and the kids."

Rachel was right. Knowing the truth would help to set Callie free from the demons that tormented her. "Rachel?"

"Yes," she said from down the hall.

"Would you bring me Clay's writing book, a piece of paper, and a pencil before you find your family?"

"I will."

Donny entered the room and sat in the chair he'd been sitting in for the last week and waited for Callie to awaken again. He was determined she would agree to be his wife.

# Chapter Forty

After a week recuperating in Rachel and Clay's house, Callie found herself being carried by Jasper to the small house where he and Donny lived.

"Y-y-you n-n-n-o I-I-I c-c-c-ould h-h-have w-w-walked th-th-this d-d-distance," she said to the big man who grinned and kept his eyes on the house ahead of them.

"You're still a bit unsteady on your feet," Donny said, walking beside them. He carried the satchel they'd left in Pilot Rock. Someone had retrieved their belongings and she now had the one new dress Gil had bought, her own nightdress and undergarments, and the dresses Darcy made for her.

"W-w-what a-a-are p-p-peop-p-le g-g-going to-to-to s-s-say." She wasn't against staying with Donny and Jasper, but she didn't want people to get the wrong idea about her.

"If you'd agree to marry me, we wouldn't have to worry about what people say." Donny turned his head toward her.

They'd discussed the fact she wasn't ready to marry anyone until she knew how much of a burden she would be on a husband. Donny, of course, said it didn't matter. But it did to her. She wasn't going to make him have to live the rest of his life caring for her. He would regret his choice and could end up finding comfort in a bottle like her stepfather. She shivered.

"You cold, Miss Callie?" Jasper asked.

"N-n-no." She stared at the cute little house as Jasper crunched up the rock walkway.

"O-o-oh!" The front windows had frilly curtains in the windows. The outside had a new whitewash. Inviting rockers sat on the porch to the left of the door. She couldn't believe two men lived in such a pretty place.

Jasper stepped onto the porch.

"D-d-down. P-p-put m-m-me d-d-down."

He set her gently on her feet. Donny stepped in front of her and opened the door. He held out a hand and led her across the threshold and into a main living area. There were two brown corduroy upholstered chairs on either side of a small, matching sofa. A large braided rug on the floor gave the room a homey feel. A small table with a lamp sat beside each chair.

She stared at Donny. Did he know the richness he lived in? Before her father died, they had a set of furniture. Her mother sold the pieces and they'd lived with mish-mashed chairs and tables. No rugs on the floor. Her stepfather drank any extra money they might have used to make their lives nicer.

"What's the matter?" he asked, standing beside her.

"Y-y-you a-a-and Ja-ja-jasper l-l-live in-in-in th-th-this ho-ho-house?"

"Yes? What's wrong with it?" His brow wrinkled as if her question confused him.

"N-n-nothing. I-I-I th-th-thought…No-no-nothing."

"There are two bedrooms. My mother and sister have been here the last couple of days cleaning and setting things up."

That explained the cleanliness and woman's touch to things. Her heart stopped. "D-d-do I-I-I ha-ha-have to-to-to me-me-meet th-th-them?"

"No. I told them when you were ready, they could meet you. I know what it's like to feel different and think everyone is staring and talking about you. I'll protect you from that. But after a while you have to get strong and stand for yourself and not let what happened to you keep you sheltered away from everyone who wants to be your friend. Or family."

She peered into his face. He was so strong for all that he'd gone through. But he had his mother and sister and all the Halseys who treated him like family. He had people who cared and would be there for him no matter what. All she had was Donny. Was he enough? Could she find her fighting self? The one who stabbed her stepfather and set out across the country alone?

"The room on the right is mine, but I'll stay in Jasper's room while you use mine." Donny led her to the back of the house. "The kitchen is to the right. See it through that door?"

She glanced to her right and saw a small, functional kitchen with a cheery yellow cloth on the table and a small vase of wild flowers. His mother and sister had gone to a lot of trouble to make the small house homey and inviting.

"I-I-I s-s-see i-i-it. V-v-very pr-pr-pretty. I-I-I l-l-like th-th-the f-f-flowers on-on-on th-th-the t-t-table."

"Clay and Rachel's two boys picked those for you."

"T-t-tell th-th-them th-th-thank y-y-you."

Donny opened the door on the right. A double bed with a quilt full of bright colors took up most of the room. Two small braided rugs in the colors of the quilt sat on both sides of the bed awaiting bare toes on a cold morning. A small bureau and tall wardrobe stood side by side with a wash stand beside the bureau. A gilded mirror stood above the wash stand at the perfect height for her.

"What do you think?" Donny asked. The worry in his voice made her smile.

"I-i-it's a-a-a be-be-beautiful r-r-room. I-I-I ha-ha-have a-a-a sn-sn-sneaky f-f-feeling th-th-that th-th-the qu-qu-quilt, r-r-rugs a-a-and m-m-mirror ar-ar-are n-n-new."

"I told them you wouldn't believe I use a mirror." He faced her. "Callie, I want you to feel at home here. When you finally accept my marriage offer, this is where we'd live. At least until I could afford something bigger."

"I-I-I d-d-don't n-n-need b-b-bigger." She didn't want anything larger. She wasn't a home maker. She was a woman who brought trouble to the people she met.

"Not now, but if we have kids…" He leaned down, capturing her lips.

She didn't want to slip into the kiss and forget she couldn't stay, but her mind and body craved the love he made her feel. His arms wrapped around her, holding her against him and keeping her on her feet. Their lips melded.

Callie sighed, giving in to the realization no one could make her feel so safe and loved. Her lips parted slightly. A heady sensation swept through her body when Donny's tongue caressed the open lines of her lips.

They'd only kissed with closed mouths until now. This new intimacy, him seeking entrance to her body, thrilled and surprised her.

When she timidly touched her tongue to his, sparks shot to her toes. He moaned and his tongue probed farther into her mouth. What should have been disgusting had her body pressing to his and her breathing coming in pants.

A door clicked behind them.

Callie pushed away from Donny. What were they doing? It was the middle of the day and she… She had wanted him to kiss her more and run his hands over her body.

She raked a gaze around the room. The bedroom door was open as they'd left it. The front door was closed. Who had walked in and seen them kissing?

Donny's hands still held her arms. "What's wrong?"

"S-s-someo-o-one s-s-saw us-us-us k-k-kissing." She wasn't sure if she was upset about allowing the kisses to go so far or mad because someone saw them and now she felt vulnerable.

"Jasper probably came to check on us, saw we were busy, and closed the door." Donny rubbed his hands up and down her upper arms.

"J-j-jasper? W-w-where is-is-is he-he-he g-g-going to-to-to s-s-stay?" This arrangement had him kicked out of the house it appeared.

"He's been sparkin' a lady in Baker City and is buying a house with the hopes of moving a wife into it."

She couldn't miss the insinuation in his comment. He was hoping to move her into this house as his wife. "W-w-why d-d-didn't y-y-you b-b-buy a-a-a n-n-new h-h-house a-a-and l-l-let Ja-ja-jasper ha-ha-have th-th-this on-on-one?"

"I know my way around this house. I'd have to learn a new one." He slipped his hand down to lace his fingers with hers. "Would you like a cup of tea or to rest?"

"T-t-tea. I-I-I c-c-can g-g-get i-i-it." She started for the door.

"You can come to the kitchen, but I'll make the tea." Donny led Callie to the kitchen. He was proud of the house. He'd worked hard to be able to buy out Jasper's half of the building. Now he'd work hard to provide for Callie and any children they had. That was if she'd ever consent to marrying him.

"Sit here." He held out a chair at the kitchen table. Callie sat. He moved to the stove and lit the kindling in the fire box.

"I-I-I c-c-can d-d-do th-th-that," Callie said nervously.

"I've been lighting this stove the last ten years. I can make hot water for tea." Once the stove was lit, he moved to the sink and pumped water into the kettle.

A knock at the front door surprised him. The Halseys and his family knew he was moving Callie into the house today and he'd requested no visitors. "I'll get the door and send them away," he said, walking out of the kitchen.

He opened the front door.

"Good to see you, Donny." He was pulled into a hug by the only Halsey he'd yet to see since returning to Sumpter. Zeke.

"Zeke, what are you doing here? Is Maeve with you?" He didn't think so. Zeke was wearing his large wool overcoat, which meant he was dressed like a dandy. Donny would have smelled Maeve's flower scent if she stood beside her husband.

"I'm alone. I was passing through on a job and thought I'd hand deliver the information I gathered for you." Zeke stepped past him.

"Can you just hand it to me? Callie's here and she doesn't want company right now." He wanted

Zeke to meet Callie, but he also had to respect her wishes if he wanted to keep her around to marry.

"I'd like to meet her. And I think she'll find the information I brought interesting." Zeke's footsteps carried him towards the kitchen.

Donny grabbed at Zeke's coat. "Let me go first." He passed the man and walked into the kitchen.

"Callie, Zeke Halsey is here to see us." Chair legs scooted across the wood floor and something crashed.

# Chapter Forty-one

Callie saw the large man standing behind Donny and heard the name Zeke. He was the Pinkerton. She couldn't stop her response to the man. She bolted out of the chair and made a break for the door.

A large arm wrapped around her. "I don't know what Donny here's told you about me, but I don't eat young women."

The man's jovial tone slowly seeped into her conscious.

"Here hold your woman, while I read my report."

The man shoved her into Donny's waiting arms. With Donny's caring arms holding her close to his warm body, she stopped shivering and stared at Zeke.

"W-w-what d-d-do y-y-you m-m-mean r-r-report?"

Donny hugged her. "I asked Zeke to look into the man you think you killed. Your stepfather."

She slid in his arms, staring up into his face. "H-h-how c-c-could y-y-you!" She wanted to slap his face and shove out of his arms, but he held her tight, holding her arms between their bodies.

"Rachel said part of the healing process was getting things that weighed on your mind off. To help you heal from the blow to your head, I wrote to Zeke asking him to see what he could find out."

Callie shook her head. How could someone who said they loved her throw her to the law? "Y-y-you d-d-don't l-l-love m-m-me. Th-th-this p-p-proves i-i-it."

"I do love you. That's why we're going to hear this together and decide what to do together. You aren't alone any more. You have me."

She continued to shake her head.

Zeke cleared his throat. "I went to Kentucky with the information you gave me and Gil's description."

"G-G-Gil's d-d-description?" She should have known Gil would have a hand in prodding Donny to go against her.

"Since I couldn't see you and give him a fair description, I asked Gil to send a description of you." Donny kissed the top of her head. Right where she had a scar and short, spikey hair.

Zeke cleared his throat again. "You didn't give me much to go on. Maeve started reading the local newspapers and stumbled upon a story about a man who was shot outside his home." He glanced over the papers to Callie.

She didn't know what he was talking about. She'd stabbed her stepfather.

"When we arrived at the town, we started showing the description and talking to the folks. Turned out the man who was shot was a Callie MacPherson's stepfather."

"N-n-no, th-th-that's n-n-not r-r-right. He-he c-c-c-ouldn't h-h-have b-b-been sh-sh-shot. I-I-I st-st-stabbed h-h-him wh-wh-when he-he—" she stopped.

"MacPherson. Now I see why you had everyone calling you Mac." Donny kissed her head again.

Zeke continued. "They all said Callie had disappeared several weeks before Mr. Draggard was found dead with a bullet hole."

Callie's emotions tumbled around inside her like a dried weed tumbling in the wind. "He-he d-d-died fr-fr-from a-a-a b-b-bullet?"

"There was mention of a recent scar on his side." Zeke watched her.

"D-d-did th-th-they s-s-say wh-wh-who sh-sh-shot h-h-him?"

"The law didn't have any idea, but there were rumors it might have been an angry father." Zeke's eyebrow rose as if he knew the reason why she'd stabbed her stepfather.

She looked up into Donny's face. A wide smile graced his handsome face.

"Callie, you didn't kill your stepfather." Donny's elation should have made her happy. But she'd lived so long believing she'd killed her stepfather, she didn't know how to respond. He'd hit the floor and not moved. She could close her eyes and see the blood and his still body.

"Callie? Callie?" Donny held her away from him. "What's wrong?"

"I think she's still trying to understand it all. Here's the report. I'll leave it on the table." Zeke walked to the kitchen door. "Will I see you at the party tomorrow?"

She'd forgotten about the party for Jeremy and Clara.

"Yes, we'll be there," Donny said, pulling her back against him as if he feared she'd run away.

"Good." Zeke watched her for a minute, then pivoted and exited the house.

Callie was numb. She'd lived like an outlaw for three years believing the law was looking for her.

Donny picked her up in his arms and carried her into the bedroom. She clung to his neck and sobbed. He sat on the bed, holding her, allowing her to cry.

She didn't know how long she sobbed, but when no more tears would come and her throat ached, she leaned back. "A-a-all th-th-this t-t-time I-I-I th-th-though-t-t-t I-I-I w-w-was a-a-a mur-mur-murderer."

"You're not. You're the kind, caring woman I fell in love with." Donny put a hand behind her head while still holding her with his other arm. "Callie MacPherson, I'm going to keep asking you this until you say yes. Will you marry me?"

She peered into Donny's face. He was kind,

loving, caring, and had believed in her even when she hadn't. How could she turn down an offer to live with him the rest of her life?

"A-a-are y-y-you j-j-just a-a-asking to-to-to n-n-not s-s-sully my-my n-n-name?" she asked, needing to know he was marrying her because he loved her.

"I'm asking because I love you and can't think of anyone else I'd rather spend my life bickering with." He lowered his head and captured her lips in a toe-curling kiss.

Her mind spun. He loves me! I'm not wanted by the law. But will he one day grow tired of a stuttering wife? How will we live? Her heart overruled her survival mode. She loved Donny and he loved her. They'd made it through tough times and together they could handle any trouble that came their way. She gave in to the kiss and enjoyed the bliss of being in love.

When he drew back for air, she asked, "H-h-how s-s-soon is-is-is th-th-the w-w-wedding?"

"Is tomorrow too soon?"

She laughed. "W-w-we c-c-can't sp-sp-spoil J-j-jeremy a-a-and Cl-cl-clara's par-par-party."

"I'll ring them up and ask if they mind sharing their day with a wedding."

Donny kissed her again.

The kiss left her breathless.

# Chapter Forty-two

Callie stood in the small bedroom of the house she and Donny would live. There was barely enough room for all the women who were helping her dress. She'd told them twice she didn't want to be fancy. Donny wouldn't see her anyway. But they'd all insisted upon helping. Darcy brought a soft velvet dress, light blue in color, with a lacey bodice and long lacy sleeves. Callie loved the dress the minute Darcy held it up.

Kelda, Hank's wife, wasn't in the room. She was in the kitchen with Aileen, Ethan's wife, finishing the wedding cake. Rachel and Maeve were in the room fixing Callie's hair in a style that would hide her scar and short hair.

Clara, Jeremy's wife, had arrived first thing this morning and helped her bathe and gave her a talk she was pretty sure a mother would normally give a daughter before a wedding night. They'd giggled when Clara told of her first experience making love with Jeremy. Callie had been embarrassed to hear the story but it also made her wish the wedding was over and she and Donny were wrapped together in the bed that stood behind her.

Clara and Jeremy had said they couldn't think of a better day to have a wedding. They were happy they were here to see it.

"I-I-I h-h-hope th-th-there ar-ar-aren't to-to-too m-m-many pe-pe-peo-ple." Her only frustration with this day would come when she had to say her vows. She wanted Donny to hear her clearly.

"Only family and a couple of close friends. Jasper, his friend, and Myrle," Rachel said.

"Wh-wh-who is-is-is M-m-myrle?" Donny hadn't mentioned this person.

"She is the woman who kept an eye on the Halsey boys after their parents died. She is family." Rachel hugged her. "Just like you'll be family after today."

There were two people she hadn't met yet that she wanted to meet. "Wh-wh-where ar-ar-are D-d-donny's m-m-mother a-a-and s-s-sister?"

"They're kind of shy. You'll see them in the front row. We Halsey women scare them with our bossiness," Maeve said. Darcy and Rachel laughed and nodded in agreement.

Callie could see where a timid person would be fearful of the women. She'd never been easily intimidated. Except for Bentine. But then she'd never run up against such a despicable person before.

Even when she thought she was running for her life, she'd never hidden completely out of sight.

A knock on the door caused everyone to pivot that direction.

Gil stuck his head in. "Are you about ready? The groom is getting antsy. Asked me to come make sure Callie hadn't climbed out a window." He winked at her.

"We're ready." Darcy and the other women stepped away from her.

Callie looked in the mirror. Tears burned the back of her eyes. "I-I-I've n-n-never l-l-l-ooked so-so-so…" She didn't have words to explain what she felt and saw.

"Remember, even though Donny can't see you, he'll know by the smile in your heart and the twinkle in your voice that you're beautiful." Rachel hugged her. "And when he drives you crazy, you come talk to me. I will completely understand."

Callie laughed and plucked at the tear on her cheek. "D-d-deal."

All the women hurried out of the room after giving her a hug.

"Ready?" Ethan Halsey stood in the doorway of the bedroom. He had to duck his head and his shoulders touched each side of the doorway. He was the oldest and biggest brother of the Halseys. She'd also discovered, the one with the softest heart. Last night after Donny had Jeremy and Clara's permission to have a wedding during their party, he'd called all the Halseys. Less than an hour later, Ethan arrived at their door offering to give her to Donny.

His kind gesture had caused Callie to burst into tears. The whole Halsey family had pulled together and made this moment happen in less than twenty-four hours.

"R-r-ready." She walked out of the bedroom she would share with Donny tonight and slipped her arm around Ethan's arm.

He patted her hand and led her out of the house, through the front door, and down the street to the park.

Donny stood to the right of the preacher who stood under a large pine tree. Jeremy stood beside Donny, and Clara stood on the other side of the preacher, waiting for her.

There were no chairs. Everyone stood. She recognized all the Halseys and their children. The older woman standing with Hank and Kelda must be Myrle. She was a woman Callie wanted to meet. At the front of all the Halseys, Jasper and an attractive Negro woman stood. Alongside of them stood a woman, of average size and stature, and a girl who appeared to be about seventeen or eighteen. They both had the same caramel brown hair as Donny. She saw the same eye shape as Donny on both women. These were her new in-laws. She smiled at them and they smiled back.

Her gaze traveled to the man standing straight and tall by the preacher. His clean-shaven face held a smile that nearly touched both ears. His unseeing eyes had crinkles at the corners as he faced the crowd.

Ethan led Callie up to Donny. He placed her

hand in Donny's.

"Who gives this woman in wedlock?" the preacher asked.

"We do!" the whole congregation said. Jasper's voice boomed louder than the rest.

Donny and Callie both laughed.

"I have a good feeling about this union," the preacher said.

Ethan returned to his place beside Aileen. Callie faced Donny. They were going to make an interesting couple. He couldn't see and she had stammering speech. But they would be a couple and they would work things out. She had no doubt about that.

The preacher ran through the vows, both she and Donny took their time answering and repeating as they were asked to do.

The preacher turned them to face the crowd. "I'd like to introduce you to Mr. and Mrs. Donny Kimball." He tapped Donny on the shoulder. "You may kiss your bride."

Donny had been waiting for this moment ever since Callie agreed to marry him. He released her fingers where their hands were laced, ran his hands up her arms, her neck, and cradled her head.

Before the Halseys and his family, he kissed her until her knees buckled. He gathered her legs over one arm and swept her up into his arms. Everyone whooped and hollered. He just grinned from ear to ear, claiming his bride.

## About the Author

All my work whether it's my romance or my mysteries have Western or Native American elements in them along with hints of humor and engaging characters. My husband and I raise alfalfa hay in rural eastern Oregon. Riding horses and battling rattlesnakes, I not only write the western lifestyle, I live it.

I love to hear from fans. You can find or contact me at:
patyjag@gmail.com
or my website – www.patyjager.net

**Historical Western Romance**
Gambling on an Angel
Improper Pinkerton
For a Sister's Love
Christmas Redemption

**Halsey Brother Series**
Marshal in Petticoats – Gil's story
Outlaw in Petticoats – Zeke's story
Miner in Petticoats – Ethan's story
Doctor in Petticoats – Clay's story
Logger in Petticoats – Hank's story

**Halsey Homecoming Trilogy**
Laying Claim – Jeremy's Story
Staking Claim – Colin's Story
Claiming a Heart – Donny's Story
A Husband for Christmas - Shayla's Story

**Letters of Fate Trilogy**
Davis
Brody
Isaac

**Silver Dollar Saloon**
Savannah
Lottie Mae
Freedom

**Contemporary Western Romance**
Perfectly Good Nanny
Bridled Heart

Windtree
Press

Thank you for purchasing this Windtree Press publication.
For other books of the heart, please visit our website at www.
windtreepress.com.

For questions or more information contact us at info@
windtreepress.com.

Windtree Press
Hillsboro, OR